MORE PRAISE FOR *TROPICAL DEPRESSION*

"The character of Murray Zemelman gives Mr. Shames a new lease on his fiction. . . . Despite its title, *Tropical Depression* flies high."   —*The New York Times*

"As tasty as a mango sundae."
                                —Bill Bell, *New York Daily News*

"Shames knows how to put his tongue in his cheek—and he keeps it firmly, entertainingly in place throughout."   —*Publishers Weekly*

"It's hilarious."   —Digby Diehl, *Playboy*

"Another winner for Shames."
                                —Thomas Gaughan, *Booklist*

"Even by Florida standards, Key West is another country. And Shames is its pop storyteller nonpareil."
                                —Betsy Willeford, *New Star Ledger*

"Laurence Shames is one of the best of the Florida Writers, and *Tropical Depression*, his fourth book, is one of his funniest and most entertaining to date."
                                —Elizabeth M. Cosin, *Washington Times*

"Nothing short of hilarious."
                                —*Pittsburgh Tribune-Review*

"He [Shames] has a nose for skirting the mundane and collaring the unusual, sewing up plotlines, stitching

TROPICAL DEPRESSION

TROPICAL DEPRESSION

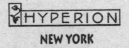

LAURENCE SHAMES

HYPERION

NEW YORK

ISBN 0-7868-8909-8

DESIGNED BY ELENA ERBER

First Mass Market Edition
10 9 8 7 6 5 4 3 2 1

for Marilyn, my wife—
absolutely, indisputably, once and for all, the best

In the writing of this book I have been immeasurably helped by a brilliant editor, a stellar agent, and vice versa. Hearty thanks to Brian DeFiore and Stuart Krichevsky, the kinds of allies that every writer dreams of having someday.

—L.S.

ONE

1

When Murray Zemelman, a.k.a. the Bra King, started up his car that morning, he had no clear idea whether he would go to work as usual, or sit there with the engine idling and the garage door tightly shut until he died. He was depressed, had been for several months. His mind had shriveled around its core of gloom like a drying apricot around its pit, and he saw no third alternative.

So he sat. He looked calmly through his windshield at the gardening tools put up for the winter, the rakes and saws hung exactingly on Peg-Board, his worthless second wife's golf bag suspended at a coquettish angle by its strap. The motor of his Lexus softly purred, nearly odorless exhaust turned bluish white in the chilly air. He breathed normally and told himself he wasn't choosing suicide, wasn't choosing anything. He was just sitting, numb, immobilized, gripped by an indifference so unruffled as to be easily mistaken for a state of grace.

Then, in a heartbeat, he was no longer indifferent. Anything but. Maybe it was just a final squirt of panic before the long oblivion. Maybe the Prozac, as dubious as vitamins in its effect these last few weeks, had suddenly kicked in.

Murray said aloud, "Schmuck! Schmuck, you fuckin' nuts?"

He reached for his zapper, flashed it at the garage door's electric eye. The wooden panels stretched, then started rolling upward, but not quite fast enough for Murray in his newfound rage to live. He threw the gearshift into reverse and stomped on the accelerator. Tires screeched on cold cement, the trunk caught the bottom of the lifting door. Varnished cedar splintered; champagne-colored paint scraped off the car; snaggled boards clawed at its metal roof. The bent garage door rose almost to the top of its track, then jammed, the mechanism whirred and whined like a Mixmaster bogged in icing.

Murray Zemelman, gasping and sweating on his driveway, opened his window and sucked greedily at the freezing air with its smells of pine and snow. He coughed, gave a dry and showy retch, mopped his clammy forehead. A shudder made him squirm against the leather seat, and when the long spasm had passed, he felt mysteriously light, unburdened. New. He felt as though a pinching iron helmet had been taken from his head and a grainy gray diffusing film swept clean from his eyes. He blinked against the sidearm brightness of a January sunrise; in his refreshed vision, the glare became a glow that caressed objects and displayed them proudly, like a spotlight that was everywhere at once.

Amazed, Murray looked at his house, looked at it as if he'd never seen it before. It was a nice house, a grand house even—big stone chimney, portico with columns—and in his sudden clarity he was able to acknowledge, not with sorrow but ecstasy, that he hated it. Yes! He hated every goddamn tile and dimmer switch and shingle. This was not the house's fault, he understood; but nor was it his. He'd worked his whole life to have a house like this; he'd paid through the nose to own it. By God, he was *allowed* to hate it. To hate the plaid-pants town of Short Hills, New Jersey, where it stood. To hate the dopey high-end gewgaws that cluttered up the living room. To hate the stupidly chosen second wife curled in bland, smug, already-fading beauty on her own side of the giant bed.

He hated all of it, and in the wake of the nasty and forbidden joy of admitting that, came a realization as buoyant as the feeling of flying in a dream: He didn't have to be there.

He didn't have to be there; he didn't have to go to work; he didn't have to kill himself. He remembered with surprise and awe that the world was big, and for the first time in what seemed like forever, he had a fresh idea.

He wheeled out of his driveway, burned rubber around a sooty snowbank, and headed for the Parkway south.

◆◆◆◆◆◆

He drove all day, he drove all night, giddy and relentless in his quest for warmth and ease and differentness.

At nine-thirty the next morning, he was draped across his steering wheel, dozing lightly in yellow sunshine cut into strips by the tendrils of a palm frond. His back ached, his jowls drooped, his hips and knees were locked in the shape of the seat, but he'd outdistanced I-95, barrelled to the final mile of U.S. 1. He'd made it to Key West.

By first light he'd found a real estate office called Paradise Properties. He'd parked his scratched-up Lexus at a bent meter and then contentedly passed out.

He was awakened now by a light tapping on his windshield.

He looked up to see a slightly built young man in blue-lensed sunglasses. The young man made his hands into a megaphone. "Looking for a place?"

"How'd ya know?" said Murray, rolling down the window.

"Jersey plates," the young man said, more softly. "Ya got a tie on. And, no offense, you're very pale." He held out a hand. "Joey Goldman. Come in when you're ready, we're putting up coffee."

Murray yawned, climbed out of the car, tried to

stretch but nothing stretched. He saw yellow flowers, flowers on a living tree in January. He sucked air that smelled of salt and iodine, air the same temperature as his face. He smiled tentatively, then dragged himself into the office.

Joey Goldman, at his desk now, regarded him. Joey had lived in Key West half a decade. He knew that almost everyone who came there, came there on vacation—and there was nothing duller in the world than a person on vacation. Some came to snorkel and drink. Others came to drink and fish. Some came to chase sex while drinking. Others just drank. But one visitor in a thousand, Joey had observed, probably more like one in ten thousand, was not a tourist but a refugee. Sometimes it was refugee as in fugitive. Sometimes it was refugee from a monster spouse or lover, or from a northern life that had finally hit the wall. Joey looked at the new arrival's houndlike bloodshot eyes, his kinky graying wild hair, his rumpled shirt and posture that somehow seemed exhausted and frenetic all at once. He decided that maybe the frazzled fellow was not there on vacation.

"So, Mr.—"

"Zemelman. Murray Zemelman."

"Some coffee, Mr. Zemelman?"

Murray nodded his thanks and an assistant brought over a cup for him.

Joey said, "What can I do for you?"

Murray held his java in both hands and gave a little slurp. "Place on the ocean."

"Onnee ocean," Joey said, "that'd have to be a condo. No rental houses onnee ocean."

"Condo's fine."

Joey cleared his throat. "What price range—"

"Someplace nice."

"You know the town?"

"Not well," said Murray. "I was here once, twelve, maybe fifteen years ago."

"Ah," said Joey.

"With my first wife," the Bra King volunteered.

"Ah. Well—"

"And yesterday I was thinking," Murray rambled. "I don't mean thinking like *trying* to think, I mean the thought just came to me, out of the blue, that maybe it was the last time I really had fun."

Joey riffled through his boxful of listings.

"The crazy things ya remember," Murray went on. "This old Spanish guy, big hairy birthmark on his cheek, like four feet tall. Had a big block of ice on a cart. Shaved it by hand, with a whaddycallit, a plane. Put it in a paper cone with mango syrup. Franny loved it. Cost fifteen cents."

Joey pulled out an index card. "You know where Smathers Beach is, Mr. Zemelman?"

Murray blinked himself back to the present. "By the airport, no?"

"Up that way," said Joey. "There's a condo there, the Paradiso."

" 'S'nice?"

"Very nice. Coupla former mayors live there. State senator lives there when he's not up at the capital."

Murray yawned.

"There's a penthouse available," Joey went on.

"Penthouse?" Murray said. "Like thirty stories up?"

"Like three stories up. We're not talkin' Miami. It's a little pricey—"

"On the ocean?"

"Across the road. We're not talkin' Boca. Three bedrooms. Three baths. Master suite has Jacuzzi—"

"Okay," Murray said.

"Okay what?

"Okay I'll take it."

"You don't wanna see it first?" said Joey.

Murray shrugged dismissively and reached into a pocket for his checkbook. "Company check okay?"

"Fine," said Joey. "It's five thousand a month and they'll want a month's security."

"I'll take three months for now," said Murray, and he wrote a check for twenty grand.

Joey took it and examined it briefly, discreetly. The company name rang a bell. "Hey, wait a second," he said. "Beauty-Breast, Inc. Murray Zemelman. I thought you looked familiar. The guy that does the ads, right? Late at night. Wit' the crown. The Bra King crown. Always wit' the women in their bras."

"*My* bras," Murray corrected softly.

"Dancin' with 'em," Joey remembered. "Bowling, playing volleyball—"

Murray nodded modestly.

"My favorite?" Joey said. "The opera one, the one

where all these women in their bras got spears and shields, and you come down, what're you wearin', a bathrobe, somethin'?—"

"Toga," said the Bra King. "I didn't know they aired down here."

"Me, I'm from New Yawk," said Joey. "Everybody here, they're from somewhere else." He opened a desk drawer, pawed his way through many sets of keys. "The Bra King," he muttered, "whaddya know . . . Okay, this is them. The square key, it's for the downstairs lock. The round one's for the penthouse. There's three buildings, like in a U around the pool. You want West. Got it?"

Murray took the keys and nodded.

Joey shook his hand, stole a final look at him, almost spoke, but realized it would be indiscreet to ask if they touched his hair up for TV.

2

Maybe it was Prozac, maybe it was glee. Was there a difference? Did it matter?

It didn't matter to Murray. Gleefully, he drove through the narrow streets of Old Town, his brain awash in juices that tickled, enzymes that made hair triggers of each synapse. Everything delighted him: bawdy clusters of coconuts dangling under skirts of fronds; purple bougainvillea that swallowed up white fences; the breath-damp air whizzing over his furry arm as it rested on the window frame. He wound his way to A-1A and clucked with pleasure at the sunshot green of the ocean, the green-tinged bottom of a distant cloud. By the time he found the Paradiso condo, his chest was tight, the unaccustomed elation strained his heart like unprepared-for exercise.

Still, his step was blithe as he moved to what he thought was the West Building of the complex and opened up the downstairs door. He got in the elevator, reveling in the naked lightness of traveling with nothing whatsoever, starting a new life without so much as a familiar coffee mug from the old. He rode to the third floor, went the wrong way down the corridor, then wheeled and found the penthouse. By a mix of filtered sunlight and flickering fluorescent, he tried his key in the door. It didn't work.

He withdrew it, tried it upside down. He went back to the first way. He finessed, he jiggled. He was stooped over the lock, one hand on the key and the other on the doorknob, when the door was suddenly, violently yanked open, pulling the Bra King halfway into someone else's unit.

Bewildered, guilty, feeling like a burglar in a dream, Murray Zemelman looked meekly up. He saw an Indian. A very angry Indian who was wearing a chamois vest with fringes and jabbing a thick finger back toward someone Murray couldn't see.

"Just forget about it," the Indian was saying. "No way you're gonna suck me into any of your greedy bullshit white-ass—"

"Tommy, Tommy," came a drawling and conciliating voice from behind a living room wall, "all I'm saying, I'm saying think about this opportunity."

"Opportunity my fuzzy red balls," said the Indian, and he turned to go. Only then did he seem to notice Murray, still half-crouched above the doorknob. For just an instant the two men met each other's eyes. The Indian's were very black and flat, so wide-spaced that they seemed to wrap around his temples; they turned down at the outside corners, gave him a look that was solemn, judging.

He hissed at the Bra King, "And you're a white asshole too." Then he pushed past him and was gone.

Murray stood there. He wasn't about to follow the Indian, and he didn't know what else to do.

After a moment, the mellow and conciliating voice turned bored and mordant and said, "The stupid savage didn't even close the door. Lock it, please, Pascal."

A muscular young man appeared in the foyer. He was wearing a hair net and a red kimono. He saw Murray standing there, rumpled and unshaven, fugitive and baffled, fraudulent key in hand, and said, "And just who the hell might you be?"

Murray had a sudden impulse to cry. What day was it, where was he, and just how exactly had he gotten there? "I'm very, very tired," he said. "I think I'm in the wrong place."

"I think that's obvious," said Pascal, who coaxed him, not gently, out the door.

◆◆◆◆◆◆

In his own apartment finally, his directions sorted out, the Bra King felt better, reassured by the sharp smell of a recent cleaning, layers of fresh towels on all the racks. He gave the place a cursory once-over, didn't really notice much. He hadn't come to Florida to sit indoors; he went onto the L-shaped balcony to suck the air and feel the sunshine and let the view nourish his resilience.

To the south—it *had* to be the south, he realized now—a parade of candy-colored convertibles streamed by on A1A; the trucked-in sand of Smathers Beach looked as moist and crumbly as the topping on a coffee cake. At his feet, the Paradiso's gracious quadrangle appeared a perfect map of the easy life of Florida. A big tiled pool shimmered a minty blue. Two tennis courts contributed a soothing geometry; a pair of cheery yellow flags waved above a putting green made of Astroturf.

Murray looked at tended plants, lounge chairs in neat rows: calming things. He told himself it would all be fine. And yet he paced. Fear of change, and loneliness, and weirdness, chafed against exhilaration. He needed to sleep; he couldn't sleep. Too much had happened; was happening. He had too much to say, too much that he could only now explain. A sort of emetic candor overtook him, he had to talk like he had to breathe. He dove into the living room to work the phone.

He sat on the edge of a huge sofa upholstered in a nautical stripe and called his second wife.

"Murray!" she said. "Where are you? I called work, I called the police. I was worried, Murray."

She didn't sound worried. In fact she sounded like she'd been placidly asleep until the phone rang.

God forbid that anything like madness, upheaval, death, or salvation should intrude on Taffy's beauty rest. God forbid that a shard of early light should violate her eyeshade, a snore or a fart or a garbage truck send vibrations past her earplugs.

"I'm in Key West," the Bra King said. "It's eighty-two degrees."

"Key West? Murray, are you out of—"

"Taffy, listen. It's over."

There was a pause. A muffled rustling of bed-clothes came through the phone. "What are you talking about, Murray? What's over?"

He looked past the parted curtains and open sliding door to effervescent sunlight. "This cocka-mamie deal we call a marriage. It's finished. Kaput. Finito."

"Murray, you're—"

"Happy. I'm happy."

A dubious silence at the Jersey end of the line.

"Taffy, allow me a spasm of honesty. Marrying you was the stupidest fuckin' thing I ever did in my entire life. No offense. I blame myself, not you. Fact is, start to finish, it had nothing to do with you. Why couldn't I just bang you on the desk like a normal human being? Once, and get it over with. Boss *shtupps* model. Happens every day, right? Zip up and get back to work. But no, for me it's the first infidelity, I have to make a big deal out of it, turn my whole life upside down. Why? Conscience, that's all. 'Cause if it was love, I wasn't such a turd for doing it. Except, Taff, let's face it, it wasn't love.

What we had, you and me, it was no big deal. Never was."

Again, a pause. Murray pictured her sweeping off the eyeshade, running a hand through the thick auburn hair that was part of what had seduced him half a dozen years ago.

"Murray," she said at last, "I'm gonna give you the benefit of the doubt. I'm gonna assume you're cuckoo. But if you're not, you son of a bitch, if you've got the faintest idea what you're saying, I am going to take you to the cleaners so bad—"

"Yes!" hissed Murray in a kind of Pyrrhic transport. "I want you to! Get a good lawyer, tell him how I took advantage of you just because you took your bra off in my office and wagged your bubbies in my face. Grab all you can. The house, it's yours. I never wanna see it again. Goo'bye."

He hung up, stared with wonder at the silent telephone, as if the instrument, and not himself, had done the talking. Truth. Flat-out, in-your-face directness—what a wild and intoxicating mystery. Where did it come from, this reckless truth, what was it made of?

He sprang up from the sofa, took a spin out to the balcony. When he got there the sun was just emerging from behind a small and fluffy cloud. The ocean twinkled, clean heat returned to the world, and absurdly, the Bra King took this as an omen. He scratched his head with gusto, was on top of things once more. He went back to the striped sofa, which was already taking on the potent feel of headquarters.

He called his office in the garment district of Manhattan, got his friend and number-two man, Leslie Kantor, on the line.

"Murray," Kantor said, "you okay? Taffy called last night. You didn't go home, you didn't come in—"

"I started to come in," the Bra King interrupted. "But the day got off to a really shitty start, so I said fuck it and retired."

"Excuse me?"

In the distance, very soft, the sound of swatted tennis balls.

"Retired, Les. Resigned. Quit. I'm in Key West. Palm trees. Coconuts."

The line went silent save for the faint scream of tearing paper. Murray had known Les Kantor for a lot of years, knew him like a book. He knew Les had retrieved his pack of Tums from his left-hand trousers pocket and was trimming down the wrapper with a perfect thumbnail. "Coconuts," he murmured at last.

"Coconuts, Les. And I'm divorcing Taffy."

"Murray, you spoken with Max?"

Max Lowenstein was Murray's psychiatrist.

"He's next on my list," the Bra King said.

"Maybe he should be first on your list."

An affectionate singsong came into Murray's voice. "Les. *Les*. You're beautiful, bubbala. So reasonable. So levelheaded. This is why I feel perfectly at peace leaving you to run things."

"I don't wanna run things. Murray, you don't just walk away like that. Milan's coming up. The big promotion with Bloomie's—"

"I don't care."

"You have to care," said Kantor.

"This is where you're wrong," said Murray. "It's where I was wrong till yesterday."

More Tums went into Leslie Kantor's mouth, the Bra King heard them clatter softly against his high-priced teeth. Then the partner said, "So Murray, what'll you do down there?"

Not until the question was asked did the Bra King realize he had no idea what he would do. He knew *where* he would do, and that was as far as he'd gotten. "I guess for awhile I'll do nothing."

"I've known you a long time," said his friend. "You're incapable of doing nothing."

Murray couldn't deny it. His only response was to chew a fingernail.

"Go fishing," Kantor suggested.

"Fishing?"

"It's as close as you can come to doing nothing and still be doing something."

"Les, I've never gone fishing in my life."

"All the better. You'll have something new to learn."

"Great," said the Bra King, "a fifty-three-year-old *shmegeggi* with a hook in his eye."

"Try it. It's very soothing. And Murray, hey, what about the ads?"

On the striped sofa in his penthouse living room, Murray Zemelman gave a little smile. He could not deny that he still liked the idea of wearing the Bra King crown, sashaying like Bert Parks among the ranks of pouting shiksas in their push-em-ups. "The ads," he said, "we'll see. If my public demands it, maybe I'll still do the ads."

"Good. You'll go fishing, you'll do the ads, when you're ready, you'll come back. In the meantime, talk to Max. Soon. Please, Murray."

"Okay, okay," the Bra King said. "I'm calling him right now."

3

Just then, some twenty feet from the southernmost point in the continental United States, a man named Tommy Tarpon, still agitated from a conversation earlier that morning, was setting up his seashells, which were displayed on a homemade plywood cart that he towed behind his ancient bicycle. His wares arranged, he sat down on a blue plastic milk crate, his back against the fence that cordoned off U.S. Navy property. Sunlight glared off the ocean, but Tommy was shaded by an enormous banyan tree whose unearthly dangling roots were lifting up the sidewalk. He sat there and waited for customers.

Some minutes later, he pretended not to watch as an oldish tourist with a green visor and red knees approached the cart of shells and nonchalantly slipped two fingers into the sunwarmed opalescent orifice of a queen helmet.

"That's how you can tell when they're sexually mature," said Tommy, when the tourist was in there two knuckles deep. "When the labium gets pink and thick like that."

Caught, the man with red knees quickly swept his hand behind his back. Tommy had seen it again and again. Women always held the shells up to their ear to hear the ocean; men always wanted to finger them, first thing. The old tourist moved to change the subject. "Is it local?"

"You bet it's local," Tommy said. "Gathered by Indians near Cape Sable."

"Is that so? How much ya want for it?"

"Seven dollars."

The tourist took some time to think it over. He peered at the flat ocean, glanced at a knot of Asians photographing each other in front of the marker that said HAVANA-90 MILES. "You a Seminole?" he said at last.

Tommy crossed his arms against his chest, put on a very Indian expression, said nothing.

"I'll give ya six bucks," said the tourist.

Tommy tugged lightly at the fringes of his chamois vest. "Eight," he said.

"You just said seven."

"Have it your way. Seven."

The tourist beamed. Now he was having fun. Haggling with a real live Indian. "Clever," he said.

Tommy smiled pleasantly, finished the thought for him. "For a Redskin. Seven bucks."

The tourist hesitated. A new concern had seized him. Did he really want a big heavy fragile seashell? He had a drive to Fort Lauderdale and four days in Orlando before flying home to Michigan. Carry a shell all that way only to get back home and find it chipped? "I'll think about it."

"Big decision," Tommy said, and he scratched his back against the Navy fence as the tourist wandered off on pink and scrawny legs.

◆ ◆ ◆ ◆ ◆ ◆

Murray had meant to call his shrink right then, but somehow he didn't do it.

He was seized by a sudden urge to go for a walk instead, smell the chlorine in the pool. Besides, by now he could no longer hide it from himself that his high spirits were extremely fragile, less a part of him than an overlay, a cheery suit of clothes that could at any moment detach itself and walk away without him. Max Lowenstein—sober, probing Max—would discover that in about ten seconds. And Murray was not so eager to have it pointed out.

So he swept off his tie, unbuttoned the top two buttons of his rumpled shirt, and rode the elevator downstairs to the pool.

He walked the perimeter of the courtyard, brushed past red and pink hibiscus in big clay pots. He watched a fat man sink an eight-footer on the putting green. Along the row of lounges, he saw slender fellows lying side by side in tiny bathing suits, women facedown with their tops undone, dollops of bosom swelling at their sides.

Murray smiled at everyone as he floated past, now and then somebody briefly smiled back. But no one smiled first, everyone seemed too absorbed in paperbacks or backgammon or cancerous communion with the sun, and by the time Murray completed his circuit, he was feeling isolated, apprehensive. His steps got heavy, it was like the instant when an airplane drops its flaps and you understand abruptly that gravity has been there all the while. For a long moment he stood still, couldn't decide which way to move his feet. He choked down panic, told himself this was not depression socking in again, just an understandable fatigue, a temporary winding down that, after all, was part of arriving someplace new.

Then he heard a soft gruff voice behind him. "First day here?"

He turned to see an old man sitting in the shade of a metal umbrella that was painted like a daisy. He was wearing a canary yellow linen shirt with topaz-colored placket and collar; oddly, he seemed to have a moth-eaten muff in his lap. Then the muff lifted up its knobby head and revealed itself to be an ancient pale chihuahua, with drooping whiskers and a scaly nose and milky eyes.

Murray said, "How could you tell?"

"For starters, ya got pants on," the old man said. "And you're curious. I seen the way ya look at people."

Murray, a little guilty, cleared his throat.

"Place like this," the old man went on, "what happens is people stop being curious. Too much coming and going. Transients. People decide, hey, this guy's only here a week, why bother gettin' to know 'im? The year-rounders, they figure these seasonal people, they dump us inna summer, why bother makin' friends? But my question, where d'ya draw the line? Everybody dumps everybody when they die, so this means ya don't bother makin' friends wit' nobody? Siddown."

For a second Murray was paralyzed by thankfulness. To have someone to sit with, this was no small thing. He coaxed his feet toward a metal chair, felt the heat of it against his butt, took a moment to study his companion. The old man's face was long and thin, his eyes were crinkly but clear and bright as marbles, he had neatly combed white hair that flashed with glints of pink and bronze.

"Bert's the name," the old man said, holding out a gnarled and spotted hand. "Bert d'Ambrosia."

"Murray Zemelman."

"New Yawka, right?"

"How'd ya know?"

"The shoes. Beautiful loafers like that, Italian I bet, you'd only find 'em New Yawk or California. And California, excuse me for sayin' this, ya'd look a little fitter."

"Very observant," Murray said.

"Hell else I got ta do? So Murray, y'on vacation?"

The Bra King didn't answer right away. He scratched his head. He opened his mouth. He giggled, not with mirth but freedom. He was in a transient place where there was not the slightest reason not to tell the simple naked truth. "Actually," he blurted, "I left my wife and quit my business yesterday."

Unruffled, the old man stroked his chihuahua. The chihuahua blinked and wheezed, short white dog hairs fluttered onto Bert's Bermuda shorts. "Ah, so you're havin' a whaddyacallit, a midlife crisis."

Murray waved that idea away. "Nah, I had that one already. That's when I left my first wife. Bought a sports car. Got tennis elbow shifting. It was stupid anyway. Leaving the wife, I mean. Really stupid. But this is something different. This one, I don't think it has a name."

Water surged along the edges of the pool, made a sound like a cat lapping milk. Bert pursed his lips and nodded. "Good. I don't like it the way everything, they give it a name, it's like it isn't yours no more. Some things, okay, I guess they gotta have a name. Haht attack. Diabetes. But stuff inside ya head? I don't see where alla that, it has to have a name."

For this Murray had no comeback, so he just looked out at the palms and the sky. The sun was getting higher, and Bert moved his chair a few inches to keep his napping dog out of the sun. Then he said, "Ya play poker, gin rummy, anything like that?"

Murray nodded that he did. Bert gestured toward a screened gazebo set back from the pool. Even empty it seemed to ring with the easy congeniality of card games, seemed fragrant with the oily richness of potato chips.

"We need a hand sometime, I'll let ya know," said Bert, and Murray nearly panted with the hope of things to do. "What apartment y'in?"

The Bra King pointed at the West Building and said, without false modesty, "The penthouse."

"Whaddya know," said Bert. "Guy who plays sometimes has the East Penthouse. Politician. LaRue's his name."

"Ah," said Murray, "I went into his place by accident this morning. Got kicked out by a geek in a hair net after being called an asshole by a screaming Indian."

The old man calmly stroked his dog. "Feather or dot?"

"Hm?" said Murray. "Ya know. Indian. American Indian. Native American, whatever they like to be called these days."

"In costume?"

"Costume?"

"Yeah. Ya know, Tonto vest, ponytail?"

"Yeah," said Murray. "That's him."

"That's Tommy," said Bert. "Sells shells. Makes himself look like an Indian for the tourists."

"Now I'm confused," said Murray. "Are you saying the man's an Indian or are you saying the man is not an Indian?"

"He's an Indian," said Bert. "I'm sayin' he's an Indian. But I'm sayin' he makes himself more like an Indian than an Indian really is, because this is the way the stupid tourists want an Indian ta look. *Capeesh?* I wonder what he was doin' at LaRue's."

"I'm surprised you don't know," said Murray.

"Why should I know?"

"You seem to know everything else."

"I know what I see," said Bert. "I know what people tell me. More'n this, I don't know." He put the ghostly chihuahua on the table, where it did a stiff-legged pirouette, its paws clicking dryly on the metal surface. Then he labored upward from his chair. "You'll excuse me, Murray, I gotta go upstairs and give the stupid dog a pill."

Slow but straight, he walked away. Murray closed his eyes a moment and listened to the watery and rustly sounds of Florida.

4

As the Bra King was trudging back up to the West Penthouse, the curtains of the East Penthouse were being tightly drawn against the high and candid midday light. The young man called Pascal—senator Barney LaRue's houseboy, secretary, and masseur—out of his kimono now and clad in purple harem pants, was dusting chairs, mixing drinks, squaring papers on his patron's desk, doing all the little things that make a meeting work.

The senator was receiving a visitor, a large contributor to his campaigns, but one whose name would never appear on donor lists and whose support, for the good of all concerned, would forever be disclaimed.

"Charlie," he was saying to this visitor, in his lush

unhurried voice. "I'm looking out for your interests. Never doubt I'm doing that."

They were sitting in his study. Recessed fixtures threw a soft glow that mostly lit up photos of Barney LaRue shaking hands with people more famous than himself—visiting dignitaries, movie stars. In every picture his blandly handsome face—too-neat silver hair, small and somewhat pointy nose, deep-set pale blue eyes—was locked in the same relentless smile, the small teeth uniform as mah-jongg tiles.

His guest sipped slowly from a glass of bourbon. "Did I say anything about doubting you, Bahney? Ya got a guilty conscience, wha'? All I said, I said a fucking hundred grand has gone from me ta you and so far I've seen dick on my investment."

The politician leaned suavely forward on well-tanned elbows. "But Charlie, that's how investments are. Sometimes they pay off, sometimes they don't."

"Mine pay off," the visitor said. He was a small man with squeezed-together features and sacs the color of liver beneath his eyes. He wore a silver jacket with a zipper, the kind of jacket race-car drivers wear.

"Charlie," said the senator, touching rum to his lips. "I promised you I'd work night and day for that bill. I never promised it would pass. And it won't pass. Sad but true. I've twisted arms, I've traded favors. They won't do it. Political reality. The churches. The tracks. This crazy coalition. Casino gambling—it isn't going to happen, Charlie."

The guest turned in his chair, addressed a massive presence that hovered a discreet distance away. Charlie Ponte did not go anyplace alone, and today his chaperone was a guy named Bruno, who had a pitted face and a frame like something for industrial use. "All that money," the boss said to his goon, "and these gutless bastards can't even pass a fucking bill."

Bruno frowned, shook his head, twirled a big globe like he might here and there punch in a continent.

Surly now, slow-burning, Ponte turned back to his host. "So you're telling me I'm fucked on that. Zat the end'a the story? You get a hundred grand and I get a lecture on politics?"

LaRue lifted up his silver eyebrows, spoke with the desperate and mendacious cheer of a salesman who didn't have what you wanted but was confident that you could be persuaded you wanted something else. "I have another idea for you. I've been working on it, free of charge."

"You're a whore, Bahney. You don't do nothin' free a charge."

The politician let that pass, leaned back in his chair. "Charlie, you familiar with the Native American Reserved Harvesting Act of 1978?"

The little mobster just glared at him, brooded about his hundred grand.

"I opposed it," LaRue went on. "Pansy liberals passed it anyway. It gives the Indians a monopoly on gathering and selling certain kinds of seashells."

"Fuck I care about seashells?" Ponte said. "Don't waste my—"

"Charlie, Charlie. Have some vision. This isn't about seashells. It's about prime retail space on Duval Street."

Ponte listened harder.

"I believe it would be useful to you to control an enterprise through which certain embarrassing-to-explain earnings might be filtered."

The mobster cooled a hot hand against his bourbon glass.

"There's an Indian in town," LaRue went on. "Sells shells on the street. Has for years. I've been explaining to him the advantages of joining forces with a wealthy backer. Opening a store. Maybe a chain of stores. The IRS, the FBI, Charlie—they're not likely to look too hard at the business of a poor downtrodden Indian. They make trouble for him, it's bad PR."

"And the Indian?" Ponte said. "He wants to do business?"

The politician pressed his thin lips together. "Not so far," he admitted. "He doesn't seem to trust me."

"Give 'im that at least."

"He'll come around," LaRue said confidently. "It just might take some time, some persuading."

Ponte glanced over at Bruno. Bruno rocked from foot to foot, cracked the joints on fingers thick as pickles.

"Not that kind of persuading," said LaRue. "Unless, of course, it's necessary. I mean logic. Reason. Having his street-vendor's license yanked."

That one Ponte liked. His upper lip pulled back, showing jagged pointy teeth. "You can do that, Bahney?"

"Maybe," said the politician. "It's city, not state. But what's that quaint saying you people have? One hand washes the other."

Ponte sipped bourbon, felt placated until he thought again of his hundred-thousand-dollar payoff, saw the neatly bundled bills flying out the window. "And how long is this persuading gonna take?"

LaRue put on that mah-jongg smile, shrugged. "He's a stubborn man."

"So am I," said Ponte, rising from the chair that Bruno swiftly moved to hold for him. "Remember that. You owe me some results."

◆◆◆◆◆◆

Shirtless now, hunkered on the sofa with the nautical stripe, Murray cradled the phone against his shoulder and related to his shrink, in great detail, the saga of the past thirty hours of his life. At the close of the story, Max Lowenstein came forth with a soft and perhaps involuntary "*Oy.*"

"*Oy?*" protested Murray. "What *oy?* Max, for months you've been telling me I'm depressed, I'm in a rut, I should do something for myself—"

"But these decisions, Murray, they're so abrupt, so radical."

"Rebirth is radical, Max—what could I tell ya? You should be happy for me, I feel alive again. Believe me, everything's under control."

"*Oy,*" the doctor said again, this time more emphatically. *Everything's under control.* That was classic Prozac-speak. It was what patients tended to say in that sometimes brief euphoric moment after the depression had lifted and just as they were poised to go manically careening like a Frisbee in a gale. *Everything's under control* they said, then went out into traffic and started handing out hundred-dollar bills. *Everything's under control*, then they climbed onto the sills of thirtieth-story windows because such great bliss could surely fly. "Murray, have you found a doctor down there?"

"I just got here, I've barely found the bathroom—"

"You need monitoring, Murray. The medication, it can be volatile."

The Bra King paused and swallowed. Something tasted off in his saliva, it had the stony taste of sudden fear. "Max, you trying to scare me, wha'?"

"I'm only trying to keep you on track. In touch."

Murray's shoulders slumped. It was disheartening to have somebody tell you you were not as happy as you thought you were, and to know in your heart he was right. The Bra King looked through the open doors to the rectangle of sunshine beyond the balcony. The light was glary, over-bright, colors burned off into scorching white just as, hardly more than a day before, they had murked and muddied into gray. For one bleak moment Murray believed that things would never, ever find their balance, never, ever be the way they ought to be.

His shrink's soft voice broke the gloomy silence. "What will you do there? Do you have friends, family, activities?"

Thanks to Les Kantor, Murray now had an answer to this question. "I'm gonna fish."

"Fish?"

"Yeah, fish. Go fishing."

The psychiatrist paused, Murray could see his hand ascending toward his bearded chin. "That's interesting. In all the years I've known you, Murray, I don't think you've ever once mentioned an outdoor activity."

"I sell bras, Max. Bras are, like, an indoor activity."

Another silence. Then: "I have an idea. Visualize something for me, Murray. Your finger on the fishing line, the fishing line going in the water. See it?"

Murray closed his eyes. "I see it. I see it."

"When you were depressed," said Max Lowenstein, "you didn't have enough voltage in your brain. Now I'm concerned you're having a little bit too much. The fishing line, it's going to be your ground wire, it's going to carry off the excess. You see what I'm saying?"

Murray pictured little lightning bolts throbbing in his head then coursing down his arm, escaping through his index finger and pulsing along his fishing line, sizzling softly as they flashed into the ocean and illuminated snapshots of big-eyed incandescent fish. "I see it, Max," he murmured. "I like it."

"Good," said the psychiatrist, "good." His voice dropped off to a slurred mesmeric whisper that was the perfect background music for his patient's deep fatigue. "Fish, Murray. And let that extra electricity escape into the ocean. And stay in touch, let me hear how you're doing."

Murray only nodded. His eyes were still closed and he forgot that he was on the phone. Blindly, he managed to hang up, and in seconds he was asleep there on the sofa, dreaming of tiny lightning bolts hissing like matches doused in a shallow sea crammed full of finned and smiling creatures.

5

On White Street Pier, a Spanish guy held a chicken head by its still-oozing neck, put it in a crab trap. A pelican stood on the rail between two fishermen, looking for a handout of bait or guts. An old man in a captain's hat squinted at the crisp horizon and took readings with a sextant.

Uneasily, Murray walked among them, his brand-new tackle box in one hand, his brand-new fishing rod in the other, and tried to look like he belonged. He found a place with some elbow room on either side of him, leaned his rod against the railing, and tried to figure out what the hell to do next.

This fishing business—he wasn't sure it was such a hot idea, but then again, it had already saved him from some anguish. He'd woken from a couple hours' sleep, dry-mouthed, barely knowing where he was. The cobwebs blew away, and behind them there was mania simmering like an empty stomach, and Murray had nothing to feed it, nothing to do. Thank God he thought of fishing, and the notion, for the moment, had given him purpose and a destination. He'd got in the scratched-up car, found a tackle store. He'd talked to a salesman, spent some money, got a bunch of fuchsia leadheads and yellow tubes and things with little feather skirts and painted happy faces. Now he was here, a beautiful place, the sun going down in back of sailboats, schooners; people around, a local feel, some action. If only he could figure out how to open the clip the salesman had tied on for him . . .

He was going cross-eyed trying to dissect the logic of the tiny mechanism, when he heard a voice, a not at all friendly voice, say: "You're standing in my spot."

He looked up to see that morning's pissed-off Indian, sitting on a bicycle, supporting himself with a thick-wristed rosewood hand against the rail. For an instant the Indian didn't seem to remember Murray, then it seemed he did, and his gaze got even stonier.

Meekly, Murray met his eyes and felt the baffled misery of the newcomer who doesn't know the rules and is afflicted at every moment by the nauseating fear that he will make some irreparable gaffe and spoil forever his chance of being welcomed. "I'm sorry," he said. "I didn't know. I'll move."

"Don't move," said the Indian. "There's no reason

you should move. I just want you to know, the spot you're in, that's been my spot for years."

Murray looked abjectly at his feet, then he looked back at the Indian, at his barrel chest and parted-in-the-middle hair. The Indian's bicycle had high handlebars, and attached to its back axle was what seemed to be a homemade cart loaded up with seashells. "Look," the Bra King said at last, "I'm happy to slide over."

"No," said the Indian. "I don't want any favors from friends of LaRue." And before Murray could answer, he stood on his pedals, rode another fifteen feet, dismounted.

Belatedly a synapse fired, Murray said, "Hey wait a second. This LaRue—I've never even met the man."

The Indian spat in the ocean. Then he started opening various compartments in his cart. From one compartment came a six-pack of Old Milwaukee. From another came a telescoping rod, a yellow bait pail, a casting net sewn up here and there with black and navy thread. He popped a beer, swilled half of it. He leaned over the railing, dipped the pail, filled it up with water.

Murray managed to open his clip. He leaned over his bright green tackle box, looked at all his silly lures, picked the silliest one and went to put it on. He hooked himself in a bad place on his thumb, a line of black blood appeared beneath the nail. He sucked it, then surprised himself by saying in the Indian's direction, "Look, I was lost this morning. I was lost, and you called me an asshole. No hard feelings, I guess you got troubles of your own. But look at it my way: I just get here, all I'm trying to do is find my apartment, some guy I've never seen before is calling me an asshole. Is this nice?"

The Indian didn't answer, got ready to throw his net. He put the end of the retrieving cord between his teeth, draped the nylon mesh across his fists and coaxed it into evenness like a baker finessing pizza dough. He drew a deep breath in, coiled his body like a discus thrower, uncoiled like a watchspring, and sent the net spinning, twirling, unfurling toward the water. Its weighted edges stretched it flat and round, it eased down like a landing bird, then settled softer than a fallen leaf onto the green surface.

Murray didn't know squat about fishing, but mastery was a thing unto itself, recognizable no matter what it was attached to. The perfection of the throw etched itself into his yeasty brain and he heard himself saying, "Jesus, Tommy, the way you did that, that was beautiful."

The Indian looked at him, somber, judging, and suspicious. "You've never met LaRue? How the fuck you know my name?"

Murray went to cast. He forgot to open the bail on the reel. The lure shot forward then quickly twanged back, it slammed into the metal railing and made an ugly clanging sound. "Your name," he said, "I hear it everywhere I go. First this morning. Then I was talking to Bert—ya know, old man with the little dog?"

The Indian's net was settling silently to the bottom. He was sitting on a plastic milk crate, finishing his beer. Very briefly, an expression almost like approval stole across his features. "Bert's okay," he said. "Hardly white at all."

Murray tried to cast again. This time he remembered the bail but forgot to hold the line down with his finger. The lure dribbled past his shoulder blade and hooked itself over the back of his Italian loafer. "That's a strange compliment."

"Not if you're an Indian, it isn't."

Tommy stood, gathered in his net with its writhing catch of pinfish. Tiny silver things with a smear of yellow along their backbones and a look of blame in their glassy eyes, they flopped in horrible displacement on the pavement. The red man gathered them up, perhaps a dozen and a half, and threw them in the pail.

Murray said, "So you really don't like white people?"

The Indian hooked a little fish beneath the backbone, cast it smoothly out toward the low and pulsing sun. "What's to like?" he said. He sat down on his crate.

Murray thought the question over, could not come up with a compelling answer. Instead, he said, "Me, I'm Jewish."

The Indian flashed him a look that very clearly said *Who gives a shit?*

Murray, concentrating fiercely, his tongue sticking out the corner of his mouth, cast again. He did it right this time. The lure arced away, flew like a tiny satellite toward the open ocean, and just kept going. Maybe he hadn't closed the clip right after all. "Some people say Jews and Indians are closely related. Some people say Indians are the lost tribes of Israel."

The Indian—compact, athletic, reticent—looked at the Bra King—ample, chatty, and a klutz. "I doubt it."

Murray bent to get a fresh lure from his tackle box.

The Indian cracked another beer, looked out toward the sun that was now as pinched and orange as a tangerine. Suddenly his rod bent double, began to twitch spasmodically. Without undue haste, he got up from his crate to fight. The reel screamed, the taut line sang as the light breeze blew past it, shaken droplets made fast rainbows. The Indian hauled and cranked, bowed and tugged and cranked some more, and at length, an eight-pound fish came over the rail, glinting silver in the sun and flapping like a flag.

The beauty of the fish, the stunning unlikelihood of someone catching it, knocked down all the rules, and Murray found himself standing close to Tommy Tarpon. "God Almighty," said the novice. "What's it called?"

"Snook," said the Indian, lowering the creature to the arid foreign ground.

"Schnook?"

"Snook. Snook." The Indian placed one foot on the fish's tail and mercifully brained it with the butt of his rod. "Good eatin'."

He crouched and worked the hook out of the

fish's lip. Catching dinner seemed to make him almost talkative. He frowned toward Murray's candy-green tackle box. "They won't take a lure when there's so much bait in the water."

"No?" the Bra King said. He rubbed his unshaved chin, frowned at his chartreuse plugs, his fruit-scented jelly worms. "Then why'd I buy all this crap?"

The Indian picked the fish up by its gill plate, said nothing for a moment. An odd change came over his face. His downturned eyes went from somber to sly, his severe mouth curled facetiously, almost urbanely, at the corners. "I don't think you want an answer to that."

Murray thought that over then answered the question himself. " 'Cause I'm a schmuck."

"Snook," said the Indian, and he gathered up his gear so he could bicycle home and eat his catch while it was good and fresh.

6

"Ah," said Bert, looking at his watch while petting his drowsy chihuahua with the other hand. "You're one a the reliable ones."

The Bra King shrugged, sat down in a hot chair near the daisy-shaped umbrella. "Used to having a routine."

"Routine," the old man echoed. "Good for the mind, good for the bowels. So whatcha been up to?"

Murray smiled ruefully, glanced across the pool. The truth was that what he'd been up to, was frantically looking for things to do. Awake at dawn, brain buzzing. To County Beach for breakfast. Duval Street for early shopping: shorts, sandals, tank tops he doubted he'd ever have the gall to wear. "Went fishing yesterday," he said.

"Catch anything?"

Murray snorted. "I ran into that Indian again."

"Loves ta fish," said Bert.

"Strange guy," Murray said.

"Bitter." The old man stroked his dog, absently brushed dog hairs from the front of his kelly-green silk pullover. "I like that in a person, bitterness. Don't envy it—makes life hard. But I respect it. Better'n this smiling bullshit like everything is hunky-dory."

Murray said nothing, looked out toward the ocean where a smudge of a freighter was riding up the Gulf Stream.

"He talk to ya?" Bert resumed.

"He talks like he's paying by the syllable," said Murray.

"Usually," Bert said. "But every now and then, ya catch it right, he talks a blue streak, like he's been storin' it up, it just comes gushin' out. I remember one time, few years ago, I got 'im in a long talk about names. About how Indian names, they mean somethin'. Tommy Tarpon—guy loves ta fish. Eddie Eagle—he's got great eyes. Sarah Bigheart, she takes care a people. White people's names— whadda they mean? Joe Mahoney—fuck does that tell ya about Joe Mahoney?"

Murray had no answer. Bert didn't need one.

"Me, my neighborhood," he went on, "we gave guys names. Guy loved eggs, we called him Benny Eggs. That way ya could tell 'im from Bald Benny. Tough Tony. Big Tuna. These are names that tell ya somethin'. My nickname, it was Bert the Shirt. On accounta my style, my habbadashery. Tells ya somethin'. Practically like Indians, am I right?"

Murray nodded. Tough Tony? Big Tuna? With the mild and woozy acceptance of the tropics, he was coming to realize that the first person to show kindness to him here in Florida was almost certainly a mafioso.

"Back when I was a kid," the old man rambled on, "there was Jewish gangsters, they had great names too. Guy put a speakeasy in a potato field, they called 'im Potatoes Kaufman. Longy Zwillman. Guy had a *schwantz* on 'im, t'ree families could hang laundry on it. Yeah. Y'innerested in poker later? Six-thirty. I think we need a hand."

◆◆◆◆◆◆

Six-thirty, Murray thought. Six-thirty, and he would have something to do. He could eat pretzels, stack quarters, shuffle cards. For several hours starting at six-thirty, the burden of gapping time would be lifted from his nervous shoulders.

Meanwhile, he caught a little sun. When his skin started feeling crinkly he retreated to the penthouse. He spent awhile walking aimlessly from room to furnished room. He sat on all the beds, peeked in all the closets as though expecting to find some exciting dirty secret. He thought of trying out the Jacuzzi in his enormous bathtub but didn't feel like getting wet just then. He paced, he looked in cupboards; time dragged, solitude weighed, and by the daintiest increments he came to understand that he was going to call his wife.

He still thought of her that way: his wife. Taffy had never been the wife but always the *second* wife, and the extra word subtracted from the title, made it suspect, like putting it in quotes. The wife had always been Franny. Even though he'd dumped her more than half a decade ago. Even though she hated his guts.

He found himself sitting on the striped sofa, the telephone at his sunburned elbow.

She didn't want him to call, she'd been quite clear on that. They had no children. She'd taken her divorce settlement in one lump sum, wanting no reason to stay in touch. They hadn't spoken since two, three years before, when Murray thought he was having a heart attack and called to say goodbye. The following day he'd called again to tell her it was heartburn. Franny had sounded only mildly relieved.

"In Sarasota, please," the Bra King heard himself saying. "A number for Frances Zemelman."

The line went silent for a moment. Murray looked past his balcony at the gleaming rectangle of sky and water. Then the operator told him she could find no listing under Frances Zemelman.

The news was one of those small sharp disappointments that bypasses the brain and instantly deflates the gut. Then Murray came back to the present, which was the deeper past of Franny's maiden name. "Frances Rudin, I mean."

A computer voice droned out the number.

Murray sprang up from the sofa, sat back down again, crossed his legs, uncrossed them, dialed. His pulse was racing. It vaguely dawned on him that his nervousness was absurd, but still, his heart hammered like that of a pimply teenager asking for a date.

His wife picked up on the third ring and said hello.

"Franny. Guess who this is?" He knew it was an asshole way to start a conversation; it was his nervousness that made him do it.

"Murray," she said. She said it like his name was some unserious but bothersome disease, like common diarrhea.

"I'm in Florida, Franny. I'm in Key West."

His wife made no reply. She was standing in her garden, a cordless phone cradled on her shoulder. She'd been working on a watercolor of spiky philodendrons. Now she watched the paint dry in the sun. It was only a so-so picture; Franny knew that and didn't mind. She was an amateur and liked it that way. She'd moved to Florida, in fact, to be an amateur, to wear gauzy cotton smocks and Tahitian-looking head-wraps and flowing colorful dresses with sandals. She ate health food, attended openings and charity events, wrote letters to congressmen, gave money to liberal and environmental causes. She dated sometimes and had taken the occasional suitor to her bed. But she was more or less content alone, painting watercolors, going to stretch class, meeting with her book club to discuss long novels.

"Franny, listen," Murray resumed, "a lot is going on with me, I thought you oughta know. I've quit the business. I've left Taffy."

"What took you so long?"

The Bra King nestled backwards on the sofa, buoyed by pillows and his wife's throaty sarcasm. "I lost some time to a bad depression."

"Murray, you indulge your moods too much. Like everything else."

"Indulgence?" said the Bra King. "This is no indulgence, Franny. I'm on Prozac."

If the statement was made for shock value, it failed entirely.

"Half the people I know are on Prozac," Franny said. "It's like the perfect Gulf Coast breakfast: Prozac and prunes."

Murray chortled softly. "Ah," he said. "Same old Franny."

This nettled his ex. "No," she said, "*not* the same old Franny. Franny has changed. Which, if you think about it, Murray, is really kind of funny. I never looked for change. Maybe I should have, but I never felt the need. *You're* the one with the big talk about change, with your midlife crisis, your dopey shiksa. But what did you change, Murray? The person you slept with. That's it. Same work. Same friends. Same attitude. My life, you turn upside down. Your own life, you really didn't have the nerve to change at all."

"So I'm a little slow," said Murray. "I'm changing now."

There was something in the way he said it that surprised his former wife. She paused, then sat down in a garden chair and tried with half-success to coax her voice to a less combative tone. "Well good for you," she said.

Murray kicked his shoes off, lay back with his wife's voice as though with her imperfect and marvelously familiar flesh. "Franny," he said. "You hate me, Franny?"

"I don't think about it very often. Not anymore."

"I do," Murray said. "I think about it all the time. I think about how screwing up our marriage is the dumbest thing I ever did. Dumb. Brainless. Wimpy. Idiotic . . ."

His wife seemed content to let him continue.

". . . Weak-willed. Childish. Mediocre . . . Franny, I'm mopping the floor with my tongue. What more do you want?"

"For you to get splinters," she said.

"Splinters," he repeated, and gave his heavy head a shake. "Ya know, what happened with us, Franny, I swear to God not a day goes by I don't kick myself innee ass about it."

His wife didn't answer for a moment, and when she did, her tone was not accusing, wasn't biting, was simply neutral around a core of disappointment. "That's just another of your self-indulgences," she said. "What good does it do?"

Murray thought that over. He exhaled loudly and his high spirits along with half his hopes seemed to fly away on the breath. "No good, I guess. No good at all . . . But Franny, I'm in Florida now, it's practically like we're neighbors. I thought it would be nice if we could see each other sometime."

"The prospect doesn't excite me," said his wife.

"Talk, at least?" coaxed Murray. "Like now? I apologize, you tell me off—"

His wife gave just the slightest laugh and the Bra King's morale went through the roof.

"I tell you you're wonderful," he rattled on, "you tell me I'm the lowest of the low . . . Can I call you, Franny?"

In her garden full of antheria and orchids, the ex-wife bit her lip, hesitated. "Free country," she said at last. "You have the number."

Murray closed his eyes as if to lock the perfect moment in. "You'll talk to me?" he said. "I'll call. I'll talk to you, you'll talk to me, we'll talk. Like human beings talking. Great, Franny. We'll talk again, the way we used to talk. Goo'bye."

He hung up, stood, threw himself backwards, spread-eagled, on the sofa. Bliss! His wife wanted him to call. Okay, she hadn't said so in as many words, but close enough; she wasn't having her number changed, she wasn't seeking an injunction.

Encouraged out of all proportion, he went out onto his balcony, let some of his excess glee seep out in the open air. He looked down at the pool, gave everyone who swam or sunbathed there his silent benediction. He looked around the courtyard, across to the beach, blessed every stone and lounge chair of the state of Florida, the place his wife lived, where he lived now, a patient and forgiving state where lives could be rethought, revised, perhaps even repaired.

7

By six-thirty his euphoria had drained him, left him wrung out, slaphappy.

He crossed the dusky courtyard, the air druggy with lingering lotions and exhausted flowers crinkling up like figs. The unruffled pool reflected a velvet sky tinged yellow in the west; darkening palms were giving up their last reserves of depth and color before becoming black cutouts for the night.

He entered the gazebo, saw Bert cradling his twitching chihuahua against the lucky shirt he wore for poker. The shirt had black spades and clubs, red hearts and diamonds, splashed on a backdrop of shimmering pearl-gray rayon; the two breast pockets were a pair of aces. "Ah, Murray," the old man said. "Say hello to Doc and Irv."

He gestured toward a tall thin man shaking corn chips into a plastic bowl, and a natty little fellow, pencil mustache, making obsessive stacks of nickels and dimes on the felt-covered table in front of him. Murray nodded, nervous as the first day of school.

"And this," the Shirt went on, "is our most famous neighbor, Senator Barney LaRue."

"State senator," LaRue said modestly. He was pouring a bottle of rum into a big pitcher that held some ice and a splash or two of lime juice, and Murray couldn't help studying him a moment. It's odd, after all, to meet someone about whom you know nothing except that someone else you've met can't stand him. LaRue reminded Murray of a catalog model, blankly handsome, sample size, the guy who sports the Crushable Fedora on page sixteen and the Three-Season Jacket on the back cover. "Gentlemen," the politician said, "who would like a daiquiri?"

They all took plastic tumblers of the cocktail, sipped them, sat down to play. Seven-card stud, quarter and a half, three raise limit. Murray played conservatively at first. This had nothing to do with winning or losing, but with the quietly desperate wish to be invited back. On the fourth hand, he took the pot with jacks and threes. It was like a rookie's first base hit, it initiated him into the game and left him breathless.

He sought to calm himself with a much bigger gulp of his rum than was good for him. He'd never been much of a drinker, even less so since he'd been on Prozac. Now the alcohol squirted through his stripped-bare circuitry, called forth sparks like salt on a wire. The light in the gazebo deepened the darkness beyond, blotted out context, he suddenly felt like he was playing poker in a spaceship. Silent thought became indistinct from audible speech. Coins looked bizarre, arbitrary, silly, like foreign money when you get the first sleepy handful at the airport.

"Your turn to bet," Bert said gently.

"Hm?" said Murray. "Check."

"Bet's fifty cents," said Irv.

The Bra King tossed two quarters.

He drank, noticed vaguely that Barney LaRue had three hearts on the table and was betting very strong. A fourth heart fell, and everyone went out. Murray went out too, just to go along, but as he tossed in his cards he was watching the senator's neck, the taut place where the throat meets the jawbone, and the jaw curves up to join the temple. He saw a subtle tinge of pink blossom through the tan and gleam just slightly at the junction with the trim silver sideburn. "He was bluffing," Murray blurted, as the senator raked in the change. "Look the way he gets a little pink there, right by his ear. That's how ya know he's bluffing."

Barney LaRue glared at him, and Murray dimly understood he'd made an enemy. He hadn't meant to, but he dimly decided he didn't care, he didn't like LaRue anyway, he couldn't put his finger on exactly why. Was it because he bluffed, or looked like a catalog model, or was it because there were times in life when you just plain didn't like somebody, and that was that?

Doc gathered cards, shuffled.

Bert, in an oblique apology, said, "Murray's been through a hell of a lot the last few days. Just decided to retire from his business."

"Yeah?" said Doc. He dealt. "What kind of business?"

"Lingerie," said Murray.

"Quarter," said Irv. "Me, I was in furniture. Low-end stuff. We called it borax. I had a saying: It may look like shit to you, but it's my bread and butter."

"Was Doc's bread and butter too," said Bert. "Call."

Doc didn't laugh, he put on a look of professional gravity. "Proctology," he said, "is a recognized medical specialty."

"But what kinda person picks it?" Murray thought aloud. "Call."

"Call your quarter and raise a quarter," said LaRue.

"God bless America," said Bert.

"Nice to hear a patriotic outburst," drawled the politician.

"Amazing country," Bert went on. "So many ways t'end up wit' a wonderful life, a condominium in Florida. One guy looks up asses for a livin', puts together a million bucks in mutual funds. 'Nother guy sells furniture ya wouldn't take the plastic off, he's got a Mercedes and a TV set the size a Cleveland. Me, I got, let's say, a checkered past, and I'm comfortable. Not only that, I'm playin' poker wit' a senator wit' a penthouse, and Murray heah, he's innee exact same penthouse from sellin' girdles."

"Bras," corrected Murray. "I'm out."

"It's not your turn," said Doc.

"Democracy," Bert intoned.

"Another fifty cents," said Irv. "Bras? Just bras?"

Murray sipped his daiquiri. The sips went down much easier now, the drink wasn't as strong as he'd thought. "Just bras," he proudly said. "We were the first to specialize that much. It was my wife's idea."

"I'll just call," said Senator LaRue.

"Straight," gloated Irv. "Made it on the last card." He swept in the pot.

Murray rambled on above the clatter of coins. "It was the early seventies. Women were burning their bras, remember? Waving 'em around their heads like rebel flags. The industry was in a tumult. I was just a salesman at the time, never even finished college. My wife was still taking classes at Fashion Institute—"

Irv shuffled the cards. "Same game. Same winner."

Murray swigged his cocktail and kept talking. "The owner of the company was an *alte cocker*, gloomy. He thought it was all over, the brassiere was going the way of the muu-muu, the poodle skirt. My wife, Franny her name was, still is, said, 'Murray, buy the bra division. Make a lowball offer, you'll get it on the cheap.'"

"Queen is high," said Irv.

"A quarter on the queen," said Bert the Shirt. "So ya bought the company?"

"Not right away," said Murray. "Any more daiquiris inna pitcher? I waffled. I was scared. I'd have to borrow, maybe I'd lose everything. I said to Franny, 'What makes you so sure the bra is ever coming back?' "

Barney LaRue looked at his hole cards. "And a quarter," he said. He leaned over and grudgingly freshened Murray's drink.

"She says to me," the newcomer went on, " 'lemme put it this way, Murray: You wanna go through life with your little pecker hanging down and flopping all day long? You wanna spend each day vaguely feeling that people are looking at you sideways, checking out the size of it, the shape? No. Politics is politics,' she says, 'but comfort and modesty will win out. The bra is coming back.' So I borrow half a million bucks and buy the bra division. These cocktails are delicious. How ya make these cocktails?"

"I'm raising," the ex-proctologist announced.

Irv frowned down at his cards and turned them over.

"An' sure enough the bra came back," said Bert.

"With a vengeance," Murray said. "The eighties. What a moment! Dress for success. The executive look. It called for a whole new line. Tits are a science. Lotta people don't realize this. Woman executive goes into a meeting with the board of directors,

she can't go in looking like she's gonna take somebody's eye out with her tits. They need a softer
look. Not too soft. Too soft, they don't look success-
ful, they look, like, pessimistic. The idea is not to
make her flat-chested but not to make her boobies
an agenda item either. Jesus Christ, did we move
product in the eighties! Whose turn is it to bet?"

"Yours," Irv said dryly.

"I'm in," said Murray. Tossed a quarter.

"Bet's seventy-five cents," said Irv.

Murray glanced at his hole cards. They blurred a
little but he could tell they didn't match. "I'm out."

"Guy gambles in bras," Doc muttered. "Cards, he
wants a sure thing."

"Don't gamble in bras no more," said Bert.
"Retired, like I said. Fifty cents ta me. I call."

"Retirement's not so easy," put in Irv, and for an
instant Murray wasn't sure if someone had spoken
or if his own new fears were murmuring to him.
"Don't kid yourself it's easy," the natty fellow said.

"One false move I get depressed," said Murray.

"Plenty a guys," said Bert, "I seen 'em like fall
into whaddyacallit, I guess ya'd have to say despair.
Yeah, despair. Lose the edge. Get old overnight.
But hey, this is gettin' fuckin' morbid."

Barney LaRue said, "There's one more raise, I
b'lieve?" He waited to see the reaction, then said,
"Well, I'll just call."

Irv dealt.

Bert paired up his queen. He stroked his dozing
dog for luck, rubbed his pockets with the aces on

them. "Queens say half a buck. Hey Bahney, the casino bill—"

"Dead in the water," said the senator.

Doc said, "The controversy."

"You got it," drawled LaRue. "My colleagues up in Tallahassee, they like controversy about as much as dead tourists piled up on Cuban rafts. I'll take a high diamond, Mr. Irv."

Irv turned over a four of clubs. He said, "So I guess that leaves us bingo with the Indians."

"They'll open up casinos soon, " the politician said. "But Indians, that's federal. State can't do a thing about it."

"An' why should it?" put in Bert the Shirt. "Poor fuckin' Indians. First time they find a way ta make some money, the state starts cryin' the blues about it. Where's the justice? Half a dollar onna queens."

"Fold," the politician said. "'Tain't about justice, Bert. It's about revenues. Thank God there's just the Seminoles and Miccosukkees."

"Who got a right—" Bert started.

"Forget right," said LaRue. "How d'you make up what's lost on untaxed gaming? You wanna see a state income tax go in?"

Doc and Irv blanched deathly white beneath their winter tans.

"While the Indians per capita get richer than Kuwaitis," the proctologist groused. "Call your half and raise a quarter."

"And in your face wit' another half," said Bert. "The Indians deserve to make a livin'."

Irv said, "Plus you have, you know, the element that comes in when there's casinos."

"Shut up about the element," said Bert the Shirt, "we're playin' poker heah. It's fifty cents. If I was you, Doc, I'd go out."

The doctor threw in half a buck.

Murray drained his second daiquiri, tongued the last drop of froth from the lip of his plastic glass. He wasn't thinking about poker anymore. He was sitting in the spaceship of a gazebo, staring at the green felt table that seemed now to lean and lurch a little, and he was wondering about this retirement thing, the abruptness of it. Despair? Old overnight? Hey, he was still a doer, a restless spirit, a hyper guy with ants in his pants. For him, there were still accomplishments ahead, projects, deals; just don't ask him what they were.

Irv dealt. A third queen fell to Bert the Shirt.

"Shoulda gone out when I tol' ya, Doc," said the former mafioso.

The other man threw in his cards.

8

The next morning Murray did not have a hangover, exactly, but things felt stale and grainy inside his head. The brain juices that had been flowing freely the past two days seemed to have sludged up, he imagined smeared rainbows on the backs of his eyes as in a puddle of oil. If he'd had aspirin he would have taken some. But he didn't, so he popped an extra Prozac.

After that the day passed pleasantly enough, though he was out of sync with it, felt like he was on a moving walkway while the rest of the world was not. At ten-thirty it seemed it should have been noon; at three o'clock he was faced with a dense wad of time before sunset. As ever, he needed an activity. He thought about fishing, imagined the ancient thrill of seeing a fish pulled from the water.

He remembered the elegant uncoiling of Tommy Tarpon as he cast for bait. He got in the scratched-up Lexus where his gear was stowed, and headed for Big Bubba's to buy a net.

It was a little early for fishing when he arrived at White Street Pier; the regulars had yet to arrive. Still, Murray was careful not to occupy the spot belonging to the Indian. He stopped maybe twenty-five feet shy of it and leaned his pole against the railing.

Then he unwrapped his net. It was white and crisp as a virgin's underpants, its obvious newness embarrassed him. He was eager to get it in the water, get some slime and seaweed on it.

He put the retrieving cord in his teeth, the way the Indian had done. He spread the mesh across his fists like pizza dough. He tried to curl up like a discus thrower but looked more like a tormented bonsai tree. He took a breath then attempted to uncoil smoothly; the motion was more like a man ridding himself of poisoned food. The net didn't spin, didn't flatten. It hit the water like a sack of trash about three feet from the pier and scared away the fish for many yards around.

Nonchalantly, with the cord still in his mouth, Murray glanced over his shoulder. No one but a couple of herons and a pelican had seen the abortive toss; it hadn't really happened.

On the second throw he did a little better; by the sixth or seventh try the mesh was spreading; by the tenth the net was landing softly. On around the twelfth toss it all came together: The fabric sprang like a flight of doves from the Bra King's hands; it opened and twirled against the flaming yellow backdrop of the sun; it hovered like a whirlybird, preparing to settle quiet as a cloud on the green surface of the sea.

Murray watched serenely as the perfect small event unfolded. He felt neither modesty nor pride, had the peculiar Asiatic sensation that the throw had nothing whatever to do with him. It was just a lovely thing.

So lovely that a sense of wonder pried open his jaws. The retrieving cord flew out of his mouth and landed with a small splash in the ocean. He was no longer attached to the net that had spun so prettily and was now slowly but inexorably beginning to sink down toward the muck.

Murray said, "Oh shit."

The crisis instantly made him a Westerner, a Manhattanite again. Synapses fired. Serenity exploded. He grabbed his fishing pole, leaned far out over the railing. The rod tip fell an excruciating inch or two short of the subsiding fabric. Faster than the mind could talk things over with the body, he had a different idea. Below the railing was a knee-high concrete wall; between the wall and the rail was about a foot and a half of empty space. If Murray squeezed himself into that groove, he could reach farther out, maybe he could grab the sinking net.

With the false agility of the desperate, the Bra King dove into the slot. His groin compressed against the hot concrete of the wall, his shoulder blades were pinned by the metal tubing of the rail. Head suspended above the green Atlantic, he flailed his rod at the disappearing net and managed to snag a strand of mesh. Pulse throbbing, he used the fishing pole like a knitting needle, poked and turned it till the fabric was attached securely. He grunted, he sweated, he savored the mindless effort.

Finally he was ready to pull in the rescued net. That's when he realized he was stuck.

He arched his back to rise; the railing pressed against his spine like a giant foot and kicked him down again. He hunkered low and tried to squirm along the wall; the concrete cinched his thigh and raked against his squashed testicles. He lifted his head; the back of it clanged softly against the metal rail. The arm that held the fishing pole soon went into a numbing cramp.

Gulls laughed. Cormorants crapped down from the tops of lampposts. The Bra King writhed and sweated. He tried to shrink himself, tried like a half-crushed bug to slink away on whatever appendage still had life. But he was going nowhere, and at length he heard a clanking squeak, as of a rusted bicycle. He turned his neck with the pained slowness of a tortoise, glanced up with popping eyes like those of a caught fish, and saw the Indian.

The Indian said, "Fuck you doin', man?"

"Fishing," said the Bra King, weakly.

"Got a funny waya doin' it."

To this Murray said nothing.

The Indian said blandly, "Want a hand?"

"Tha'd be great."

In no special hurry, Tommy Tarpon climbed off his bike. A practical man, he first took the rod from Murray and gathered in the sodden net. Then he grabbed the Bra King by the belt and an ankle, and set himself to yank. "Tuck your head," he advised.

He didn't say it quite soon enough. He reared back and hauled. Murray came free with a scraping sound, then clunked his skull on the metal rail. There was a ringing, the Bra King couldn't tell which side of his brainpan it was on. But he stood and faced his rescuer, looked him in the eye. "Thanks," he said. "You're very kind."

The word had an odd effect on Tommy Tarpon. It seemed to make him impatient, elusive, as though it was an accusation. He went to his bike without a word, rolled it to his spot.

Murray leaned against the railing, a little unsure of his legs. His clothes were splotched with sweat, a soft breeze tickled the wet places. He watched the Indian go through his ritual: the telescoping rod, the six-pack, the milk crate, all taken from his cart of shells. He watched him make his one casually perfect throw of the net. He watched him gather in his bait.

He was still leaning motionless against the rail when Tommy had filled his yellow bucket and made his first cast toward the lowering sun. The Indian glanced quickly over at him, said, "Didn't you say you were fishing?"

Murray had sort of forgotten about fishing. His back ached and his arms were tired. Besides, he was embarrassed to throw his net with the Indian watching, and he knew now that his lures were futile. He just shrugged.

Tommy Tarpon turned toward him so slightly that he could not have seen him with more than the very edge of his wraparound eye. "Take some bait from the pail," he said. He said it not grudgingly, exactly, but as if some force, some necessity beyond his conscious preference was pulling the words, the offer, out of him. "I have more than I need."

The Bra King hesitated, suddenly feeling shy. A pinfish was a tiny gift, but a gift nevertheless. And gifts were not to be taken lightly. They made connections, they were connections; exchanges that led to more exchanges. At length Murray sidled slowly toward the bait pail and reached in.

Minute creatures swam between his fingers as through the tendrils of a reef. He managed to grab one, it jerked and struggled against his palm, he was shocked and humbled at the amount of life contained in such a puny package. He lifted it into the air, winced with remorse as he pressed it onto his hook. He cast the skewered fish into the ocean, let it swim around in fatal circles, waiting for a bigger fish to come and eat it and be hooked in turn.

After a moment, without looking over, Tommy said, "I'm sorry I cursed you out the other morning. Had nothing to do with you."

Murray just said, "Hey, no problem."

They fished. In the distance, schooners full of tourists scudded by in front of the pulsing orange sun.

Tommy said, "The Paradiso, place makes me edgy. Much too white for my red ass."

"Yeah," considered Murray. "I guess it's pretty white. Where d'you live, Tommy?"

The Indian leaned back on his milk crate, swigged his beer. "Toxic Triangle."

"Excuse me?"

"Corner of the harbor no one wants. Across from the electric company. Next to what used to be a field of oil tanks. Water's full of beer cans. Dock's falling down. Good place for an Indian."

Murray focused on the small doomed tugs of his baitfish. His line lay across his index finger, he felt the excess voltage of his brain throbbing down his arm and out into the sea. "So it's true what Bert says," he thought aloud. "You really are a bitter guy."

The Indian sucked his teeth, spat in the ocean.

Then Murray yelped, lurched, set his feet and arched his back against the sudden violence of a bending, twitching rod. Line screamed off his reel, water roiled fifty yards in front of him as a hooked fish bolted in rage and terror from the pain in its lip and the inexplicable weight against its progress. "Holy shit," the Bra King said. "I got one, Tommy? Fuck I do now?"

"Let 'im run," the Indian said calmly. "Keep your rod tip high and let 'im run."

The fish sprinted, Murray could feel its zigs and zags. Beads of sweat popped out on the angler's forehead, a blue vein stood forth in his neck.

"Now start to reel," said Tommy. "Pull back gently, then quick forward, and reel in what you've gained."

Murray, breathing heavily, leaned and reeled, arched and bowed, the motion reminded him of old men *dahvenning* in synagogue. He won back half his line, then the fish took off again. The grinding process started over.

"He's getting tired," said the Indian.

"*He's* getting tired? I'm gonna *plotz*."

"Get 'im just a little closer and I'll gaff 'im."

The Bra King didn't know exactly what that meant, but it sounded like a good idea. He tugged and grunted, and Tommy produced a medieval-looking tool from a compartment of his cart. He leaned over the rail, finally caught the played-out fish by its gill plate, and horsed it up onto the pier.

"Redfish," he pronounced. "Six, seven pounds. Gotten rare around here. Good eatin'."

Murray, huffing, amazed, looked at the defeated creature hanging from the gaff. Its eye was flat and glassy, its gills heaved, showing brick-red membranes. "First fish I ever caught."

"I figured that."

"Want 'im?"

There was a pause. The sun hit the horizon, began to spill across the ocean like a broken yolk. The Indian looked flabbergasted and once again mistrustful.

"Your bait," Murray said.

"That was nothing. I gave you the bait."

"So I'm giving you the fish."

Tommy shook his head. "Your fish."

"I couldn't have caught 'im alone. Take 'im."

The Indian stood firm, looking at the changing colors of the dying creature.

"Look," Murray went on, "you helped me, I'd like you to have 'im."

Tommy regarded Murray, pushed his lips forward in a thoughtful pout. Who was this clumsy headlong stranger who talked too much and tried too hard, who seemed to be empty of malice and of bias, who fished with an ignorant purity and seemed as displaced as he felt himself to be? Who was this odd awkward man that would offer another a fine rare fish, the first fish he'd ever caught? The Indian gazed unblinking at the fiery horizon, then said, "Tell ya what. I'll take half the fish."

The Bra King had his breath back now, was mopping his brow with his forearm. "Half, whole, whatever you like."

The Indian hesitated another moment, scoured Murray with his judging eyes. Finally he said, "I'll take half, you take half. But if ya like, we'll leave the halves together, we'll grill 'im on the beach."

Murray couldn't talk. It was not uncertainty but the thrill of the new that stopped his mouth. A fish; an Indian; a campfire on a Florida beach he'd fled to by himself. Finally he said, "Ya mean we'll gather driftwood—?"

"Driftwood?" said Tommy. "Fuck that. Ya got a car?"

Murray nodded that he did.

"You'll go to the grocery, get some charcoal, the kind ya just light the bag. And while you're at it, grab a bottle of bourbon, Scotch, whatever. Something brown. Driftwood. Jesus, you really are a piece of work."

9

The demolished fish lay on a picnic table in a tiny unwalled hut at County Beach. Its head was still on above a naked skeleton. Its eye was seared opaque white, its tongue stuck out in a gesture of unconquerable defiance. Embers glowed softly in the barbecue grate nearby, red-hearted ash floated away on a mild breeze. Tommy poured bourbon from a bottle that had gotten pretty light.

Apropos of nothing very recent, he said, "Yeah, you're right, I'm bitter."

Murray nodded agreeably. He was smashed. He said, "Ya know, before I moved here, I really didn't drink much."

"I did," Tommy said. Then he added, "Aren't you?"

The Bra King ran a hand over his stubbly and slightly numb jowls. "Aren't I what?"

"Bitter," said the Indian. "I'd think anybody with a brain would be bitter."

Murray swigged liquor from a plastic cup, gazed off at the last mauve residue of sunset. Then he said, "No. I'm not bitter. I'm depressed."

Tommy Tarpon plucked a bone from the fish's carcass, picked his teeth with it. He knew the place Murray lived. He'd seen Murray's car.

"Fuck you got to be depressed about?"

"That isn't how it works," said Murray. "You don't get depressed *about* something. Not necessarily. You just get depressed."

"For no reason?" said the Indian.

"There's reasons," Murray said, "there's reasons. But the reasons are, like, a little indirect. Ya pay a shrink to figure 'em out."

"Then they go away?"

"Who said they go away?"

The Indian squinted off toward the purple ocean.

"But this bitter thing," Murray resumed, "you telling me you got reasons, crystal-clear, ya know just what they are?"

"You bet your ass I do," said Tommy.

But he didn't elaborate and Murray let it drop. They were solitary men at a dubious and bashful point along the road of possibly becoming friends. They weren't quite ready to talk about their reasons.

The silence went on longer than was comfortable. Then Murray said, "Hey Tommy—the Paradiso, you so much don't like it, how come you were there the other morning?"

Tommy drank bourbon, leaned out beyond the roofline of the tiny hut to glance up at the brightening stars. Bitterly he said, "I was summoned. I was summoned, and like a fuckin' jerk I went. Curiosity, I guess."

"Summoned why?"

"So LaRue could try to fuck up my life."

"Fuck it up how?"

Tommy plucked another fishbone, ran it along the skeleton, it made a sound like a fingernail on a comb. "Murray, stop asking me so many questions."

"Do I ask a lotta questions?"

The Indian didn't answer. In the quiet they could hear the soft hiss of tiny wavelets seeping down through sand.

Murray said, "If I didn't ask questions, your tongue would stick to the roof of your mouth, you'd get lockjaw, something."

Tommy coaxed a morsel of fish from the skeleton, absently scarfed it down. "Okay," he said, "okay. He wants me to open a store."

The Bra King rubbed his chin, scratched his ear, he didn't see what was so terrible. "A store? Zat all? Jesus, Tommy, the way you made it sound—"

"He just wants to use me."

"Use you how?"

"I don't know how," Tommy admitted. "But I'm not stupid. He's doing me a favor? Bullshit. Something he wants, some white-ass scam, he needs an Indian."

"Why an Indian?"

Tommy squeezed air furiously past his gums. " 'Cause Indians get certain crumbs that whites can fuck them out of. Cigarette concessions. Boating rights. The way it works, Indian front man signs the papers, white backers pull the strings."

Murray said, "Just 'cause it's a good deal for the other guy doesn't mean it's a bad deal for you."

"It would totally fuck up my life. Look, the way it is now, I do what I want. I sell a few shells; I fish. A store, there'd be schedules, records, cash registers, burglar alarms. All that white bullshit."

Murray considered. He'd seen some retail operations in this town. "That white bullshit," he said, "might make you pretty rich."

Tommy leaned low across his arms. "I don't wanna be rich."

Murray blinked at this novel sentiment, frowned down at his knuckles then looked straight at the Indian's eyes. "You sure?"

For a second Tommy didn't speak, Murray saw the slightest give in his bleary but steadfast gaze, saw for the first time a fleshly wrinkle in his bedrock certainty. "I don't wanna be rich," he said, "if it means I'm gonna be owned by these scumbag assholes who I hate."

The Bra King ran a hand through his hair, then sniffed his fingers and realized that they smelled like fish. "I still don't know what scumbag assholes—?"

"I don't know what scumbag assholes either," admitted Tommy.

"Then how do you know—"

"Murray, there's no shortage of scumbag ass-holes. Look, only Indians can sell these shells. One of our crumbs. That's why they need me. No Indian, no ball game."

"So that gives you some leverage—"

"But who's really gonna win this game?" Tommy interrupted. "The guy who's gonna win is the money guy, some turd who's in tight with LaRue. They'll throw me a few bucks, sure. But you think they're really gonna let me win?"

"Let you win?" said Murray. "*Let* you win?" He surprised himself by feeling suddenly feisty. He grabbed the bourbon bottle, poured himself a slug, briefly felt like someone else, someone tough and leathery. "Tommy, no one ever *lets* you win, I don't care if you're an Indian or a Jew or the fucking czar of Russia. You win because you win, because you find a way. And once you've won, you look back on all the scumbags who you know in your heart were rooting against you, working against you, and you think: How sweet it is, all you bastards can kiss my hairy ass."

He slammed his cup down, soaked his fist with whiskey, the klutzy denouement pulled him back to who he was. He looked at Tommy, saw a faint and furtive smile slip across his solemn mouth.

"Aha," he resumed. "Telling 'em to kiss your ass. You like that part."

The Indian's face was growing vague, but he did not seem drunk, just weary. "Yeah," he said, "I like that part. But Murray, I don't wanna spend my life sitting in a fucking store, and I can't stand the idea that my tribe dies out as the flunkey of these asshole scumbags."

"Maybe there's some other way," the Bra King said.

"Some other way what?"

"To make you some money without being a flunkey of asshole scumbags."

"Forget about it, Murray. I'm fine as I am."

There was a silence. The two men sipped liquor, looked at embers whose dusty glow rose and fell as though with the beating of some ghastly heart.

Then the Bra King said, "Hey wait a second. What's this about your tribe dying out?"

Tommy said bitterly, "It's not important."

"Of course it's important," Murray said. "Ya mean dying out, like, extinct?"

The Indian looked away.

"Jesus," Murray said. "Like how many people ya got in this tribe?"

Tommy just stared at him.

"You telling me," said Murray, "the tribe—"

"—is me," said Tommy.

"Jesus," Murray said again, and he looked at his friend like he was seeing a ghost, a prophet, a dinosaur. "What's the name of this tribe?"

Unconsciously, Tommy squared his shoulders, lifted up his chest. "Matalatchee. People think I'm a Seminole, but that's not even close. We're a branch of the old Calusas. The original Florida Indians."

"And proud of it," Murray thought aloud. "So

you're not gonna be a flunkey and you're not gonna live on crumbs."

"No," said Tommy. "I *am* gonna live on crumbs. Seashells. But my own way. My way of saying, okay, you fuckers, this is all you're leaving me, this is all I need."

Breeze shook the palms, fronds dryly scratched. Murray put bourbon to his lips, had the sudden feeling that if one more sour drop passed his gullet he would surely retch. Instead of drinking, he said, "Jesus, Tommy, you don't make things easy for yourself."

The Indian didn't answer that. He put his hands flat on the table, lifted himself from the slatted bench, and said, "I'm tired, Murray, I'm going home."

"Just like that?" the Bra King said. Instantly he felt desolate, it took very little to remind him he was lonely and out-of-place and discombobulated. "We haven't finished our conversation."

Over his shoulder Tommy said, "No one ever finishes a conversation. That's why I think it's really better not to start one."

"But your tribe," said Murray, "the Hookasookie."

"Matalatchee," Tommy said. He walked to where he'd parked his clunker of a bike, and climbed aboard. With no farewell he rode away over the lumpy sand, his cart of seashells rattling with every bump.

10

Late the next morning, wrapped in the shade of the banyan tree, Tommy Tarpon leaned back against the Navy fence as a man in a turban and a woman in a sari approached his cart of shells. The man's face was the color of tree bark, as gray as it was brown; the woman took such tiny steps she seemed to be moving on mechanical feet. She picked up a lightning whelk and held it to her ear to hear the ocean.

The man smiled pleasantly, gestured toward the merchandise. "Verry beauteeful," he said. "These shells, some are same from Indian Ocean. Some I do not recognize. You are Indian?"

Tommy tugged the fringes on his vest, nodded wearily.

"We are Indian too," said the woman in the sari. "You give us good price."

Tommy had yet to make a sale that day. "Dollar off for Indians. Find one you like. Seven bucks."

The wife listened to more shells, the husband slipped his fingers in a few. They were still deciding when a fat man in a sweat-splotched shirt approached the cart.

"Tommy," said the fat man, "I need to see your license."

The fat man's name was Fred, and Tommy had known him, distantly, for many years. He was a native, a Conch, whose patronage job consisted mainly of drinking coffee and eating greasy fritters as he made languorous and random rounds of Key West's souklike streets.

Tommy cajoled. "What the hell, Fred, you think I'm new in town?"

"Gotta check it," the inspector said, without a hint of humor. "See it's up-to-date."

The Indian shook his head, produced a tattered document from a pocket of his chamois vest.

Fred screwed up his face to squint at Tommy's license, gave it back, then unclipped a tape measure from the moist and crinkled waistband of his pants. He placed the end of the tape against the cart of shells, ran it out toward Whitehead Street. "Y'only got a four-foot setback from the curb. That's a violation, Tommy."

The Indians, sensing the unease that goes with other people's problems and that spoils a vacation, sidled away, their money still securely in their pockets. "Perhaps we come back later," said the husband.

Tommy watched the sale depart, then said, "What is this bullshit? You see me here every goddam day for I don't know how long—"

The fat man wasn't listening. He'd pulled a stub of pencil from his shirt, licked the blunt and smudgy tip of it, and was writing out a citation. "Twenty-five dollars," he said. "Pay it at the courthouse. Another violation within a year, they take away your license."

Tommy was on his feet now. His hands were on his hips and veins were throbbing in his neck. "Who's they?" he said.

"Ya know," said Fred. "The board." He scrawled demerits on paper that went soggy in his pudgy palm.

"Come on," said the Indian. "Gimme a name. Who's leaning on you to do this?"

The fat man didn't answer, didn't meet Tommy's eye. He put the citation on the cart, coaxed a wad of his trousers out from between his sweating buttocks, and walked away.

Tommy stewed. He stewed, he paced, he used his hip to bump his cart back one more foot, bring it grudgingly to code. He sat down on his milk crate, calculated how many hours he'd be sitting there to make the money to pay the goddam fine. He stewed some more, was still stewing when his attention was grabbed by the appearance of something unlikely and in fact ridiculous: Murray on a bicycle.

He was barreling down Whitehead in yellow running shorts and a lime green tank top, and he was ringing his bell like a berserk Good Humor man.

Never-worn white tennis shoes gleamed against the pedals; wraparound sunglasses made blue mirrors of his eyes. Wobbling, briefly unable to remember where the brakes were, he dropped his feet like landing gear and scraped to a halt in front of the cart of shells. "Tommy, yo," he said. "Do I look local or what?"

Tommy regarded him, blinked at the suggestion of titty where some men had muscles, at the hairy, pale and skinny ankles protruding from the sneakers. The Indian was in a vile mood and he could find no words.

It didn't matter. The Bra King didn't need an answer.

"I woke up this morning," he went on, "I felt terrific. By rights I should've had a hangover. But I didn't. Pill last night. Two pills this morning. Beautiful. I went out and bought a bicycle."

Tommy didn't see the connection. He just nodded grumpily from atop his milk crate.

"And the clothes—bought 'em days ago. Didn't have the *baytsim* to put 'em on."

"*Baytsim?*" muttered the Indian.

"Yiddish. Means eggs. Ya know, balls."

"Ah," said Tommy. "*Oopoppi.*"

"Say wha'?"

"Balls in Matalatchee."

"Whaddya know. So anyway, with the clothes, today I figured screw it. This town, I've seen plenty a guys wearing tank tops that shouldn't be wearing tank tops, and I say to myself, Dignity. Just what the hell is dignity except ya have less fun than the goofballs who aren't dignified. Am I right?"

Tommy hadn't noticed that Murray's style was cramped by excessive dignity. He said nothing.

"And how are you?" the Bra King finally got around to asking.

"Lousy," said the Indian.

Murray took a moment to study him, saw slightly bloodshot eyes, tense skin stretched across the forehead. "We hit it pretty hard last night."

"Nothing to do with that," said Tommy. He told Murray about the summons. "Fuckers are harassing me, threatening to take me off the street."

Murray frowned, looked past the southernmost marker, scanned the horizon for hints of Cuba. "Convincing you to get a store?"

"Tha'd be my guess," said Tommy. "Scumbags."

Inexorably, the Bra King said, "Alla more reason we gotta talk." He climbed off his brand-new bike, yellow shorts hiking up to show a flash of bright blue underpants. "I'd like to sit a minute. Mind if I sit a minute?"

Tommy didn't say yes, he didn't say no. He seemed resigned, as to the pitch of a vacuum cleaner salesman who's wedged that first ameboid foot between the door frame and the door.

Murray moved around the cart of shells and sat down on the sidewalk, his back against the fence that cordoned off the Navy property. When he was settled in, he said, "Crumbs."

He let the word hover there until Tommy gave in and said, "Crumbs what?"

Tourists milled, scooters clattered past. Murray said, "What you said last night. About how you make your living. And it dawned on me that if you're gonna be so goddam pigheaded about making your living offa crumbs, at least y'oughta pick a crumb that's worth some money."

Tommy hadn't felt hung over before. Now, listening to Murray, he was getting a headache. "I have no idea what you're talking about."

Somehow, propelled by medication and a lifetime's worth of ambition, busyness, the Bra King had gotten to his feet, was pointing, pacing. "I have a plan, Tommy. A plan for you to win. Win big. Your own way. No scumbags. You can tell 'em all to kiss your ass."

The Indian leaned back against the fence. He didn't believe it for an instant.

The Bra King was undaunted by the lack of a response. "The other night I played poker," he said. "I'll level with ya: LaRue was in the game. I didn't like him. He bluffs and his neck gets pink. Anyway, I got polluted. Which is weird, 'cause before I came here, I had liquor bottles, dusty, they lasted me for years. So we're playing poker, talking this and that. Politics, retirement. Then all of a sudden guys are talking about casinos, about how only Indians can open 'em—"

Now Tommy reacted. He raised his hand like a traffic cop, pulled his face away like he was fending off some terrible contagion. "I know all about that, Murray. Forget it."

"Now there's a crumb that's worth something. No taxes. No competition. A license to print money."

The Indian crossed protective arms against his innards, resolutely shook his head.

Murray paced, his reflective glasses glinted in the sun. "Come on, Tommy, ya read about it in the papers. That tribe in Connecticut. Or down here, the whaddyacallit, the bingo Indians."

"Miccosukkee," Tommy said. "Look, they've been recognized for years, the states are stuck with them. But any new tribes, they bury you, they fight you to the end."

"So fight 'em back."

Tommy gave a bitter snort. "It's the whole fucking government. You don't have a chance."

"You don't have a chance," Murray mimicked. "Tommy, I don't understand this attitude you have, this getting even by giving up."

"Who said I think I'm getting even? Murray, listen, it's impossible, they put you through a million hoops."

"Like what kinda hoops?"

"Like you gotta prove you're a tribe distinct from all the others."

"Okay, okay," said Murray. "Didn't you tell me you're the last of the whaddyacallit, the Kalamooties?"

"Matalatchee," Tommy said. "It doesn't stop there. You gotta prove there's tribal lands."

"So is there?"

Tommy looked off at the ocean, hesitated, then nodded, reluctantly, like he was making some terrible admission. "There's a little island, ten acres maybe, about four, five miles offshore. There's some shell heaps, some remains of tools—"

"So what's the problem?" the Bra King said.

"Everything's the problem. Murray, fuck I know about casinos?"

"So ya hire people—"

"And then they own you."

"No!" said Murray. "You own them! You're the boss. It's a beautiful thing. Get used to it."

Pleasure scudded very briefly across Tommy's face, was quickly canceled by his accustomed look of impending calamity. "Forget it, Murray, this kind of battle, it's not for me. It's for the big tribes that have money for lawyers—"

"Ya need a lawyer?" Murray blurted. "I'll give ya money for a lawyer."

Tommy looked at him, bewildered, suspicious, moved. His voice got soft and thin. "Why would you do that? Why would you give me money for a lawyer?"

Murray stalled in his pacing, rubbed his fleshy chin. "I gotta have a reason? Call it tribal loyalty. It'd be a *mitzvah*."

"Fuck's a *mitzvah*?"

"Ya know, a good deed that ya do just because ya wanna do it. Look, you helped me catch a fish. I don't like to see a guy get screwed."

"I'm gonna get screwed anyway," said Tommy.

"Why ya gettin' all negative on me?"

The Indian didn't answer that. He leaned back on his milk crate, blew some air out past his pouted lips. Then he rose, slowly, deliberately, and started lifting the hinged sides of his cart of seashells.

"Tommy, hey," said Murray, "I'm bothering you, I'll leave. You don't have to close up the business."

"You're not bothering me," said the Indian. "In fact I want you to come home with me, have a beer."

The Bra King, nothing if not sociable, said, "Hey, that's great, I'd love to have a beer."

Tommy climbed aboard his clunker of a bike. "You see Toxic Triangle," he said, "maybe you'll figure out why I got this lousy attitude."

11

They pedaled along Whitehead Street, past Hemingway's house and bailbondsmen's offices, then turned up Fleming and crossed the rude clutter of Duval into the residential precincts of Old Town. Ancient pine and cypress planks bellied out along the sides of pampered dwellings; buttery allamanda crested over the tops of picket fences; gingerbread trim hung from eaves and porches. Matched palms swayed on tiny, perfect plots; pastel shutters shaded windows otherwise naked to the passing world.

Another zig and zag took them across William Street to Caroline, then past the chandlery and bookstore and the restaurants that catered to the yachting crowd.

But one block farther on, the avenue grew strangely desolate, not sinister but forsaken or maybe simply overlooked. On the land side of the street, a mostly empty parking lot sprawled behind a bent-up chain link fence. On the water side, a weedy vacant lot coughed limestone dust on every breeze. Ahead loomed the electric company, with its red-and-white striped smokestacks, its clustered pylons and crisscrossed wires carrying juice away.

Tommy hung a left in front of it, onto an unpaved little road with big gray stones that rattled Murray's teeth. In the scrub along this byway, lizards slunk and a rooster strutted. A cat sat in an abandoned refrigerator without a door; a dog peeked out from under the rusted chassis of a ghostly truck. The road wound around a low abandoned building with long jagged tears in its corrugated roof, and ended at a narrow dock of warped and cracking timbers.

Tommy climbed off his bike. Murray looked out at the green water blazing in the midday sun, and at the bizarre armada of Toxic Triangle. Homemade houseboats were tied up here and there, they looked like grown-up versions of the rafts kids made with popsicle sticks. Old dismasted sailboats with laundry hanging from their lifelines bobbed next to retired fishing craft whose cockpits were shaded with tarpaulins or thatch.

"Mine's at the end," said Tommy. "Corner lot. Walk your bike, the dock gets pretty dicey."

They went single file down the narrow pier and Tommy stopped in front of something that used to be a shrimp boat before it was half-sunk. Now its broad stern was partly underwater and its bow thrust upward at a jaunty angle, like an airplane taking off. Plastic lawn furniture was bolted to the splintery planking of its tilted deck, and its small square pilothouse was raised on shims so it was almost, but not quite, plumb. The odd dwelling was linked to land by three frayed ropes and a two-board gangplank.

"So whadda ya think?" asked Tommy.

It was a test, and Murray knew it was a test, and without hesitation he said, "I think it's fabulous."

The Indian scanned his face for some sign of the facetious. "Fabulous?"

"Fabulous!" the Bra King said again. He gestured at the harbor, the sky, the gulls and frigate birds wheeling. "Look at this view! I pay through the fucking nose for waterfront, and I gotta look at a road, a sidewalk, a hot dog vendor, before I see a drop a water. *This* is waterfront."

The Indian raised an eyebrow, undid the leather cord that held his ponytail. "See below?" The tone was that of a dare.

Murray just stepped onto the gangplank.

They went through the pilothouse and down a companionway ladder to the slanted cabin. There was no horizon there, it was like walking in a funhouse. Dusty fractured light streamed in through glassless portholes, a hammock hung at an inexplicable angle between two posts. A propane fridge and cooking ring stood on a yellow table with two short legs and two long ones, a cracked mirror dangled cockeyed from a rotting beam. The rear section of the chamber was a floor-level aquarium. Saltwater lapped softly against a wedged-in plank. See-through minnows swam in and out.

Murray pointed at the tiny fish swimming around in Tommy's living room. "This is, like, part of the ocean?"

Tommy nodded. "Sometimes, something big enough swims in, I eat it for dinner."

"Everything ya need," said Murray. "Beautiful."

"Yeah," said Tommy. "Great." He produced a six-pack from the little fridge and they took it up on deck.

They sat in the lawn chairs, whose incline made Murray feel like an astronaut. He looked across the harbor to the manmade islands, Christmas Tree and Tank. He looked a dock away, a mere few hundred yards, to Land's End Marina, where hired hands were cranked up stately masts in bosun's chairs, rigging halyards, changing spreader boots. "Some big boats over there," the Bra King said.

"And some shitass deathtraps over here," said Tommy.

Murray said nothing for a minute. He sipped his beer, looked sideways at his host, saw that he was scowling.

"Tommy," he said at last, "maybe this is like some Indian thing. But where I come from, if you invite somebody to your home, it's because you're being friendly. It's not because you're trying to talk him out of being friends."

The Indian looked at him, looked away, sipped beer.

"And it just so happens," the Bra King said, "I like it here."

Tommy shook his head. "I'll say one thing for you, Murray. You're not a snob."

"Hey. Litvak trash that made a couple bucks. What I got to be a snob about?"

Tommy looked at Murray's clothes, his wrap-around sunglasses. "Not much, I guess."

"Right," said Murray. He drank. The sun beat down on his head. He said, "So anyway, about our plans for the casino—"

"There are no plans," said Tommy. "Give it a rest."

Murray couldn't. He struggled up out of his chair, tried to pace on the sloping deck, hit a skid and ended up hugging the pilothouse. "Tommy, Tommy, you're killing me, you're breaking my heart. A chance like this—"

The Indian stared at him. Old hopes, ideals long ruined and rancid, were souring his stomach and hardening his face and making his voice more steely and scornful than he meant for it to be. "Whose chance?" he hissed. "Whose chance is it, Murray?"

Instantly the Bra King's shoulders slumped, he labored heavily back into his chair. "Hey," he said, "now you hurt my feelings. Whaddya think—you think I'm one more white scumbag looking to horn in?"

Sunlight flashed off the water. The Indian's eyes were solemn, judging.

Murray felt fat and flaccid now in his absurd green

tank top. "I'm not a scumbag," he said. "I'll tell you what I am. I'm a *yenta*. Ya know what means a *yenta?*"

The Indian shook his head.

"A meddling busybody pain innee ass. But a scumbag? No. To that I take exception."

Tommy Tarpon stared off at the harbor, unaccustomed words were clogging up his mouth. At last he said, "I'm sorry. I wasn't calling you a scumbag. It's just that—"

"Just what?" coaxed Murray.

"Just that," the Indian tried again, "I'm not used to—"

He stalled, he spluttered, and suddenly Murray understood.

"Ah, I get it," the Bra King said. "You'd feel more comfortable if I was being a selfish prick. Right?"

"I'd know more where I stood," admitted Tommy.

Murray pulled himself out of his seat, did a bear-like little dance along the tilted deck. "Well, I am. Okay? I'm doing this for me. But it's not about money, Tommy. Thank God, money I don't need. I need a project. The truth? I'm bored outa my mind down here, I'm going off my gourd."

Tommy said, "I've noticed."

Murray started snapping his fingers. "I'm used to action. Deals. Phones ringing. Guys saying it's life or death, they have to talk to me."

"So that's what you want," said Tommy, "have a vacation then go back up north."

Murray pictured snow shovels, his second wife. "Did I say that's what I want? I said that's what I'm used to. I'm not going back."

Frigate birds wheeled overhead, a cruise ship bellowed as it entered the harbor.

Murray sat back down, resumed. "Listen, I have an idea. Whaddya say I ask some questions, look into getting you recognized? It seems too involved, we drop it. It seems doable, you let me help."

"Who you gonna ask?" said Tommy.

The question took Murray by surprise. He was winging it, hadn't got that far in his manic scheming. He said the first thing that occurred to him. "LaRue, I guess."

"LaRue? He's the last person—"

"Who else do I know in politics?" said the Bra King. "Look, it's just a few questions. Rules. Procedures."

"I fucking hate LaRue."

"I've picked up on that," said Murray. "You don't have to talk to him. I will. I won't even say it's about you."

The Indian frowned down at stale water dotted with beer cans and slicks of rotting weed. "I got a bad feeling about this," he said.

"I got a terrific feeling about it," said the Bra King. "Look, lemme talk to him, that'll be my project. You're worried about me horning in? Don't worry, here's the deal: I try to get you recognized. It happens, that's it, I back off, my part's over, you do what you want. Deal?"

The Indian crossed his arms, looked out across the harbor that was swollen with currents, seamed with wakes. A flight of ibis flapped by, he watched their gawky progress. When he turned toward Murray his face was settled, composed, and deeply solemn. "No deal," he said. "I get recognized, we're partners. All the way."

"I'm not asking for—"

"Shut up just one second, Murray. Partners. Yes or no?"

12

"This is in reference to a Native American?" said Barney LaRue.

It was four P.M. They were talking in the old cypress house on Eaton Street where the senator kept an office. Golden light slanted in through French doors that backed onto the garden, it gave a sacramental aspect to the table on which LaRue lay naked save for a small towel draped across his oiled buttocks. Pascal was giving him a massage.

"An Indian, right," said Murray. "Native American, whatever." He sat on the edge of a vinyl chair, hands dangling between his knees. He was a little nervous. He didn't know from politics and he was unaccustomed to negotiating with naked men.

"This Indian," said the senator. "What's his name?"

Murray cleared his throat. "I'd rather not say for now."

The politician just slightly raised his head of lavish silver hair. The sheen on his skin revealed to Murray a pale thin scar between his jawbone and his ears, the place where flesh had been snipped, pulled taut, and sutured back together. "Why the hell not?"

Murray fidgeted. He couldn't very well say *Because he hates your fucking guts.* Instead, he said, "He's private, shy. And if nothing comes of this, he'd rather have it be like nothing ever happened."

"Nothing comes of what?" said LaRue impatiently. "What's the story on this bashful Indian?"

Pascal pummeled the senator's back, a hollow oomphing sound squeezed forth from his chest.

"He's the last surviving member of his tribe," the Bra King said.

The senator winced as the masseur's thumb all but disappeared between his glistening shoulder blades. "Not quite so deep there, Pascal." Turning his attention back to Murray, he said, "You know, about as many people claim to be the last member of their tribe as claim to be descended from the Romanovs. It's this odd prestige in having all your relatives be dead."

"I think this guy's for real," said Murray.

LaRue didn't answer for a moment, just let himself be knuckled. Murray looked at Pascal. Pascal had thick black eyebrows and blond hair with dark roots. He worked in a tiny undershirt that showed most of his lean smooth chest. Something was shining on his left nipple, and after a moment Murray realized it was a silver stud in the shape of a dog bone.

"So say he is," the politician said at last. "What's he want from the government? Freeze his sperm? Name a rest area after him?"

"He says there's a tribal island—"

"Aha!" said the senator, lifting up just slightly on an oiled elbow. "Let me guess. Miami Beach? Key Largo, maybe?"

"Nah," said Murray. "Nothing like that. A tiny little island, four, five miles off the highway, no one lives there, nothing's on it."

Pascal pressed an elbow into his patron's lower spine. A coo of tormented pleasure escaped the senator's well-formed lips. "And the Indian has decided this island should be his."

Murray nodded.

"How old's this individual?"

Murray shrugged. "Forty-four, forty-six."

"Forty-six. And one morning he wakes up to the sacredness of tribal heritage and real estate."

"He's always known the situation with the tribe," said Murray. "He hasn't done anything about it 'cause, no offense, he thinks the government would screw 'im."

LaRue squirmed beneath his slipping towel, could not suppress a fleeting smile. "Of course the government would screw him. The government would *have* to screw him. Case like this succeeds, it spawns a dozen more. Tax rolls shrink. Businesses complain. Country can't afford to keep handing out these private franchi—"

He broke off mid-word, his brain having caught up with his mouth and discovered an idea suddenly shining bright as a dime in the street. For a moment he lay still, letting the notion ripen until it twinged his loins, then he shoved Pascal aside with a fist to his unyielding stomach, and, with surprising grace and quickness, spun to a sitting position on the table, deftly rearranging his towel so that Murray saw no more than a coy flash of silver pubic hair. "And you're this Indian's attorney?"

"Me?" said Murray. "No. I was in the garment industry, remember?"

"Of course," said LaRue, though he hadn't remembered. All he remembered about Murray was that he was a lousy poker player who couldn't hold his liquor and couldn't keep his mouth shut. A harmless buffoon. A pushover. "But he has a lawyer," the politician gently probed. "Advisers."

The Bra King sat there in the other man's office, surrounded by diplomas and certificates and photos of the powerful. He suddenly felt uneasy, exposed, as if by some macabre transference he'd become the naked one. He cleared his throat, said softly, "Just me. For now at least."

"I see. And if he's recognized, and gets this island, what's he want to do with it?"

Murray squirmed, his rear end made an inelegant sound against the vinyl seat. "I'd rather not say for now."

That was answer enough for Barney LaRue. He nodded solemnly, squelched a grin and put on a most compassionate expression. He leaned slightly forward, gleamed like a big basted bird in the softening light. Murray could not help noticing a subtle surge of pink along his neck, a tawny flush where the jaw met the ear. "Florida's Indians," the senator intoned. "Grave historic wrongs to be corrected. What can I do to help?"

◆◆◆◆◆◆

As soon as Murray was out the door, Barney LaRue cinched his towel around his waist, went to his desk and dialed the number of a waterside restaurant in Coconut Grove.

"Hello, Martinelli's," said an unctuous voice on the other end of the line.

"Do you have *stringozzi?*" asked LaRue.

"No, sir. No *stringozzi.*"

"Then let me have the shark."

"How you like it, sir?"

"In a suit. A sharkskin suit."

"Hold on a minute, I'll put you through."

The line went silent. LaRue drummed manicured fingers against his blotter, looked past the French doors to the jasmine and hibiscus in the garden.

Finally a gruff voice said, "Yeah?"

"Charlie? Barney. These passwords, Charlie, they're asinine."

"Maybe I should start wit' a prayer and a pledge

allegiance," said the mobster. He swivelled in the enormous chair that dominated his office-fortress at the back of Martinelli's, looked through narrow windows of bulletproof glass at the smeared red and green channel markers of the Intracoastal. "Whaddaya want?"

"You always assume I want something," said the senator.

"You always do," said Ponte.

"Actually, I'm calling to make you rich."

"I'm rich already. Course, I'm a little less rich from dealing with certain deadbeat politicians."

"I'm gonna make that up to you, Charlie. More than make it up."

"I'm listening."

LaRue paused, let his oiled back slide deliciously against the leather of his chair. "I think maybe first we should talk about price."

"Price?!" The single percussive syllable came popping through the phone. "You have the fucking balls—"

"No scenes, Charlie," LaRue interrupted. "No tears. What I'm offering, it's the bargain of the ages."

The mobster tapped a hard shoe against the floor, felt a tightness in his throat.

"All I want," the senator resumed, "is, oh, say fifty thousand if you're interested, another two hundred when the deal is done, and let's say five percent of everything when you open your casino."

"Casino?" Ponte said. He said it softly, wistfully, the word hung in the air like a whore's perfume on a muggy night. "Bahney, ya told me just the other day—"

"Forget what I told you the other day. And forget about the gambling bill. You know what would happen if the legislature passed that bill? Caesar's, Harrah's, all the big boys—"

"I'd hold my own with them."

"I'm sure you would," purred LaRue. "But who needs the competition? What I'm offering now is ten times better."

Ponte said, "So offer it."

LaRue leaned back, watched purple shadows swallow up his garden. "What if I told you there was a tribe of Indians—"

"We been through this bullshit wit' the Indians," Ponte cut him off. "The Seminoles, the Miccosukkees, they got their deals in place."

"A tribe of Indians," LaRue went calmly on, "a *new* tribe of Indians, that needed your expertise, and yours alone, to open a casino a short boat ride from Key West. You grasp the possibilities of that, my friend?"

In his office scented with seafood and garlic, Charlie Ponte indulged himself in a secret and tentative smile. He grasped the possibilities. Craps tables, slots, cocktail waitresses in fishnet stockings. A take in the tens of millions, easy. A big hotel, of course. Call girls. A lending service for the compulsives. "So what's the story on this tribe?"

"Well," said LaRue, "officially speaking, it's not a tribe just yet."

Ponte stashed the smile. "So you're jerkin' me around like usual."

"The tribe is just now seeking recognition. A representative was just here, Charlie, to ask my help. It's very much in your interest that I give it. That's why you're going to front me fifty thousand dollars."

"Pigs get fed," said Ponte. "Hogs get slaughtered."

LaRue ignored the bromide. "You see," he said, "if the state opposes the petition, it can be tied up in the courts for years, forever. If I can persuade my colleagues to let it pass, you could have your tribe in a month or two. I'll personally deliver it."

The mobster ran his tongue along his gums, sucked his pointy teeth. "And how many more assholes I gotta buy off then?"

"Excuse me?"

"How many fuckin' Indians to split the pie? What about lawyers? Consultants? Other backers? Tell me what I'm walkin' into here."

The senator paused, purred, caressed his own smooth anointed chest. "Charlie," he said, "here's what I believe you people call the beauty part. The tribe, Charlie? It's exactly one guy."

Ponte swivelled, squinted at the Intracoastal lights. He wanted badly to believe he'd heard right. "One little Indian?" he whispered.

"One little Indian," confirmed LaRue. "With one little Jew running interference for him. No lawyers, Charlie. No other backers. Just this one pushover lunatic who doesn't know jack shit about politics or gambling or any other goddam thing, as far as I can tell."

Ponte flushed with happiness, sweated at the hairline, spun in his chair until he was tangled in the phone cord. "One little Indian," he murmured. "One little Jew." Then a sobering thought occurred to him. "Bahney, this Indian, he trust you any more than the Indian wit' the seashells?"

"This Indian doesn't have to trust me. This Indian needs me."

"Poor bastard," Ponte said.

LaRue chuckled. Then something occurred to him. Key West was not exactly awash in Indians. "Be funny if it was the same damn Redskin."

"Not so funny if he's stubborn as you say and you can't persuade his ass."

"On this he'll persuade himself," said the senator with smiling confidence. "So we do business, Charlie? I get my fifty thousand?"

"One little Indian," Ponte said again. "Jesus, Bahney, either you're fuckin' me big time or you're almost makin' this too easy."

TWO

13

Some weeks later, at the beginning of February, Murray and Tommy, counterbalanced by a very large and enthusiastic woman from the Bureau of Indian Affairs in Washington, were bouncing along on the low gunwale of a very old skiff as it plied the shallow waters between Key West and the ancestral Matalatchee homeland, a place denoted on modern charts as nothing more than a nameless smear ringed by the tiny dots that indicated mangroves, but known to Tommy as Kilicumba, "the dry place in the wet."

The craft was piloted by an old acquaintance of Tommy's, an ageless, grizzled Cuban sponger and fisherman named Flaco, who carried in his head a full-color chart of the shoals and channels of the backcountry and who saw in the water things that no one else saw. Flaco didn't like to share his knowledge, which was, after all, his livelihood. This disinclination had given him a long-standing habit of silence, a way of peering narrow-eyed at the horizon as though there were nothing in the world to say.

But that didn't stop Murray from talking.

He looked around the woman from Washington, through the pellucid emerald water to the sandy bottom dotted here and there with tufts of turtle grass, and he said above the whine of the outboard, "Beautiful, beautiful. Water's so clear, you'd think it's a foot deep."

"It is a foot deep," Tommy said.

"Beefteen eenches," Flaco muttered grudgingly. He stared at the horizon, sinewy strands of flesh hanging from his unshaved chin.

Murray stared too, saw golden flats where egrets stood, azure fingers of deeper water where tides had scoured away the sand. In the distance, low and featureless mangrove islands seemed to float above the surface, to hover atop a silver vacancy as though nested in metallic wool. Murray saw those islands plain enough, but the island that he pictured was one that wasn't there. Tommy's island, he felt somehow sure, would be very different, would gleam with sugar-white beaches, undulate with arching palms. Freshets of cool water would come cascading over shining rocks, ripe mangoes and papayas would fall from shading trees onto soil so luxuriant that it would not bruise the fruit.

"Lotta bugs in the mangroves," Tommy said to the woman from Indian Affairs. "Good thing you're dressed for it."

Her name was Estelle Grau, and in fact all she needed was a neckerchief to be dressed like a perfect scoutmaster. She wore crisp creased khaki pants and matching long-sleeve shirt, orange boots laced up above the ankles, and a pith helmet with a chin strap. On her knee was a waterproof clipboard, and around her neck a Leica camera. "Field work," she said, in a happy husky voice. "It's what I like. Mosquitoes, I imagine."

"Mosquitoes mostly," Tommy said. "Six, eight kinds. Spiders, land and water. Scorpions, of course. Ants—red, green, black. Sometimes hornets, not always. A pretty iridescent fly the Indians call *wakita malti.*"

"What a lovely name," said Estelle. "What's it mean?"

"Scratch till you bleed."

Murray looked down at his bare arms, at the hem of his Bermuda shorts halfway down his tender thighs, at his insteps pink and naked in his boat shoes. He noticed quite suddenly that even Tommy and Flaco were covered up.

"Snakes?" asked the woman down from Washington, in the calm tone of the naturalist.

"Some swimming rattlers," Tommy said. "A few coral snakes and cottonmouths. But not many. The alligators eat the rats, don't leave 'em much to feed on."

"Alligators?" Murray said. His tone was not that of the naturalist.

"Small ones," said the Indian. "Four, five feet. They don't bother you unless you step in a gator hole."

Murray smiled, nodded.

" 'Course," continued Tommy, "gator holes are pretty hard to see. Small, ya know, just like little puddles. Lotta times, leaves are floatin' on 'em, they look just like the ground. Hard to get your leg back sometimes."

Murray looked at his legs, imagined himself with only one. Morbidly, he turned the thought into an ad idea: Pegleg Pete, in which the lame but virile Bra King would command a galleonful of buxom pirates in lingerie . . .

In the meantime, the little boat droned on, scudding through the muddy spots left by fleeing stingrays, past the channel-edges where patient barracuda waited motionless, invisible to everyone but Flaco.

At length they neared an island that was slightly larger than some they had passed, a shade taller than most perhaps, but basically looked like all the others. Tangled mangroves waded out along an indistinct shoreline. Cormorants perched on low branches and spread their pterodactyl wings to dry. There were no palms, no beach, no hint of fresh water; no crests of land poked out above the mat of shrubbery, and the closest thing to a harbor was a vague cove where current had made a dent in the vegetation.

Flaco now steered gingerly toward that notch in the shore, already trimming up his engine. Fifty feet from land he turned the motor off and lifted it. The little boat coasted slowly toward the island then gently ran aground with a scratch and a squeak. "Ees island of Indians many long time before," announced the boatman.

A cloud of mosquitoes came promptly forth to suck blood from the visitors.

Murray waved them from his face, took cautious breaths of overripe air that smelled like anchovies and sulfur, and revised his expectations subtly downward. Okay, so there were no freshets, no cascades, no mangoes. But, the Bra King told himself, Miami must have looked like this to early visitors, men of destiny who beheld the flat and soupy land and saw not a pestilential bog but a paradise needing just a little spiffing up, a coat of paint, some bug spray. Besides, this was a historic moment, a homecoming, a reclaiming. Murray remembered that he had brought along a disposable camera to record the occasion.

"Wait a second, wait," he said to Tommy, as Tommy was preparing to jump overboard and drag the skiff closer in to land. "Lemme get this picture."

Mosquitoes strafed him as he fished the cardboard camera from his shirt pocket. He fixed Tommy in the viewfinder, and he saw things he'd never seen before in the Indian's face. Emotion locked his jaw, his Adam's apple shuttled up and down in his thick and fibrous neck. He looked toward his tribal island, and his eyes pulsed with a wry but stalwart pride that wrestled with and triumphed over the worldly knowledge of how small, how meager was the thing that he was proud of.

Murray took the picture. Tommy deftly slid from the gunwale into ankle-deep water.

All of a sudden the Indian looked extremely short. He had disappeared up to the middle of his thighs.

The Bra King, horrified, watched his friend subside, become a lopped-off torso in the sunshine. "Oh my God, my God," he said. "He stepped in quicksand, it's all my fault."

Tommy was immobile as a fly in pancake batter, but not especially concerned. "It's not quicksand. It's Florida. It's muck. Gimme a hand, somebody."

Estelle Grau reached across. She offered a wrist and Tommy held on and kicked free, wiggling like a worm in close-packed dirt. Soaked but undaunted, he found a firmer footing and dragged the skiff along the sand and baby mangroves.

The others stepped ashore, though shore was merely relative. Hot water, instep deep, was trapped among the maze of roots and vines; the upward slope of the land was so slight as to be imperceptible. Flaco, armed with a machete, moved to the front of the group and began to hack a path through the unbroken foliage.

The visitors advanced slowly; mosquitoes and *wakita malti* had ample time to find them. Murray bent to rub his shin; his hand came away black with scrambled bugs and red with his own bright blood. Frogs croaked out a steely alarm. Something slunk by and gave a soggy rustling to the rotting leaves; there was a muted splash nearby as a bashful gator took refuge in a hidden hole.

By tiny increments the land grew higher, drier, mangroves became chest-high, head-high, and at last provided a canopy of shade. Murray was squashing a mosquito in his ear when once again the world abruptly brightened; he looked up from his welted feet to see that the bushwhacked path had given onto a clearing. Silver sunshine and perfect silence rained down on the open place. In the middle of it were two flat-topped pyramids made of seashells. The pyramids were about twenty feet long on each side; they ended in mesas maybe twelve feet square.

There was something eerie and arresting about the place, something chastening and ghostly, and for a moment no one spoke. Flaco let his machete hang at his side. Murray allowed the bugs to feast on him while he tried to puzzle out the meaning of Tommy's doleful and unflinching gaze. The Indian was staring at the blunt-topped monuments with what seemed a diffuse but nagging grief, the futile kinship a traveler feels when coming upon a graveyard full of strangers, or of ancestors who might as well be strangers.

The woman down from Washington broke the spell. "These are perfect middens," she announced. "Absolutely classic. The shape, the siting. Calusa-style, not Seminole."

For all her bulk and all the heaviness of her scout-master's boots, she suddenly seemed weightless. She floated toward the pyramids, produced a GPS receiver that pinpointed their latitude and longitude. From another pocket came a tape to measure the middens' exact dimensions. Notes were made, photographs taken, shell samples withdrawn for testing.

Tommy Tarpon crossed his arms and strolled the perimeter of the clearing like a king perusing his domain. Flaco absently hacked at things. Estelle Grau took compass readings, fiddled with her clipboard. Murray did an unavailing little dance to keep the insects guessing, stamping his feet and waving his arms. Finally he crushed a cluster of mosquitoes near his jugular, and said, "I hate to be a party pooper, but two more minutes, I need a transfusion."

"Almost done," said the woman down from Washington.

She analyzed; Tommy gazed. Then the Bra King led the way back to the skiff, skirting puddles that might have held gators, tromping through leaves that might have hidden snakes, breathing heavily, splashing muck, and smacking himself all over as he ran.

14

"So it wasn't what you expected?" Tommy said.

They were sitting on the tilted deck of his houseboat, thrown back in their plastic chairs like astronauts, drinking beer. Murray was caked in a pink lotion, he looked like he'd been dipped in Pepto-Bismol. The lotion was supposed to stop the itching but did not. "Well," he said. "Let's just say it doesn't look like a resort."

"No, it doesn't," Tommy said. He peered off toward the next marina, where the masts and rigging of the wealthy gleamed vermilion in the sinking sun.

"Those wha'd-she-call-'em, middens—what are they about?"

The Indian drank beer. "No one knows, exactly. Maybe religious. Maybe just trash heaps. Either way, a way of making high land, ya know, for storms."

Murray considered, tried to think of anything but his ravaged skin, exerted every ounce of discipline to keep himself from scratching. "You spend a lot of time out there?"

The question surprised Tommy, he looked at Murray sideways. "I'd never been there in my life until today."

Murray was confused. "I figured, when you were growing up—"

"I grew up in the Everglades," said Tommy. "On a reservation with the Seminoles. Course, my mother made sure I understood we weren't Seminoles. So I was, like, an outsider, twice. She told me about Kilicumba; we never went. I didn't even know which island it was. Flaco did."

The Bra King gave in and scratched his arm. He knew he shouldn't but for the moment it was heaven. He was going to ask Tommy why he'd never visited the island, but then he didn't need to ask, he knew.

"Ya know," he said instead, "I'm always hearing stories about Jewish guys who don't feel Jewish, or don't want to, don't want the burden of it. All of a sudden they go to Israel, they're *dragged* to Israel by their wife or something, and they have these, I dunno, these revelations. The tour guide takes 'em to the Wailing Wall, they figure big deal, next thing they're standing there sobbing. They're on a street in Haifa, bored stiff, they suddenly start singing Jewish songs, they get a yen for borscht. They come back home, join a *schul*, start sending pledges to the UJA. Go know."

"What's borscht?" asked the Indian.

"Cold beet soup."

"Sounds disgusting."

"Ya put sour cream in it," Murray said. "It gets pink, like this shit I got all over me."

"Y'ever been to Israel, Murray?"

"Me?" the Bra King said. "It's the last place inna world I'd go."

"That's how I felt about Kilicumba," Tommy offered.

"Besides," Murray said, "I'm inna *shmatta* business and I'm a neurotic hypochondriac—how much more Jewish I gotta feel?"

"What's a *shmatta*?" asked the Indian.

"*Shmatta*. Ya know, a rag. A garment."

They drank beer, and watched old wooden schooners ferry tourists out into the ocean for sunset.

"But what I was thinking," Murray said, "I was thinking about the power of a place . . . I was thinking, this afternoon, I was watching you, trying to imagine what you felt out there. I couldn't do it. So I figured, say it wasn't an Indian place, say it was a Jewish place—what would I feel? The truth—I have no idea. What Jewish would I think about? Hebrew school? Charlton Heston playing Moses? Then I thought, wait a second—if you're supposed to feel something, and all you can do is think about what it is you're supposed to feel—that's not right, something got, like, too thinned out along the way, left too far behind. Ya see what I'm saying?"

Tommy looked at his friend, the wild hair, the pinwheel eyes. "Murray, you still taking pills?"

"Of course I'm taking pills. I'm a Jew, I'm taking pills. Come to think of it, why am I feeling so Jewish today? Ya know what it is? I saw you out there being an Indian, it made me feel more like a Jew. Is that screwy?"

"You see me being an Indian every day," said Tommy.

"Ya mean the ponytail, the vest? Due respect, Tommy, that's just bullshitting around." He pointed across the harbor, toward the backcountry. "Out there you were an Indian. I saw the pride. I saw the loss. But what I was saying, I'm saying I watched you out there, I thought about this thinning out, and suddenly I had the name for our casino."

He leaned far forward now and scratched his legs ecstatically. Dried pink lotion flaked beneath his fingernails, blistered skin began to ooze.

"I don't think there's ever gonna be a casino," said the Indian.

"Don't get negative on me, *bubbala*."

"*Bubbala?*"

"*Bubbala*. Like Jewish *kemosabe*. But look, what's the problem? LaRue's leaving us alone, this Estelle person's handling everything, ya don't even need a lawyer—"

"There's just so many steps. All the approvals, the complications."

"So we take one step at a time. Don'tcha wanna know the name at least?"

Tommy finished his beer and popped another. A chicken squawked in the weeds. "No," he said.

Murray fought off feeling miffed. "Why don't ya wanna know the name?"

"I'm, like, superstitious, okay? If there's ever a casino, you'll say the name, I'll tell you if I like it."

"He doesn't want to know the name," Murray said to the sky. He leaned back in his tilted chair, feeling like an astronaut.

"And this *bubbala* thing," said Tommy. "I don't know about this. Who ever heard of an Indian called *bubbala?*"

◆◆◆◆◆◆

That night, Murray took a long and itch-relieving soak in his master-bath Jacuzzi, then, from bed, he called his wife.

He wanted the atmosphere to be just right. He fluffed up all his pillows, made sure he had an unobstructed line of sight through his open curtains, past his balcony, to the yellow moonlight gleaming on the Florida Straits. He put a glass of milk and a little stack of cookies on the nightstand. Then he dialed.

"Franny? Murray," he said, when she picked up. "'Zit too late to call?"

"In hours," she said, "or years?"

He relished her tartness, burrowed deeper into his pillows. "What reflexes!" he said. "Bustin' my chops before y'even say hello. How are you?"

"Hold on," she said. "I've got *Streetcar* on the video, lemme turn it off."

Murray blissfully ate half a cookie. When his wife came back to the phone, he said, "Marlon Brando? Marlon Brando you'll turn off for me?"

"Him I can always turn on again. How's your depression?"

"Much better," said the Bra King. "It's been days since I've been publicly catatonic. Only problem, I'm getting low on pills."

"Maybe you could stop the pills by now."

"What're you, crazy?"

"Zinc is good for mood things," Franny said.

"Zinc is good for making garbage cans not rust," said Murray. "Medicine, they don't put it on garbage cans. Medicine, the doctor calls a fancy drugstore, you pick it up, there's a price tag says a hundred dollars stapled to the bag."

"I thought you might be more open-minded than you used to be, Murray. You told me you were changing."

Too late, the Bra King realized he'd been losing points. He frowned at his half-eaten cookie, squirmed against his pillows. "I am changing," he insisted. "Just not about zinc."

"What about, then?" asked his wife.

Murray thought and sighed, looked out the window at the moonstruck water. "I haven't checked the stock tables for three, four weeks. How's that?"

"I'd call it less than a breakthrough."

"Ooh," the Bra King said. "I got one: I bought a bicycle, I hardly use the car anymore."

"Really?" Franny said, and he could tell she was

impressed. "You must look pretty funny on a bicycle."

"I guess I do. I haven't really thought about it."

"Haven't thought about it? Murray, that's progress."

Now he was happy, he rewarded himself with the rest of his cookie. "Yeah," he said, "I guess it is."

There was a silence, it went on long enough for Murray to fear that he was losing his momentum. He groped for more evidence to lay before his ex, more proof that he was not the same old cranky selfish lout he knew she took him for.

"But wait," he said, "I haven't told ya the best one. I have a friend down here, guess who he is?"

"How should I know who he is?"

"He's an Indian. Great guy. Bitter. He's got a claim against the government, I'm helping him pursue it."

"Helping someone, Murray? You?"

"Hey," he said, "what's right is right. With all the shitty things that have been done to these people?"

For a moment Franny said nothing. Suspicion edged into her voice. "Murray, I was married to you for twenty-one years, the most political thing I ever saw you do was buy stamps. All of a sudden you're an activist?"

"I'm not an activist," the Bra King modestly replied. "It's a personal thing, one individual."

Franny paused again, put a skeptical finger on her lower lip. "There's a business angle in this, isn't there?"

Murray's voice was a low wail of offended virtue. "Franny! The guy wants this little island where his ancestors lived. It's got whaddyacallit, mittens on it."

"Middens," said his wife.

"See, I knew you were interested in this stuff. This is why I'm telling you. Tommy, this guy's name is. You'll like 'im, you'll meet 'im when you come down here."

"Who said I'm coming down there?"

"Franny," Murray coaxed. "Wouldn't it be nice to see each other?"

"Not especially."

"Come on, you'll bring me zinc, magnesium, I'll suck the iron out of a steak knife."

"I'm going back to Marlon Brando now."

"Marlon Brando? When you could talk to me?"

"Sweet dreams, Murray, and don't get cookie crumbs in the bed."

"How d'ya know I'm eating cookies?"

The phone clicked softly in his ear, it was almost like a kiss good night. He drank some milk, happily he looked out at the ocean. He was making progress with his wife; he had no doubt that he was making progress.

15

A couple of mornings later, Estelle Grau, dressed not for field work but the office, appeared at Barney LaRue's Eaton Street headquarters.

She sat in a straight-backed chair across the desk from the senator, pulled her khaki skirt down snug across her ample knees, settled her clipboard against the mesa of her thighs. "Your constituent," she announced robustly, "seems to have a legitimate claim."

LaRue smiled like he'd just been paid a personal compliment. Estelle couldn't help noticing how uncannily the smile matched the many others that grinned back from the pictures on the walls, the overflow of pictures that would not fit on the walls of the study in his penthouse.

"The Matalatchee do seem to be an offshoot of

the Calusa," she went on, "perhaps a variant in name of a former Gulf Coast tribe called Apalachee. The main branch of the Calusa was pretty well wiped out by 1800—mostly from diseases brought by the Spanish. But a few sub-clans hung on, mostly living in the Everglades. That lasted until the Second Seminole War of 1835. The clans didn't want to fight alongside the Seminoles, who historically were enemies. They couldn't flee north against the white army. So they trickled south into the Keys. There were probably never more than a few hundred individuals."

LaRue feigned interest. He'd had a lot of practice feigning interest and did it very well. He cocked his head at the attentive angle of the Victrola dog. He disciplined his perfidious eyes to stay wide open. Now and then he nodded.

"Reservation records at Pine Hammock show quite clearly that Tommy Tarpon's family were not Seminoles," the woman down from Washington went on. "Shells taken from the middens on the island the applicant calls Kilicumba have been out of the water at least a hundred years, probably a hundred-fifty. It's very persuasive, all in all. So I'll be recommending to the Secretary that he recognize the tribe and cede the land to them. To *him*."

Barney LaRue was still feigning interest in the fate of Florida's Indians, his smile alternating with pouts of fellow feeling. But his mind had started wandering, he was getting a number of steps ahead of himself.

"What if he dies?" he blurted.

"Excuse me?"

The senator seemed as surprised by his question as was his listener. For just an instant he was non-plussed. He cleared his throat, strove to sound like he was being neither more nor less than thorough. "I mean, if the tribe consists of just one person . . . "

"One person who's very much alive," Estelle Grau said. "So let's take one thing at a time. What I need to know from you, senator, is how much opposition to expect from the state."

LaRue unfurled his smile, light glinted off his mah-jongg tile teeth. He was once again composed and confident. "Expect none."

The woman from Washington shifted largely in her seat, rearranged her skirt with a touching jumbo daintiness. "None?" she said. "Senator, in all my experience with these things—"

Handsome, almost avuncular in a leering sort of way, Barney LaRue leaned across his desk. "Ms. Grau," he said, "I have been a Florida legislator for twenty-seven years. I know how to get things done in Tallahassee. You do your part in Washington. I assure you that in a case like this, where there are grave historic wrongs to be corrected, issues of justice at the forefront, the state of Florida will not stand selfishly in the way."

◆◆◆◆◆◆

Days passed; weeks passed.

In Washington, Estelle Grau rode herd on the bureaucratic beast that would process Tommy Tar-

pon's application. In Tallahassee, Barney LaRue
sweet-talked, bluffed, and horse-traded with his colleagues. In Coconut Grove, Charlie Ponte waited
to be handed the Indian who would lead him into
the promised land of casino gambling.

The clipped month of February phased over into
March, and in Key West the weather grew more
reliably perfect. The breeze blew gentle but rock-
steady from the east, as though pushed along by
some slow colossal fan; the mercury hit eighty-two
and stuck there, like all the thermometers had suddenly broken. Spring Break began, and Smathers
Beach was paved in first-rate bodies from third-rate
schools. Sometimes, when old man Bert the Shirt
walked his stiff-legged dog along the promenade,
Murray tagged along, and the two of them would
appraise the youthful flesh—the buoyant chests,
the thong bikinis—with the wistful calm of gal-
lerygoers who'd been priced out of the market.

In the lengthening sunsets, Murray fished with
Tommy, excess wattage crackling from their nervous brains, coursing through their fishing lines,
vanishing like half-seen phosphorescence in the
water. They had reached a point in their friendship
that allowed for times—not many—when even the
Bra King felt he didn't have to talk.

Then, one morning in the middle of the month,
Tommy was asleep in his hammock when he heard
somebody call his name.

The voice was smooth yet faintly needling, mellow yet commanding as it filtered through the

houseboat's soggy planks. "Tommy!" it said. "Tommy Tarpon! Come out here, friend, and hear the news!"

Tommy was badly rested and slightly hung over. His eyes itched and his scalp felt like a garment that had shrunk up in the dryer. He waited for one more shout, to make sure he wasn't dreaming. Then he climbed out of the hammock, blinked against the slanting light from the glassless portholes. He labored up against the slope of the floor, and climbed the companionway ladder in his underwear.

Standing on the dock was Barney LaRue. He was wearing a blue pinwale suit and a beautiful red tie. His teeth gleamed and his upswept silver eyebrows shone bright as tinsel in the early sun. "Congratulations, Tommy," he said. "You've been recognized."

Tommy wasn't quite awake. "Recognized?"

"You're a tribe, man. A sovereign nation. You've got your island."

The Indian stood there, tired and numb, in his underwear on the top step of the ladder. It was great news, soiled somewhat by the bearer of the tidings, and Tommy was confused. Now that he'd got what he wanted, now that it appeared, for once, that the system wasn't going to screw him, he didn't know what to say and he didn't know what to feel. Pelicans flew low across the water, trees swayed on the islands across the harbor. He was sovereign, and nothing looked different from the way it looked the day before.

"Get yourself ready," the senator ordered. "We're having a press conference."

"Press conference?" said Tommy. "I don't want a goddam press conference."

LaRue spoke as if coaxing a sulky child. "Of course you want a press conference. Come on now, they'll be here in fifteen minutes."

"Here?" Tommy squinted out at the rock-strewn scrub of Toxic Triangle, the ruined boats, the chickens, and the lizards.

"Rags to riches," the senator intoned. "The American dream."

"I want Murray here," said the Indian.

"Murray?" said LaRue. He said it like the name just faintly rang a bell. "What's Murray got to do with it?"

"He's my friend. He started this whole thing."

LaRue looked down at his watch. "There isn't time to get Murray. Now Tommy, please get ready, unless you plan to make your television debut in your BVDs. And do something about your hair. Make it look more Indian."

Dazed, Tommy Tarpon descended once more into his spookhouse of a cabin. Light slanted in, fish made tiny splashes in the sunken stern. He approached the table with two long legs and two short legs, threw water on his face from a chipped white basin. He regarded himself in the mirror that hung at an inexplicable angle from a peg. Vaguely, he wondered how it was that, back when he was one more bum, nobody ever woke him up and told him what to do, and now that he was sovereign, he was immediately being swept into things he didn't like by people he couldn't stand. He thought of resisting, but lacked the clarity of mind to do so; it was all too new, the granting of his application was too bafflingly at odds with the bleak logic of his pessimism. He picked up his comb, parted his blue-black hair precisely down the middle. He tugged it taut in back, tied it with a leather cord into a small ponytail. He pulled on blue jeans and the chamois vest with fringes.

By the time he appeared topsides, a small delegation of the media was assembling. A truck topped with a satellite dish had parked at the foot of the Toxic Triangle pier. Vans painted with radio call letters were scattered here and there. Young men with bandannas tied around their heads were hefting cameras, TV correspondents were having their noses powdered against the morning glare. A reporter from the *Herald* read the paper and ate a bagel. A representative of Key West's own daily, the *Sentinel*, came clattering up on a rusted blue bike.

Tommy looked at the gathering press and got the beginnings of a stomachache. He walked discreetly to the far end of the dock and peed in the ocean.

Producers milled, framed angles with their hands. Microphone booms swung overhead like cranes. Finally a woman with a pencil behind her ear positioned Tommy and the senator in front of the half-sunk houseboat.

As cameras rolled and pencils scratched at notebooks, Barney LaRue announced the recognition of the Matalatchee nation, then delivered a brief homily on the American traditions of fair play, of honoring agreements, of seeing justice done. He introduced Tommy Tarpon, "the last survivor, a tribe of one, a man who had nothing but his pride, his dignity, and his unshakable faith that America would in fact do right by him."

It is a rare thing to see an Indian blush, but Tommy's face was now as red and blank as a slab of fresh-caught tuna. His hands clenched and unclenched, he was sweating inside his chamois vest. Dead airtime accumulated and he uttered not a word.

"I guess we're ready for questions," said LaRue.

"Senator," said a correspondent for a local cable station, "if I understand correctly, tribal recognition is a federal matter. How can you be sure the state won't challenge the decision, as it has in other instances?"

The politician smiled benignly, stroked his red silk tie. "This is where high ideals and practical politics meet. Later this morning, a bill will reach the governor's desk. It deals with water rights for citrus growers, and the governor will certainly sign it. As a rider on that bill, there's a provision saying that the state will not contest any federal grants dealing with ten acres or less of offshore land."

"What's offshore land got to do with citrus?" somebody asked.

The senator gave a sly shrug and everybody but Tommy understood that it was time to laugh.

"What's the procedure from here?" asked one of the radio reporters. "Will there be a formal treaty?"

"Of course," LaRue said gravely. "There'll be a signing at the courthouse, Thursday afternoon." Less gravely, he said, "Cocktails after."

"Question for Mr. Tarpon," said the woman from the *Herald*. "Will you live on the island? Lease it out? Are you planning, perhaps, to bring gambling to the Keys?"

Tommy shifted from foot to foot, sweat squished in his sandals. "I live here," he said. He pointed to the half-sunk boat and there was defiance in the gesture. "As far as gambling goes—"

"No plans have been made in that direction," LaRue interrupted. "Any other questions?"

The reporter from the *Sentinel* sidled a foot or two away from the group. He was a gangly fellow with frizzy brown hair, resolutely casual in khaki shorts. He held a ninety-nine-cent spiral notebook and a chewed-on plastic pen. "Senator," he said, "your positions on minority issues are well-known. In 1990, you voted against more funding for inner-city schools and day care. In 1992, you introduced a bill seeking to curtail Seminole rights to sell tax-free cigarettes. Why are you suddenly this man's champion?"

LaRue shot his questioner a look like a gob of spit, but by the time he spoke the wallpaper smile had returned. "This is hardly the place to discuss my past voting record, though I assure you I had solid reasons for every position I took. Suffice it to say this man's case is different."

"That's what I'm asking," pressed the *Sentinel* reporter. "What's different about it?"

The senator squinted at the journalist, but the journalist's gaze had now been captured by the eyes of Tommy Tarpon. The two skeptical men shared a glance, traded something wordless, like ants do when they touch antennas. Overhead, gulls wheeled and cackled, from the weeds came the idiot complaining of a chicken.

Barney LaRue cleared his throat, cranked his smile one notch wider. "Thank you all for being here," he said.

16

The reporters dispersed, LaRue slipped away.

Tommy jumped onto his bicycle, unburdened lately with its cart of shells, and rode as fast as he could ride. Trees blurred, cats dodged from his path as he headed through Old Town and around the cemetery toward the Paradiso condo.

It happened that Murray was having a crisis of his own that morning. He'd turned his Prozac bottle over, and the last two capsules landed in his palm. This should not have surprised him, but it did; like a drunk who can't believe his glass is so soon empty, he suspected some subterfuge or a glitch in the laws of nature. He put the vial to his eye, shook the air inside it. He ate the green and cream-colored capsules and started pacing.

Now he dove onto the sofa with the nautical stripe and called Max Lowenstein.

"Murray," the shrink scolded, "you don't think I keep records? You shouldn't be out for another month. You been upping the dosage, Murray?"

"Well, I, uh, sometimes—"

"Murray, let me ask you something. If a cardiologist prescribed a pill for your heart—"

"I see what you're saying. But come on, I know how I feel."

"That," said the psychiatrist, "is open to debate. But okay, how *do* you feel?"

"Great, Max, I feel terrific."

"Then why more pills?"

"I dunno. Security blanket. I'm a nut, Max. Who knows that better than you?"

The intercom buzzed, Murray jumped at the unaccustomed sound. He excused himself to answer it, pushed the button, asked who was there. When he heard it was Tommy, he rang him in, left the apartment door open, went back to the phone.

In his absence, Lowenstein's qualms had deepened. "I'm really not so comfortable," he said, "prescribing for a patient I've had so little recent contact with."

"I understand, Max," said Murray, his cajoling tone edging over into pleading. "But really—"

"What have you been doing with yourself?"

"Fishing. I went fishing like we talked about."

"Good."

"It was good, Max. The electric thing, it was a really good idea."

"Don't flatter me to get your pills. Go on."

"Well, I went fishing and I met an Indian and we're friends and we're going into the casino business."

"*Oy.*"

"What's with this *oy* bullshit again? I tell you all good things, you tell me *oy.*"

Just then Tommy knocked softly on the open door, stepped into the apartment. Murray didn't really see his friend's flushed skin and clenched expression; he just pointed to the phone in case the Indian didn't notice it was glued against his ear.

"The casino business with a bunch of Indians," Max Lowenstein was saying. "I'm sorry, but to me, this sounds bizarre, grandiose, maybe clinically manic."

"It's a new challenge," said the Bra King, his pleading now thinning out to desperation. "Besides, it isn't a bunch of Indians, it's one Indian. He's a tribe. The last of a tribe. Here, he just came in. Say hello."

"I don't want to say hello."

But Murray had decided this would be a good idea; if Max heard what a sane calm person Tommy was, he'd come across with the prescription. "Wait, I'm putting him on."

"Murray," said the shrink, "this is totally inappropri—"

The Bra King didn't hear him, he was thrusting the receiver in Tommy's face. "This is my shrink. Tell him everything's okay."

Lowenstein's voice squawked faintly, told Murray

to get back on the line. A telephone voice a foot away always sounds like it belongs to a midget.

The baffled Indian took the instrument, said softly, "This is Tommy."

"Tommy, hello. Please put Murray—"

"I just want you to know that Murray and I are partners and everything's fine. He calls me *bubbala*."

Murray was pacing. Tommy handed him the phone, he took it on the fly, like a runner in a relay race. "There Max, ya see?"

Max didn't see. "Murray, allow me to lapse into the vernacular. This whole thing sounds crazy."

Murray stopped short on the carpet, yearning for his pills. He thought of a new approach. This was not conniving. But people learn what works, which words and actions will be approved by whom; and sometimes, in people of goodwill, this learning deepens, becomes not just a stance but a new conviction, and through it, a person has been changed. Murray remembered what had worked with Franny.

"Max," he said, in a voice full of affronted virtue. "I wanna help this guy. This makes me crazy? He's got one chance to really beat the odds. I've gotta keep my pecker up to help him."

Lowenstein was quiet for another moment, then he muttered, "Altruism as a side effect. Live and learn."

"Did I say altruism? I said this guy's my friend."

"Okay, Murray, okay," said the psychiatrist. "I'm not sure I should be doing this, but I'll FedEx down a new prescription. Don't take more than I tell you to take."

Murray punched the air triumphantly, winked at Tommy. He gave Max the address. And he didn't promise about the dosage.

◆◆◆◆◆◆

Serene now, imagining the reassuring slide of capsules down his gullet, the Bra King sat down on the sofa, said to Tommy, "And how are you?"

The Indian took his turn at pacing. "Fucking pissed," he said. "Fucking humiliated."

The Bra King was surprised, focused finally on Tommy's tortured countenance. "And you waited all this time to tell me?"

"Fucking hypocrite comes to my boat—"

"What hypocrite?"

"LaRue," said Tommy, like it was perfectly obvious. "Scumbag wakes me up, says dress up like an Indian. Me, I'm too confused, groggy, I don't have the balls to tell 'im stick it up your ass, like a fucking circus dog I do it."

"I don't get it," Murray said.

Tommy trenched the carpet, veins stood out in his neck and a steely gleam came through the russet of his forehead. "Tells me there's a press conference. Stands me up in front of cameras, a buncha jerkoff journalists—"

"Why?"

"Why?! Murray, because I'm recognized. And this fucking douchebag—"

The Bra King was off the sofa now, he was not aware of rising. "Recognized!"

"—this fucking hypocrite smiling like an ass with teeth—"

Like a linebacker, Murray put himself in Tommy's path, grabbed him by his taut broad shoulders. "Recognized!" he said again. "Tommy, that's great. You won, man. You're a tribe, you got your island."

"I shoulda told him—"

The Bra King shook him. "Forget that bullshit, Tommy. You won. You're sovereign. That's the last time they can fuck with you."

It finally seemed to get through to Tommy. The tension went out of his arms, Murray felt his shoulders drop. He took a deep breath, looked down at his feet. He traced a dreamy little circle around the living room, through stripes of sunshine and stripes of shade, then he sat crosslegged on the carpet. His face was tilted downward, he lifted nothing but his eyes to glance briefly through a thicket of brows at Murray. He looked away, bit his lower lip, began to cry. Big tears collected at the corners of his downturned eyes, they swelled and then burst suddenly, staining his cheeks like the beginnings of rain on brick. For a moment there was no sound, just this tearing that was silent as a seeping sponge, then he gave a short whimper followed by an extravagant, razzing sniffle, which was followed in turn by a choked and giddy laugh whose catharsis started with the sinuses.

"Fuckin' A right," he said when he could talk. "We won, Murray! I never in a million years thought those fuckers would give it to me, I never believed it for a second ... And LaRue, this horse's ass, he's up there talking about my unshakable faith. Douchebag! ... Jesus, I'm exhausted, Murray. I am just wrung out."

He blew his nose then sat there limp, his wet eyes puffy and ecstatic.

Murray said, "What say we have a bottle of champagne?"

◆◆◆◆◆◆

They went downtown, drank bubbly in the hot sun on empty stomachs. When the first bottle was gone it was getting on toward other people's lunchtimes. Trays of food went by and made them hungry. They ordered some, with another bottle to wash it down. By this time the day was seeming improbably long, and Murray, wobbly on his shiny bicycle, went back to the penthouse for a nap.

He fumbled around the empty apartment, wandered aimlessly from room to room as he shed his clothes. Finally he drew the bedroom curtains against the bright and blaming daylight, and he tumbled into bed.

He didn't remember reaching for the phone, suddenly the receiver was in his hand. He dialed his wife in Sarasota.

"Franny," he said. "Great news, Franny."

Smells of alcohol and fried food bounced off the

mouthpiece and back into his face. Apparently his ex could smell them too.

"It's two o'clock, Murray. You becoming a lush down there or what?"

"Little celebration," the Bra King slurred. "Tommy got recognized. The Matalatchee are a tribe."

"That's nice, Murray. Murray, listen, I have the women from the book club here. It's not a good—"

"I thought you'd be more interested," Murray whined. "Activist and all that."

"I am interested," she said, but from the way she said it, Murray could picture her leaning away, ill at ease, looking through a doorway to make sure her guests were comfortable without her.

"The book club ladies—they there right now?"

Franny sounded exasperated. "They're in the garden."

"Good. I wanna proposition you."

"For God's sake, Murray."

"Two days from now, there's gonna be a treaty signing. A historic occasion. I want you to be there, spend a few days with me."

"A few days?! Just like that I'll spend a few days with you? Murray, what kind of girl do you think I am?"

"Franny, we were married twenty-one years!"

"And we've been divorced for six."

The Bra King squirmed against his pillows, his shoulders looking for those six years of lost comfort, the memory of being home. "I know, I know. But look, this treaty, he signs a piece a paper, it says he promises he won't declare war on the United States. How often you get to witness someone promising he won't attack your country? Besides, dammit Franny, I'm proud of this, I want you to be there."

She hesitated, the pause was as full of promise as something gift-wrapped. She sighed. Then she said, "Murray, I have to get back—"

"Please, Franny," Murray said, but he said it only by reflex. His hopes were dashed, he knew he'd been turned down, the phone in his hand had taken on the tragic aspect of a broken doll.

When she spoke again, it was almost in a whisper. "Maybe I'll come. But I'm staying in a hotel."

Murray sat bolt upright in his bed, stared cross-eyed at the wand of sunshine that gleamed between the panels of the curtain. "You'll come?!"

"I said maybe."

"Franny, I'm thrilled! But a hotel? C'mon, I got a penthouse heah."

"How many bedrooms?" asked his wife.

"Three."

"I'll think about it, Murray. Maybe I'll come. Maybe I'll stay in a guest bedroom. When's this treaty thing?"

"Day after tomorrow, four o'clock, the court-house."

"Maybe I'll be there."

"What maybe? Tell me, I'll make arrangements, I'll pick y'up."

"I'm going now, Murray. *Anna Karenina* is waiting."

"Anna Karenina," the Bra King said, though the phone had already clicked down in his ear. "Marlon Brando. What about me? I'm the one who's waiting. I'm sitting here, Franny, I'm blotto, I'm waiting."

17

The courthouse in Key West was a stout and square brick building in a town of flimsy, leaning wooden homes, a monument to order and solidity in a place whose charm and wonder was the lack thereof.

Fortunately, though, the structure's august appearance did not stand up to close inspection. Decades of ferocious sun and tropical cloudbursts had cracked and pitted its mortar, had flaked the paint on its phony fluted columns. Fecund trees dropped leaves and fronds and seed pods faster than the maintenance crew could pick them up, and the lawn and even the courthouse steps were generally strewn with spent and rotting greenery. Groaning air conditioners sought to filter out the tropics from the shut-up building, but even so, there was something dislocated, contrived, in the stock-

ings and pumps worn by the lady lawyers, the mail-
order suits and ties modeled stiffly by the prosecu-
tors. In all, the building felt less like a sanctum of
domestic government than like an embassy of some
foreign nation whose mores were peculiar, whose
costumes were quaint, and whose exotic capital
was very far away.

At a quarter to four on the day of the treaty signing, Murray and Tommy stood in the courthouse
hallway, shuffling their feet and cracking their
knuckles.

"Nervous?" Murray asked.

By way of answer, Tommy burped then wiped
his damp palms on his pants. They were khaki
chinos, the only pants he had aside from a couple
of pairs of jeans. With them he wore his one blue
shirt, a shirt of such vintage that the collar was not
worn away, but cracked from so many years of
being folded. He'd had his hair trimmed and he
wore it parted on the side: damned if he'd dress up
like a minstrel Indian ever again, for Barney LaRue
or anybody else.

"How 'bout you, Murray? You nervous?"

"Me?" the Bra King said. The courthouse wall had
a molding at eye level, it was one of those crazy
things old public buildings always had. He plucked
at it, it rocked against its ancient nails. "Wha' do I
got to be nervous about?"

He hadn't told Tommy about Franny. Franny he
was keeping as his own delicious secret, as if there
could be nothing more sweetly clandestine and
illicit than a rendezvous with one's own re-

romanced wife. Besides, with every passing minute he became more devastatedly sure that she would not appear, and whether you were sixteen or fifty-three, it was embarrassing to get stood up for a date and have your buddies know about it.

At five minutes to four, Barney LaRue, dressed in summerweight mohair and with his skin aglow from a lunchtime facial, came halfway down the marble stairs that had fossil footprints worn in them. "They're ready for us," he announced.

Tommy looked at Murray. Murray cast a surreptitious look back toward the door. They headed up the stairs.

LaRue led them into the book-lined chambers of Judge Walter Beasley. Beasley was a burly man, with a trim gray beard and a sardonic manner on the bench. He'd put on robes for the occasion; if you looked closely, you could see that a seam was opening on his shoulder, threads as curly and black as pubic hairs were twirling toward his neck. Maybe fifty people were packed into the room. Estelle Grau was there. There were legislative assistants and judicial assistants and members of the press. Tommy recognized the gangly reporter who'd asked LaRue questions that the senator didn't like. The two were nodding at each other, when LaRue steered Tommy toward a lectern next to the judge's desk. He made a point of leaving Murray behind, tossing him overboard in the middle of the throng.

At one minute to four, Judge Beasley cleared his throat and asked for quiet.

Murray watched Tommy, blinked, and tried without success to smile. He was excited and yet he suddenly felt extremely blue, blue and utterly, insanely removed from what was going on, as if he'd had too many Manhattans at a catering hall and wandered into the wrong affair. He was standing between strangers, in a room that seemed to tip. He felt for his friend a tenderness that yet remained melancholically distant. Tommy looked scared, less like the guest of honor than like something about to be carved up for dinner. A depressed Jew and a bitter Indian, Murray thought: What sort of lunatic confluence had made them friends? How had Murray persuaded Tommy that this moment was his destiny? How had Tommy *let* him? And where the hell was Franny?

The judge droned on about the importance of the occasion and about the authority that was vested in him, and Murray winked at Tommy while silently he called himself a yenta, a lonely man with not enough to do but stick his nose in the affairs of other lonely men. Had he ever done a deed that was truly kind, or did he only meddle? Did he trust himself to know what friendship was, or was he only keeping busy? And where the hell was Franny?

Beasley adjusted his shredding robe, produced a document in a leather binder. Tommy coughed softly into his fist. Then the door to the judge's chambers opened, very slowly. It made just the tiniest squeak against its hinges, and only Murray turned around. Standing in the doorway, half-hidden by a maze of other people's chins and shoulders, was Frances Rudin Zemelman Rudin. She was wearing white silk pants and a big red shirt whose tails reached down to her knees. Her curly brown hair was flecked with gray, she wore big silver earrings and a necklace made of amber.

"Franny!"

Murray thought he whispered it, but still somebody shushed him.

His wife slipped across the room as the judge, reading through elegant half-glasses, intoned a bunch of sentences that started with "Whereas."

She stood next to him now. She wasn't tall, she wore flat shoes, he remembered exactly where the top of her head came to, the exact angle at which he had to hold his neck to see her face. She used herbal creams and hair stuff, she smelled like rosemary and peaches.

Tommy saw her standing next to Murray. He narrowed his somber eyes, and smiled.

Walter Beasley ran through a few more Whereases. Then he pronounced, "Therefore, in recognition of their mutual sovereignty, this treaty is hereby concluded between the United States of America and the Matalatchee Nation of Kilicumba Key, Monroe County, Florida, each side pledging to respect the territorial prerogatives of the other and to live together in peace."

The judge swept off his glasses, held the treaty's final page up for display. "The document, as you can see," he said, "has been signed by the President himself. It will now be executed, on behalf of the Matalatchee Nation, by Mr. Tommy Tarpon."

He put the treaty on the lectern and handed

Tommy a pen. The already quiet room went into a deeper hush. Murray thought Franny was standing closer to him now, though he might have just imagined it. Tommy pulled back the sleeve of his old blue shirt that was frayed where the ancient folds had been, and signed the treaty. Everyone applauded.

The judge held up his hands for quiet. "The document still needs witnessing," he said. "May I ask Ms. Estelle Grau, of the Bureau of Indian Affairs, and Mr. Barney LaRue, state senator from Monroe County, to serve as witnesses?"

The woman down from Washington strode with her large slow grace to the podium and witnessed Tommy's signature. But as she moved to hand the pen to Barney LaRue, the Indian intervened and took it.

"Your honor," he said, bashfully, but less so than he could have said it five minutes before, "if I'm a sovereign and all, I'd like the second witness to be my good friend Murray Zemelman."

Judge Beasley shot an awkward look at Barney LaRue. The rebuffed politician quickly hid the hand that had been poised to take the pen, and managed a strangled smile, he looked like he was swallowing his gums. "Well, I see no reason—" the man in robes began.

Franny put her hand on Murray's back, urged him forward to accept the offered honor. He floated toward the lectern in a kind of transport, like a religious man being called upon to read the Torah.

He signed the treaty, he embraced his friend, and through the thin applause that followed, he looked out to see his wife clapping near her chin, looking truly proud, and older than he remembered her, and very lovely.

18

After the signing, the thirsty guests filed out and headed by car and cab and bicycle and scooter to a cocktail reception at Barney LaRue's penthouse.

Murray had driven the scratched-up Lexus with the Jersey plates, it was parked under a tree that had dropped a yellow fuzz all over it. There hadn't yet been a moment to introduce Franny and Tommy, and only now he presented her as his wife.

"Ex-wife," she corrected, shaking hands. "He dumped me for some brainless floozy. Nice to meet you. And congratulations."

It was not a chatty ride. Everyone was slightly drained, felt more than slightly awkward. Tommy sat in the back, fidgeted with the ashtray in his armrest.

At some point the Bra King said, "Your bags, Franny, don'tcha have any luggage?"

"I left it at the airport," she said. "I still haven't decided if I'm staying."

Tommy smiled to himself and looked discreetly out the window. The Straits were calm and had the sheen of green aluminum.

"Of course you're staying," Murray said. "Ya shlep all this way to turn around again? Tomorrow I'll rent ya a bike, we'll find the guy who makes the sno-cones. Remember the sno-cones, Franny?"

She remembered the sno-cones, she looked down at her short unpolished fingernails, neat hands folded in her lap. "Don't get nostalgic on me, Murray. It isn't fair."

He drove to the airport, he fetched her bags. When he dropped them in the trunk the whole car rocked.

"Weighs a ton," he said, getting back behind the wheel.

"I brought you some vitamins and things. That Prozac, Murray—enough already."

The Bra King let that slide, drove to the airport exit. It was opposite the ocean, he looked at water while waiting for a break in traffic. Thinking aloud, he said, "You care about me, Franny. You want me to be well. Ya didn't care, ya wouldn't carry all that stuff."

Franny looked away, fingered the chunk of amber in her necklace. "So Tommy," she said, "how's it feel to be a nation?"

◆◆◆◆◆◆

Pascal the masseur, Pascal the secretary, was now Pascal the caterer. Dressed in a tuxedo shirt and lavender bowtie, he greeted guests, poured drinks, delivered hors d'oeuvres and little cocktail napkins on a silver tray.

Franny Rudin accepted a glass of champagne and maneuvered around the leather sofas and glass-topped coffee tables toward the balcony, away from the cigarette smoke and the jabbering. Murray and Tommy took their glasses of bourbon and followed. But the party almost instantly tracked them down. Everyone wanted to wish Tommy well, to shake the hand of a real live Indian and be able to say they'd met a sovereign. The guest of honor made agonized attempts at chitchat, smiled till his cheeks were cramped, and when Pascal appeared with a fresh tray of drinks, he grabbed a big one with the secret panic of the socially overwhelmed. He watched people blowing smoke in one another's faces, straining to look fascinated by one another's stories.

"So this is what white people do for fun?" he asked.

Franny was nursing her champagne, looking out across the swimming pool, the putting green, the screened gazebo. Murray was leaning near her on the rail, smelling her hair on puffs of breeze. Neither felt qualified to answer.

The gangly journalist came by to introduce himself.

"Arty Magnus," he said, and he held out a cool

longfingered hand. His hair was thick and frizzy, his expression wry and skeptical, not a smile and yet not quite a smirk; he was one of the few who didn't say anything stupid or demand that Tommy respond with something stupid, automatic, and for this the Indian was grateful.

"I didn't think you'd be invited," Tommy said, "after the questions you were asking the other morning."

Arty leaned close, spoke softly. "The press is always invited, no matter how much the host or hostess hates them." He sipped his drink. "And they always go, no matter how much they hate the host or hostess."

Tommy pulled on his bourbon. "You hate the host?" he whispered.

"Sometime we should talk," said the reporter. He looked over his shoulder. More people were streaming toward Tommy, their eyes slightly droopy with drink, their hands soggy with condensation. "But for now I'll leave you to your public."

A fidgety Murray moved closer to Franny, just barely brushed her hip with his own. "I'm dying to have some time alone with you," he said.

His wife looked off at the water, at people walking, running, skating on the promenade. "I don't mind some insulation."

"How about a nice quiet dinner? Candlelight, a corner table in some little garden?"

"What about Tommy?"

Murray frowned, chewed an ice cube, felt the

idiot frustration of a teenager trying to be suave, thwarted in a make-out quest by a little brother he couldn't shake. "Maybe he'll get tired."

Franny had been packing, traveling all afternoon, the word brought on a yawn. Murray watched her closely in that extravagantly intimate instant before she brought her hand up to her mouth; by sunset light he saw her crowns, her gold and silver fillings, remembered with love the way she sometimes dribbled from one side or the other before the novocaine wore off.

"He won't get tired earlier than me," she said.

Murray hid his disappointment in his glass. Behind them the party buzzed, made clacking, whirring, scratching sounds that swung between the festive and the infernal.

Then Barney LaRue strolled out to the balcony, still uncreased in his perfect summer suit. His presence somehow muffled the party noise, he carried with him a pampered smell of body oil and rich shampoo. He barely glanced at Murray, he made no acknowledgment of Franny. He handed Tommy another drink, pushed it on him really, then stood almost rudely close, assaultingly close. "I'd like to speak with you a moment," he said.

Tommy looked at Murray. Murray raised an eyebrow, took a half-step forward.

"Not you," the politician said. He said it softly but with the inexorable certainty that he would be obeyed. The Bra King stalled, his weight spread indecisively between his feet.

The Indian gave a rueful look, shrugged at his friend, and carried his bourbon toward the living room with its whorls and wreaths of smoke.

Franny turned back toward the sinking sun. "I hate this party," she said. "Do we have to stay much longer?"

19

Tommy followed LaRue through the ranks of half-crocked functionaries and local busybodies and hangers-on. He followed him down a hallway, past a bathroom with a couple of people lining up to use it, around a bend in the corridor to where the dimmered lighting didn't reach.

LaRue paused momentarily before a closed door. His heart was racing. To be doing this here, now, with a judge in the living room, the press nosing through his home—the sheer nasty baldness of it was as bracing as an ice cube on the scrotum. He gave a furtive glance around, quickly opened the door to his study, hustled Tommy through in front of him.

Inside, sitting at the politician's desk, occupying his regal chair and smoking one of his cigars, was Charlie Ponte, the Mob boss of south Florida.

"Hello, Chief," the mafioso said to Tommy.

"I'm not a chief."

"Sure y'are," said Ponte.

"A chief is elected," Tommy said. "It's an honor to be a chief."

The little man kept on. "You're a chief, I'm a chief. Bahney here, he's a chief. The losers out there"—he jerked a thumb toward the living room—"they're a buncha fuckin' Indians."

Tommy sipped his drink, looked around, noticed Bruno. Bruno was standing hugely in the shadows; he twirled a giant globe, which seemed to fascinate him the way a brightly colored beach ball entrances a gorilla.

"Mr. Ponte's going to be your partner," said LaRue.

Tommy said nothing. Ponte blew a smoke ring, fingered it as it hovered near his face.

"That island of yours," the mobster said. "Handled right, it's an extremely valuable piece of real estate."

"I know that," Tommy said.

"Of course you do," said LaRue. "I'm sure you're very smart about these things. So you'll see the advantage of having a professional like Mr. Ponte on your side."

"I already have a partner, thank you."

LaRue ignored the comment.

"You'll be building a casino," he announced. "Once it's open, you'll get twenty thousand a month, no strings. You'll sign papers, you'll be around for ceremonies. That's all you have to do."

"I'm not interested," said Tommy.

"Listen, Chief—" said Ponte.

"And please don't call me that."

The mobster took a moment to collect himself. He pulled down on the waistband of his silver-zippered jacket, he put on a ghastly smile that stretched the liver-colored sacs beneath his eyes. "All right then," he said pleasantly. "Not Chief. Fuckstick. Listen, Fuckstick, the deal we're offering, the partnership—"

"I have a partner. I told you that."

Ponte stubbed out the cigar on the senator's desk blotter. Bruno sidled closer to Tommy, it was as if a tree had lifted its roots and walked. Tommy smelled B.O. and aftershave.

The mobster pulled his eyes away from the stubborn Indian and asked LaRue: "This partner—'zit the crazy Yid ya tol' me about?"

The senator nodded that it was. Then he looked vengefully at Tommy. "The one who witnessed the treaty. Meddlesome type. Always underfoot. A nuisance."

Ponte rocked in his seat in some ghoulish parody of mirth. "Ya know," he said, "I almost gotta laugh."

Bruno took this as a cue, he came forth with a constipated high-pitched titter that set Tommy's hair on end and started perspiration trickling down his spine.

"A fuckin' nobody," the Boss continued. "A kike amateur. But okay, okay. Ya got a lot on your mind just now. I unnerstand. So take a little time, think things over—"

"There's nothing to think over," said Tommy.

Ponte glanced at Bruno. Bruno leaned down toward the stocky Indian and threw an arm around him, the gesture was almost lovey except that Tommy's collarbones were bending in like the ends of an overdrawn bow.

"I think there is," the mobster said.

Bruno gave a final squeeze then slacked his grip. The Indian felt his skeleton rearranging.

LaRue smiled, never raised his voice. "Tommy," he said, "we realize this is all very new for you, a period of adjustment. But a lot of things will be much easier once you understand we own your red ass now."

Tommy pursed his lips, thought that over. He'd had a lot to drink. He was scared but not as scared as he should have been. He'd come around to being in that bar-brawl frame of mind where there was something sickly fine about being threatened, hit, because it gave you a cherished opportunity to hit back. "You own my ass," he mulled, "you can kiss it anytime you like."

He spun like a halfback, got free of Bruno's grip. The big man made a move toward him, but Ponte, with a lifted eyebrow, called him off. Tommy yanked open the study door and skittered through it, falling prey to the comforting but dangerous illusion that he'd won the skirmish, that the first round was his, that maybe his opponents would retreat.

He wanted badly to believe that, but still, outrage

and a seeping dread overtook him in the hallway, caught up suddenly like the panic of realizing you are choking on a piece of steak. All at once his temples were pounding, the bones in his legs felt fused. He lumbered through the maze of hallways, across the crowded smoky living room; he recognized no one, bodies looked warped and wavy, faces were masks with black absences for eyes and smeared red gashes for mouths.

He could barely breathe, he struggled toward the balcony for air, trying vainly to calm himself as he went. He saw Murray standing very close to Franny, whispering to her, their faces silhouetted in the dusk, and instantly he knew what he and his partner had to do: They had to meet this enemy together, stare him down, show him their resolve, and do it now, before the will of the adversary had time to gather and to crest.

The Bra King watched his friend approaching, saw the wild eyes and sweat-darkened blue shirt. "Tommy, what's goin'—"

"Murray, come with me a minute."

"Wha—?"

"Just come with me. Right now."

Murray pulled his brows together, handed his empty glass to Franny.

He followed Tommy in his headlong ramble through the thinning party, down the lighted hallway, past the bathroom, around the bend to where the corridor was dark. Without knocking, with only the briefest hesitation for a gulp of air, the Indian threw open the study door.

The room was dim, and, standing by an open window, drawing deeply on a glowing joint, was Pascal the houseboy. Mingled with the smell of hemp was the memory of a good cigar and the lingering feral stink of Bruno, but no one else was in the room.

The affronted young man in the bowtie put a hand on a hip and fixed the intruders with a petulant glare. "Do you mind?" he said.

"Tommy, talk ta me," said Murray.

The Indian said nothing for a moment, his face was twisted with rage and confusion and fear and relief. "Never mind," he said, in what he took for triumph. "The chickenshits are gone already."

They gathered up Franny and were out the door without saying their goodbyes.

20

That evening they had a romantic candlelit dinner for three.

They sat in a quiet garden under an enormous breadfruit tree. Bougainvillea flowers, thin and dry as tracing paper, chattered softly against a lattice-work fence. Overhead, a tired Orion was laboring up the steep late-winter sky, his brilliance dimmed by an eggshell-white half-moon.

They got their drinks, and after they'd clinked glasses, Murray said, "So Tommy, ya wanna tell me what went on in there?"

The Indian didn't want to. With great difficulty he'd composed himself, he didn't want to get riled again. He'd persuaded himself he'd handled the confrontation very well; but that belief was fragile, he didn't want to mess with it.

"I probably made more of it than it deserves," he said.

"Made more of *what?*" asked Murray.

Tommy sipped bourbon, said nothing. It wasn't the time, the place, he didn't want to go into it in front of Franny.

"What was it you made too much of?" Murray pressed. "This is what I'm asking."

"I just had to talk to one person too many. Let's leave it at that."

"So who was the one person?"

Tommy shook his head and blubbered his lips like he was under a too-cold shower, then turned to Murray's ex. "Franny, can I ask you something? When you were married to this guy, was he always in your face like this?"

"Constantly," she said.

"Always yammering?"

"Except when he was sulking."

"Always pushing, pushing into things the other person doesn't wanna talk about?"

"That's Murray," Franny said.

The Bra King, drinking wine now, was just slightly juiced; he heard, or thought he heard, or longed to hear a note of unquenchable fondness, of acceptance, in Franny's voice. It put a lump in his throat and he hid behind his menu.

Tommy and Franny, on terms now, Murray's relentlessness a bond between them, carried on just fine without him.

"Your necklace," said the Indian. He was suddenly voluble, happy to talk about anything except LaRue and Ponte and Bruno. "Amber. The Matalatchee word for that is *tahtukahti.*"

Franny tried to say it.

"No," said Tommy. "More bite in the *ts.*" He leaned forward, pressed his tongue between his slightly parted teeth, then squeezed a little burst of air out of his throat. He made a sound that was more than just a consonant but wasn't quite a syllable. "Ttuh."

"Ttuh," said Franny, but hers wasn't quite as hard-edged as the Indian's, it didn't really pop.

Tommy demonstrated again. This time he used his hand to show how the air climbed up his neck and blurted with a small explosion from his face. "Ttuh."

"Ttuh," said Franny.

Now Murray could no longer resist joining in.

"Ttuh," he said. But he had too much moisture in his mouth and his puff of air was too diffuse, he made a soggy sound, a little like a fart.

"Watch," said Tommy. Both hands now pantomimed crisp, dry, and percussive air. "Ttuh."

"Ttuh."

"Ttuh."

"Are you ready to order?" the waiter said. He'd been standing near their table for quite some time.

By the time the mango cobbler arrived for dessert, the tension had mostly drained from Tommy. He and Franny felt that they had known each other for awhile, and Murray had moved even closer to forgetting he had ever been divorced, as if the last six years had been nothing more than some numb extended business trip, an emotionless sleepwalk to strange hotels in vague cities. Now he felt the wordless relief of the end of roaming, the bone-deep ease of the return.

"Murray," Tommy said, pulling him out of his thoughts, "ever been to the Everglades?"

"Hm? No," the Bra King said.

"Amazing place. Flattest place on earth. Slopes one inch per mile."

"Really?" Franny said. She looked at him with wide eyes, an interested forehead.

He sipped the port that Murray had ordered all around. "But that tiny slope," he heard himself continuing, "is enough to make the whole bottom half of the peninsula a huge slow river. Grasses, sedges, swamps that seem stagnant but aren't. A gigantic spongy filter. Roots sucking in minerals, caterpillars getting minerals from leaves, the minerals make the colors for the butterflies. Same with flamingoes. Need certain plankton from certain alkaline waters to make them pink. Amazing place."

"Jesus, Tommy," Murray said, "you know a lot about it."

The Indian got shy, couldn't remember how he'd started on the Everglades in the first place. He hid behind his glass a moment, then amazed himself by saying, "I was gonna be a biologist."

"Gonna be?" said Franny.

"Three years at Gainesville. Scholarship."

"You never told me," Murray said.

"Bad for my image," said the Indian. "Don't let it get around."

"How come you didn't finish?" Franny asked.

Tommy shrugged, waited for the accustomed bitterness to grab him by the throat, was surprised to find its grip was not so suffocating now. "Something happened. Not interesting. Something happened and I quit." He tossed his napkin on the table, leaned back in his chair.

"So what happened?" Murray asked.

"I said it isn't interesting."

"Yeah, but if it made you quit—"

"There he goes again," Tommy said to Franny.

◆◆◆◆◆◆

On the sidewalk Murray said, "Lift home?"

Tommy said he'd like to walk. He went to shake hands with Franny. Franny hugged him, then he wobbled off into the mild night.

Driving back to the Paradiso, Murray said, "The way you draw people out, Franny, it's amazing. I'm like the guy's best friend, me he tells nothing. The way you do it, it's really great."

"Don't butter me up," she said. "I'm sleeping in a guest room."

The Bra King let that pass. "It's your face," he said. "The way there's a lot of open space between your features, places where a person's eyes can rest. To look at you is very restful."

"Great," she said. "Some women are exciting, stunning, sensual. Me, I'm restful."

"Restful lasts longer," Murray said. "Besides, you're all those other things too."

Franny started to laugh but the laugh caught in her throat. Her face flushed, her eyes burned, she squirmed in her bucket seat. Then she said, "Damn you, Murray. You've still got this, this doglike charm. Droopy eyes. You always miss someplace when you shave, you know that, Murray? And you say these crazy things, these lunatic attempts at compliments . . . You're like this big sloppy, shedding, drooling dog."

They were riding up A-1A by now. The moon was high above the Florida Straits, its light on the water was a silver arrow that tracked them as they drove. Murray whimpered ingratiatingly like a retriever pup, gave a softly growling little bark.

"Cute," said his former wife. "Adorable. I'm still sleeping in a guest room."

◆◆◆◆◆◆

Tommy Tarpon made his way through quiet streets, saw cats skulking under porches, their haunches higher than their heads, heard tree toads murmuring, contentedly nested in people's orchid boxes. The air was moist enough to put a pearly coating on windshields, an opal smear of halo around the streetlamps. The Matalatchee sovereign was tired beyond thought, his brain hummed with edgeless

impressions of ceremonies and hypocrites and enemies and friends.

He reached Caroline Street, absently ran his hand
along the chain-link fence that corralled the parking
lot. He crossed toward Toxic Triangle, did not take
special notice of the dark Lincoln parked against a
crumbling stretch of curb on the far side of the road.
He walked the rocky path to the dock, kicking
pocked pieces of limestone. Chickens squawked as
a raccoon sneaked through the weeds. Music from
downtown rolled around the harbor, arrived sounding cottony and baleful.

He strolled to the end of the pier, peed in the
ocean; his stream called forth little sparks of phosphorescence. Then he stepped onto his half-sunk
houseboat, climbed along its tilted deck, went down
the companionway ladder to the dark funhouse of
a cabin. He climbed into his hammock, almost
serene or at least exhausted, and was asleep before
his bed of net had stopped its swinging.

21

The Bra King, still hoping that things might turn out otherwise, dropped his ex-wife's heavy luggage in the bedroom next to his, while she poked around the penthouse with the cool eye of a realtor.

He found her in the kitchen, peeking into cupboards. "Nice place," she said, with no particular enthusiasm. "For a rental unit. Heavy Scotchguard, dishes that bounce. But pretty nicely done. Too big, really. Of course, you always had to have a bigger place than you really needed."

The Bra King didn't take offense, he was too pleased to have his wife within his own four walls. With pride he swept open the mostly empty refrigerator. "I shopped today," he bragged. "I got some fruit, wouldya like some fruit?"

"We just had dinner," Franny said.

"You like fruit," Murray informed her.

"Do I have to like it right this second?"

Undaunted, Murray led the way to the living room, parted the curtains that gave onto the balcony and the ocean view. "Sit on the couch?"

She eyed him like he was selling Turkish rugs, then moved sideways toward the sofa with the nautical stripe. Murray followed, they sat down at the same moment. They weren't kids, their buttocks had gone a little soft, and flesh spread when they sat, the spreading made their hips touch. Murray put his arm not quite around her but behind her on the back of the settee.

"Franny," he said, "I'm so glad to see you, I'm so glad you came."

Grudgingly, she said, "It's nice to see you too, Murray."

They took a couple breaths, listened vaguely to duct noise from the hallway. Then Murray said, "Let's neck."

"Don't be ridiculous," said his former wife.

"Why is that ridiculous?"

"Because everything you say is ridiculous, Murray."

But, to his amazement, she tucked her head against his chest, rested her face in the soft place between his shoulder and his ribs. Her earring traced an imprint in his skin, he felt her warm breath through his shirt. Cautiously, tentatively, he reached toward her short brown hair, stroked it, smelled rosemary and peaches. He closed his eyes, absorbed her nearness, and almost all of him would have been perfectly content, ecstatic, to go no further, to leave things just exactly where they were, to sit there clothed and on the couch, forever.

◆◆◆◆◆◆

Hanging plumb in his hammock, snoring softly, Tommy barely felt the boat rock. Very faintly he heard the squeak of stretching dock lines. The dangling mirror clattered softly on its peg, disturbed water gurgled briefly at the stern. A woozy puzzled moment passed; the Indian shifted slightly and fell back into a deeper sleep.

In the next instant, a splintering crash, an intimate explosion, brought him wide awake.

Something had gone very wrong, his boat was caving in on top of him. The pilothouse seemed to have been lifted off its shims as if by a tornado; glass shattered in its one remaining window, sun-peeled timbers came raining down the companion-way. By the time Tommy had spun out of his hammock and found his footing on the sloping floor, the bulk of the ruined structure had tumbled down and wedged itself tight in the hatch, blocking off the only exit. Tommy shouted; there was no one near enough to hear him, no one who could have heard him above the sudden orgy of demolition on the deck. Sledgehammers rang off metal fittings, the sound was like the bells of hell. Rotting boards, soft and spongy as decayed teeth, were stove in by murderous iron.

The doomed craft listed now to starboard, Tommy struggled for balance. In the tumultuous gloom of the cabin, he saw a faint and sickening gleam as an ax-blade bit through the bruised skin of the hull, just below the waterline. The weapon was withdrawn and instantly the ocean started sluicing in, gushing crazily, as from a ruptured hydrant. More blows fell; lewd gashes scarred the houseboat's sides, an infernal hiss of water drowned out even the hard smack of the axes. Tommy felt warm but clammy liquid lapping at his feet, covering his ankles, crawling up his calves. The intruding sea floated the table with the two short legs and two long ones; Tommy's gas ring became a weird memento, a piece of flotsam, his old chipped basin bobbed madly on the monstrously displaced tide.

Then, as suddenly as it had started, the attack was over. Tommy felt adrift, understood that the dock-lines had been chopped, the sinking boat set free to wallow some yards out.

In the cabin, clamor gave way to deathly silence, the airless silence of the ocean floor, as the subsiding craft settled down below the level of its gashes. There was no more hissing now, but rather an inexorable ooze—less the boat sinking than the ocean rising, less the ocean rising than the ceiling coming down, heavy and relentless as an apple press. Choking back panic, Tommy floundered through water climbing quickly past his groin, up his torso, rib by rib. He waded to the ladder that, mockingly, led upward to the dead-end passage of the blocked companionway. While ocean flowed through glassless portholes, he dragged his sodden body up the rungs, his few possessions floating past and his hammock lolling like a bank of seaweed. Pressing his back against the heavy snaggled boards that glutted the hatch, he strained upward with all his might, bent nails and bits of glass clawing at his skin. He stared down at the black water coming up to meet his face, and savored bitterly the insanity of drowning in your living room, ten feet out to sea, in a sea that wasn't even ten feet deep.

◆◆◆◆◆◆

Suavely, with exquisite gradualness, Murray was moving his right index finger toward what he remembered as an especially arousing place on Franny's neck, when the phone rang.

The phone was on a table right next to the sofa, it sounded very loud. Franny twitched as though in answer to a fire alarm, her head sprang off his torso.

The Bra King muttered, "No one ever calls me," as the instrument rang two times, three times. Irritably, he leaned over and picked it up. He spit out a grouchy hello and got a response that was brief and to the point.

"Murray? Tommy. My house sank."

"What?"

"It sank. They sank it."

"Who sank it, Tommy, wha'?"

"Murray," said the Indian, who seemed to be shivering. "Not now. I'm wet."

"Wet?" said the Bra King. Cozy and dry in his penthouse at midnight, he just didn't get it.

Exasperated now, Tommy said, "Wet, Murray. Those scumbags from the party, they just about drowned me."

"Hold on a second," Murray said, and he pressed the phone against his stomach. "His houseboat sank," he said to Franny.

"Oh my God," she said. She was sitting upright on the edge of the sofa, on her somewhat flushed face a look of concern for her new friend, mingled with the ruefully wise expression of a woman who realizes she has narrowly avoided a big mistake. "What'll he do?"

The Bra King raised the phone to his mouth, asked Tommy that.

The sovereign hadn't had much time to think about it. But he'd been neglecting his sales of shells; he had very little cash, and neither bank account nor credit. "I'll guess I'll go sleep on the beach for now."

"That's out of the question," Murray said. "Where are you?"

"Caroline Street. The pay phone by the grocery store."

"I'll drive over, bring you some money. You'll go to a motel."

"You can't do that," said Franny.

"Hold on," said Murray, and pressed the phone to his belly again. "Can't do what?" he whispered.

"Send him to a motel. After what he's been through all day and night? You'll bring him here."

"Here?" said the Bra King, whose glandular optimism in regard to his ex-wife had flickered but hardly gone out.

Franny simply nodded, the way good people do when they know beyond a shred of moral doubt that they are right.

Murray winced but brought the phone back to his face. "You'll stay with us awhile."

Tommy paused. Key West nights were mild but not that mild, his teeth were chattering just slightly. "Jesus, Murray, I don't want—"

"It's all settled," said the Bra King. "I'm heading over now."

Tommy paused again, said, "My bike and shells, the cart, it's all I have, can I throw them in your trunk?"

After they hung up, Murray asked Franny if she wanted to come along for the ride. She said no, she was tired, she was going to bed, and Murray knew she meant in a bedroom of her own.

He went downstairs and climbed into the scratched-up Lexus.

The moon was low, the breeze was still, and on the quiet ride crosstown, the Bra King reflected on something Franny had said: that he always wanted a bigger place than he really needed. Well, maybe that had been true when he'd arrived, a lonely refugee with neither friends nor prospects. But now the showplace at the Paradiso was turning out to be just right. A room for him; a room for a former wife who thought it was ridiculous to neck with him; a room for a sovereign but suddenly homeless Indian.

THREE

22

Murray had shopped, but he'd done so like a bachelor, sparsely and forgetfully; and of course he hadn't known that they'd be three—or even, confidently, two—for breakfast.

So the morning meal was improvised and incomplete. There was coffee but no tea, which Franny now preferred. There was cereal but no eggs, and to Tommy breakfast didn't really seem like breakfast without eggs. There was toast but no jam, fruit but no yogurt. On the other hand, there were plenty of pills. Franny took A's and E's, and calcium for solid bones, and manganese for healthy hair, and deodorized garlic to keep her memory alert. She offered Tommy C's and beta carotene to counteract the stress that he'd been under. On Murray she urged zinc, and to humor her he ate some with his orange juice but took his Prozac also.

They were sitting at a plastic table—perfect for a rental unit—on the balcony. Unsullied morning sunshine slanted low across the ocean, it lit up just one side of the joggers and walkers and skaters on the promenade. Franny wore a yellow terry robe; her hair was wrapped up in a bright red towel. Tommy was wearing the jeans he'd almost drowned in and a blue tank top borrowed from Murray's dubious assortment of Key West duds.

"We'll have to get you some clothes," Murray said, around a bite of toast.

Tommy was chewing granola. He only nodded somberly.

"Such a shame," said Franny, pulling a section off a tangerine, cleaning it of stringy pith. "How d'you think it happened?"

Tommy shrugged, glanced under his eyebrows at Murray. "Lotta things go wrong with boats."

The fib hung in the air like the smell of greasy cooking, made everyone uneasy. After a moment the Bra King said, "There's nothing we can't talk about in front of Franny."

Maybe Franny was flattered, but mostly she looked baffled. She bit a piece of tangerine, it squirted down her chin.

Tommy put down his spoon, let it rest against the edge of his bowl. "People boarded," he said. At the thought of the violation, skin moved at the outside corners of his downturned eyes, flesh twitched across his hairline. "With axes, sledges."

"Jesus Christ," said Murray.

"Why would anybody—?" Franny said.

"They smashed the hull," the Indian went softly on. "Cut the dock lines."

Murray nervously slurped coffee. "The guy you talked to at LaRue's?"

Tommy pursed his lips and nodded. "Tha'd be my guess."

"Does someone wanna tell me what the hell is going on?" said Franny.

For the moment they ignored her.

"Who was he, Tommy?"

"Name was Charlie Ponte. Little guy, shadowed eyes, slicked-down hair. Had a bodyguard or something with him, a monster."

"*Oy*," the Bra King said. "Mafia?"

"Murray, I'm an Indian. Fuck I know about the Mafia? Excuse me, Franny."

"Someone better tell me what this is all about," she said.

Murray inhaled deep and loud, blew air out past his flubbery lips. "LaRue," he said. "Fucker was setting us up the whole time."

"I hate to say I told you so," said Tommy.

"I still don't understand—" said Franny.

"This Ponte guy," Tommy said. "He's sitting there in LaRue's office, he's telling me, like it or not, he's my partner in the casino."

Murray looked down at his lap.

Franny said, "Casino? *Casino?!*"

There was a soft breeze from the south, it carried faintly the slap and hiss of wavelets that could now be heard in the mortified silence. Tommy, unaware that he had blundered, blundered on.

"I tried to tell 'im I already had a partner," he said. "I tried to tell 'im forget about it."

Franny was glaring at Murray, and Murray was trying to decide if he would crawl under the table or throw himself over the railing to the concrete and the shrubbery three floors down.

"So what I think happened . . . ," Tommy rambled, and then he abruptly stopped.

He stopped because Franny had thrown her tangerine at Murray, was on her feet almost before it bounced off his chest and started rolling warpedly around the table. Her hazel eyes were wide and righteous, naked and unsparing in their morning lack of makeup, and Murray shrank under her gaze, quailed like a timid circus bear being scolded by its trainer. She spit out a sound that was midway between ha! and hm, was illusionless and sharp as the crack of a whip.

"I should have known!" she said. "Murray the activist. Fat chance!"

"I never said—"

"I should have known there was a business angle somewhere."

"Franny," whined her former husband, "you've got this all—"

She talked right over him, her severity leavened somewhat by the towel on her head, which had shifted in the course of her tirade and was tipped now at a rakish angle. "A casino. Cigarette girls. Slot machines. How tacky. How typical."

"Now Franny, listen—"

"You should be ashamed," she hissed. "Now I understand, I see it all. First you take advantage of Tommy. God knows what you've got him into. Then you use Tommy to try and take advantage of me." She recoiled and shook like she had a giant bug inside her robe. "Christ, Murray, I'm not saying this would've happened, but it might have happened, I might've actually ended up in bed with you again." She shuddered, made a disgusted sound. "At least I'm spared that."

She fell silent, crossed her arms against her midriff, realized her pique was not yet spent. "And now you've got the Mafia involved. Terrific."

"We don't know it's the Mafia," said Murray, though in his heart he did.

"Sleaze goes to sleaze," said Franny.

Murray winced, turned to Tommy for respite. "This Ponte person, he say anything else?"

Tommy picked up his cereal spoon, suspended it between his index fingers. He didn't answer the question right away. Instead, he said to Franny, "I don't think you're being fair."

Franny tried to straighten the towel, the knot loosened and it was more cockeyed than before. "Fair? He lures me down here with some cockamamie story like he's angling for the Nobel Prize, then it turns out he's exploiting you so he can make a trillion bucks and be a bigshot. *That's* fair?"

"He's not exploiting me. And this isn't about money."

"No, of course not. So what is it about?"

"It's about," said Tommy, and then he realized he didn't quite know. "It's about . . . What it's really about is two guys needing something to talk about, something to do. It's about getting to be friends."

That slowed Franny down. She sat again, absently picked up the tangerine and ate a slice. Less strenuously, she said, "Other people, they're getting to be friends, they go bowling, they rent videos, they find things to do that don't involve the Mafia."

The Indian shrugged.

Murray said, "Tommy, please, what else did this guy say?"

"He said he'd pay me twenty grand a month to be the front man. Sign papers, smile at customers."

"Twenty grand a month?"

Tommy nodded.

The Bra King thought it over, but not for long. "Take it."

"No way," said Tommy Tarpon.

"It's a lot of money."

"We're partners, Murray. I didn't start this thing to end up being someone's flunkey."

"A quarter mil a year," said Murray. "And nobody gets hurt."

There was a silence. Breeze rattled palms, there was splashing in the pool, convertibles went by on A-1A.

Then Franny said, "Hurt?" She said it in a different voice from any she had used so far that morning.

But now it was Murray whose tone was turning strident. "Yeah: *hurt*. The Mafia—ya think all they do is whimsical little pranks like sinking people's houses?"

Franny reached into her bag, pulled out some C's and beta carotene.

"Gimme a couple a those," said Murray.

"So now whadda we do?" said Tommy.

"I tol' ya what ya should do."

"Forget about it," said the Indian.

Murray looked off toward the ocean. He suddenly felt very heavy in his plastic chair, he was uncomfortably aware of the weight of his jowls pulling down against his cheekbones. At last he said, "Ah shit."

No one picked up on the comment, and after a moment, Murray sighed and rambled on, griping to the heavens.

"I'm tryin' to do the right thing here, I really am. So wha' do I accomplish? I make friends with a guy, right away the Mob is after 'im. I bring Franny down, I try to show her I've really changed, she ends up thinking I'm a dirtbag."

"I never said you were a dirtbag," said his former wife.

"Cheeseball then."

"Cheeseball, maybe." She took the towel off her head. Her hair had mostly dried, it stood up here and there in spiky little curls. "Murray, listen, I'm sorry for what I said. It's just that . . . "

"Just what, Franny?"

She cast a quick shy look toward Tommy, decided to proceed. "Just that, dammit Murray, I was starting to feel close to you again. I didn't want to hear about money, deals, casinos."

Murray didn't meet her eye. "I didn't want you to hear about those things either, Franny. I wanted it to be . . ."

He broke off, blotted his loose mouth on a napkin, let out a slow and quavering sigh, started pushing back his chair. "I'll take you to the airport."

She sat there in her yellow robe. Breeze tickled her damp scalp, and suddenly she was blindsided by a feeling that seemed to come not from inside her but rather to be carried like the seed of something on the air: She didn't want to leave yet.

She licked her lips, then spoke softly. "You said you'd take me for a sno-cone."

Murray fiddled with silverware, for a time he couldn't talk. "Franny," he said finally, "I don't know what's gonna happen here. It could get crazy, dangerous."

His ex-wife didn't answer and she didn't change her mind.

The Matalatchee sovereign got up to clear the table.

"The sno-cone guy," he said. "This time of year he works on Leon Street, over by the school."

23

The Spanish guy who'd made the sno-cones fifteen years before was making sno-cones still. He still had the hairy mole on his left cheek, the stubby two-wheeled cart painted lumpy red and lettered with blotched and leaning letters. The only difference was that he no longer dragged the cart behind him rickshaw-style. By now he'd attached the shafts to a motorized tricycle, a cartoonish thing with a pull-start motor the size of a sewing machine.

The sno-cone man had been diminutive a decade and a half ago, and age had made him even smaller. He worked in baggy blue jeans, a boy's size, not a man's; they were held up by an ancient belt that went around him almost twice, and the legs were rolled into makeshift cuffs above a pair of elfin shoes. His neck had shrunk to a sinewy stalk, his face was pulling inward like a piece of air-dried fruit.

Strangely, though, his arms had gotten longer.

When he worked his plane across the scarred surface of the hundred-pound block of ice, the motion seemed to go on and on, his shoulders stretching as though on springs, his elbows extending like they were made of rubber. Six long sweeps was all it took to shave ice enough to overfill a paper cone.

"So, Meess Lady," he said to Franny now, "you like'a maybe *guanábana*, coco, papaya?"

Franny was wearing linen shorts, standing astride her rented bike. It had been a long time since she had a sno-cone, it would probably be a long time before she had another one. She put a thoughtful finger to her chin. "Do you still have guava?"

"Fo' course I got guava," said the sno-cone man. "What kinda sno-co' man, he no have guava?"

He stood on tiptoe, grabbed from a shelf a bottle of red syrup. "You like a leetle or a lot, nice lady?"

From fifteen years before, Franny remembered the sweet and gooey last slurp of a sno-cone, when the stinging ice was gone and nothing remained but a shot of viscous syrup that instantly turned warm. "Pretty much," she said.

The tiny fellow poured it on; with a courtly nod he handed over the paper cone. Then he turned to Murray. Murray ordered mango. The sno-cones now cost half a buck.

They took them into the shade of a mahogany tree, put their bikes aside and sat down on a patch

of grass. Across the street was a middle school; a
few tardy kids were straggling back from lunch.
Stylish in their baggy pants and high-top sneakers,
they reaffirmed the Lilliputian measure established
by the sno-cone man and his tricycle. The smallness
made the world seem new and safe and innocent,
seemed to speak of young love and discovery and
second chances. Murray slid closer to Franny on
the grass.

A huge dark Lincoln, grossly out of scale with
everything except the overarching trees, turned
onto Leon Street.

It advanced with the slow malign momentum of
a ship adrift in fog, then parked in back of the sno-
cone cart. The driver left the engine running, it sent
forth a bad smell and an arrogant whine.

Franny frowned her disapproval, waved away
exhaust fumes. Murray sucked ice and tried to reason away the beginnings of dread as he watched a
huge man unfold himself from the car.

He was wearing a dark blue suit and opaque
glasses, and he seemed the largest creature for many
miles around. His suit was vast and yet it could
barely contain him; a seam stretched open across
his billboard of a back, tormented polyester crinkled
up between his leg of mutton thighs. He pulled
fabric out from between his buttocks and loomed
above the sno-cone man; it seemed implausible
they belonged to the same species.

The giant grunted out an order for a sno-cone,
grape.

Franny could see no reason why his engine

needed to be running all this time. Before Murray could shush her, she said, "Excuse me, would you mind turning your car off while we're eating?"

The huge man looked at her with just a hint of unbelieving smirk. He turned away.

"That's rude," she said. She said it to Murray, but she believed in the power of peer pressure, she said it loud enough for the gargantuan to hear. Murray, feeling slightly queasy now, put a discreet finger to his lips.

The Spanish guy gave Bruno his sno-cone.

Bruno took a quick suck of ice. He seemed to notice it was tasty and had another. Then he walked leisurely through the shade toward Franny and Murray.

Sitting on the ground, the Bra King watched him approach, saw massive tubes of leg, the rude wrinkles of a crotch under the eaves of a hard and bearlike belly. He thought of getting to his feet, seemed not to have the time or will to do so. He sat, telling himself that nothing was wrong, the giant was not the person who'd scuttled Tommy's boat, there was more than one gorilla in town, he would surely veer away.

But now the huge man was standing directly over him, humming tunelessly and shifting his weight from foot to monumental foot. Meekly, lifting nothing but his eyes, Murray looked up, saw stubble and razor rash on the other man's neck, tangled black hairs webbed inside his nostrils.

The giant gave a mordant smile, then emptied his sno-cone on Murray's head.

He didn't throw it; he inverted it carefully, then squeezed and twisted the paper cup against the Bra King's skull, leaving it there a moment, like a dunce cap. Melting ice and syrup trickled through Murray's hair and down across his forehead and his neck, he flicked purple ice onto the grass and tried to process what had happened.

Franny's indignation ripened much more quickly. Without even seeming to take the time to aim, she flung her sno-cone at the giant. It caught him square under the chin and exploded like a small frozen firework across his face and suit.

Time stopped for a moment, red ice hung motionless in a starburst pattern. The breeze went dead and the air refused to carry sound. Bruno looked down at Franny in her linen shorts, her little sneakers and her half-socks with pom-poms holding them above her shoes. For awhile it seemed he might stampede her, stomp on her, break her ribs with the sharp toes of his shoes. Instead, he hovered indecisively, his upper lip pulled back from his teeth, then he wheeled back toward the sno-cone cart.

He picked up what was left of the ice block, maybe sixty, seventy pounds; he hoisted it above his head like it weighed no more than a basketball. Then he advanced on Murray and Franny like a cannon being trundled into place.

The Bra King didn't remember getting to his feet, but he was standing now, some unsought and eva-nescent gallantry had propelled him between his ex-wife and the goon. His feet were parted shoulder-wide, his soft hands curled into useless unaccustomed fists. But Bruno kept advancing, and Murray's courage quickly eroded, he was backing away with his eyes kept squarely on the dripping projectile that was aimed at him. Bruno trudged forward, Murray skulked back, moving from shade to remorseless sunshine. Finally, with a shot-putter's bestial grunt, Bruno lurched and flung the ice.

It hit the Bra King in the gut, he caught it like an old-time boxer training with the medicine ball. The impact quickened his backward steps; with the missile still seeming to chase him he retreated on the brink of falling until his spine collided with the trunk of a coconut palm. The tree stopped his body an instant before it stopped the ice; the block squeezed the air out of Murray, it exited quickly from everywhere at once with a symphony of unpleasant noises.

He crumpled, dazed and empty, to the ground. He looked up and saw clustered yellow coconuts, shards of sunlight squeezed between their pendant forms.

Bruno, in no great hurry, got into the Lincoln and drove away.

Franny ran to her fallen ex, knelt on the ground and gently, even lovingly, mopped syrup from his brow. She asked if he was all right and he labored mightily to answer with a reassuring wheeze.

She stroked his sticky hair and shook her head. "God," she said, "all I did was ask him to turn his motor off."

"Some guys," the Bra King gasped, "they like their motors on."

"I mean, was it so terrible what I said?"

Murray writhed in search of oxygen, squinted through palm fronds at the bright blue sky. "Betcha a sno-cone," he managed, "that's not what it's about."

24

Murray's ribs ached, his deflated lungs hung slack in his chest, shapeless as used condoms, but at some point it dawned on him that the ice attack provided a perfect pretext for getting Franny into the master-bath Jacuzzi with him. After some hemming and hawing she agreed to join him for a soak, though the woman he'd slept naked with for twenty-one years now insisted they wear bathing suits.

They were still soaking when Tommy came home from selling shells.

Murray called out to him, summoned him to the boudoir.

The Indian hesitated. He'd heard tales about the kinky rich, their threesomes, foursomes, their bondage rings in marble walls, their alabaster sex toys and household pets dressed up like maids and butlers. With some misgivings he walked into Murray's bedroom with its unmade bed, its wavy linens suggesting carnality. With considerable unease he stepped through the open doorway into the steamy baronial bath. Mostly with relief, he saw the chaste straps of Franny's one-piece, the decidedly ungoatish look on Murray's jowly face.

Striving for a sophisticated nonchalance, the sovereign lowered the lid on the toilet seat and sat down on the pot. "So how was your day?" he asked.

"Not terrific," said the Bra King. "I was assaulted with a frozen confection."

"Excuse me?" said the Indian.

"I think I met your gorilla. About six-six, wedding-cake black hair, cheap suit from the Fat Boys' store?"

"Sounds like him."

"He hit me with a piece of ice the size of Brooklyn."

"Knocked the wind right out of him," said Franny. "Could've ruptured his spleen."

"*Oy*," said the Indian.

"*Oy*?" said Murray. "Now I'm hearing *oy* from you?"

The red man shrugged. "People you live with, you pick up their mannerisms."

"We've lived together half a day," said Murray.

Tommy didn't answer, though something in his look said, yes, but it would be much longer.

Just then the phone rang.

"Want me to get it?" Tommy asked.

"Sure. See if the cord'll reach."

The Indian grabbed the instrument from the bed-side table, said, "Zemelman residence."

"Christ," said Les Kantor, "he has a houseboy now?"

The comment offended Tommy. "I'm not a houseboy, I'm a sovereign nation. Hold on, Murray's in the bathtub."

He dragged the phone in, Murray put the receiver against his dripping ear.

"Murray? Les. What kind of nuthouse you running there?"

"Nuthouse? An abode of bliss. Guess who's in the bathtub with me, Les?"

"I'm not sure I wanna know."

"Franny."

"You have to tell everyone?" she said.

"She'll talk to you?" said Kantor.

"You bathe with people you're not on speaking terms with? What's up?"

"Just got back from Milan," said the acting CEO of BeautyBreast, Incorporated.

"Ah," said Murray. "And how was the show?"

"Uninspiring. Whole fuckin' world's in a doldrum. But there's one thing I think we have to talk about. If you don't have time right now—"

"For you, *bubbala*, I have time."

Tommy Tarpon, sitting on the toilet, flanked by fogged mirrors, tried not to look miffed. He thought *he* was *bubbala*.

Les Kantor said, "The news from Milan, I'll give it to you in one word: Nipple."

"Nipple?"

"Nipple. Designers are showing a lot of it. The whole silhouette: nipple."

"Don't tell me the braless thing—"

"No, thank God, it's not the braless thing. Just the opposite."

"What's the opposite of the braless thing?" Murray asked.

Franny sank down lower in the tub, submerged until she was nothing but a curly head protruding from the vaporing water.

"Look," explained Les Kantor, "designers are showing nipple, but the women, it's not the seventies, they're not making statements with their tits, it's just a style, a look, the nipples are really built into the bra. You see what I'm saying?"

"Ah," said Murray. "Falsies for the nineties."

"Right, but it's gotta sound more elegant than that. *Faux aureoles*, something like that. Anyway, we gotta work up a whole new line, new slogans, new commercials. You on board on this?"

"Sure."

"Come on, Murray, say it like you mean it."

"Sure, sure. Only, Les, I got an awful lot going on—"

"Murray, please, we gotta move on this. I'll call you in a day or two, okay?"

"Okay."

"Tell Franny I said hi."

Murray hung up, feeling strangely elated. His ex-wife in the tub; his old partner on the phone; his new partner on the toilet. Bras; casinos; romance: It was almost enough distraction to occupy every splayed-out tendril of his juiced-up brain. "Now where were we?" he said.

"Where we were," said Franny somberly, "is trying to figure out what to do about these large strong people who seem to want to hurt you."

"Right," said Murray. "This what's his name, this Ponte, I think we gotta find out more about him. Maybe we should talk to Bert."

"Bert?" said Tommy. "Why Bert?"

" 'Cause I'm not sure, but I'm pretty sure that Bert is Mafia."

Tommy crossed his legs, crinkled up his brows, reflected on the arcane and infinite oddness of the white man's world. "You shitting me?" he said.

❖❖❖❖❖❖

Habits stick to lonely men like barnacles to boats, and Murray knew that Bert the Shirt, with sunset approaching, would be sitting in his folding chair, ten yards from the lapping shoreline of Smathers Beach, his sneakered feet half-buried in the coarse imported sand, his eyes fixed placidly on the western horizon, his dog half-conscious in his lap.

The Bra King wasted no time on pleasantries, but

said to the old man's back, "Bert, we really gotta talk to ya."

Bert was hard to startle; his reflexes weren't slow so much as yogic, things registered but with the urgency skimmed off like the fat on soup. He swiveled calmly, the teal blue silk of his shirt shimmering as it crinkled around his skinny neck. "Ya put it that way," he said mildly, "ya make me feel important. Hi Tommy. So what's on your mind?"

But now that he had Bert's attention, Murray couldn't find a tactful way to start. "Well," he fumbled, "what it is . . . from, like, a coupla things you've said, a coupla hints you've dropped, I sort of got the impression that maybe, in some way, direct or indirect, I know it's not something you'd usually talk about—"

"Spit it out," the old man said.

Murray nuzzled sand with his feet.

Tommy said, "You Mafia, Bert?"

The old man stroked his dozing dog, short white hairs the length of eyelashes rained down on his clothes. "Ya gotta love this Indian," he said to the chihuahua. Then he said to Tommy, "Was. I was Mafia."

"Was?" said Murray. "I thought the way it worked, you're in, you're in."

"You're in till ya die," the old man said. "Me, I died."

"Say wha'?" Tommy said.

"Twelve, fourteen years ago. Courthouse steps. Haht attack. The graph went flat, they lemme out

. . . Where you're standin', Murray, I can't see the sun."

The Bra King stepped aside, orange light replaced his shadow across the old man's long thin face.

"But inna meantime," Bert continued, "why y'askin'?"

"Tommy and me," said Murray, "we're thinking of going into the casino business, and—"

"Don't," the old man said.

"Don't what?" asked Murray.

"Don't fuck with the casino business. The casino business, ya gotta understand, certain people feel it is their God-given right to milk that kinda thing. Other people try to get involved, they get extremely upset, it's like their whole world seems outa whack."

"We're already involved," said Tommy. He told the old man about the meeting in Barney LaRue's study, about Ponte's offer, about the sinking of the houseboat and the battering with the sno-cone.

Bert the Shirt petted his dog, said, "*Oy*."

"You too?" the Bra King said. "*Oy* is like a Jewish thing."

"My ass," said Bert. "It's a New Yawk thing. I lived in New Yawk sevenny years, I'm entitled to say *oy*." He paused, then added, "hypocrite cocksucker."

"Ponte?" Tommy said.

"Nah, Ponte is what he is. LaRue. I hate guys like that. He wants ta be a crook, let 'im be a crook, but be honest about it. Don't go gettin' other people ta do the dirty work."

"Dirty work?" said Murray. The phrase conjured distasteful images of piano wire, car compactors, garbage dumps.

The Shirt just stroked his drowsy dog.

Tommy pressed. "So Ponte—he's a killer?"

The sun was poised an inch above the water, Bert refused to take his eyes off it. "All I'll say, I'll say he ain't a guy ya wanna be enemies with."

"How about business partners?" Murray said. "I've been telling Tommy, just take the deal."

The Shirt waited till the sun hit the horizon, till its reflection leaped up and made it no longer a sphere but a fat cylinder of flame.

"The trut'?" he said at last. "I don't think he'd be terrific as a partner. He's one a these guys, ya think ya have a deal, two weeks later he wants a better deal. Pretty soon he thinks he's better off wit'out a partner. And the partner goes away."

"Where's he go?" asked Tommy.

The old man pointed toward the sky. "Look the way that one little cloud, it's already gettin' purple onna bottom. Sittin' here like this, I love it."

"But Bert," said Murray, "we don't want 'im for an enemy, we don't want 'im for a partner—what's that leave?"

The old man serenely stroked his dog as the water took on the dull flat sheen of green aluminum and the sunset ripened to a madman's canvas of billowing reds and acid yellow. "It don't leave nothin'," he said. "This is why I'm tellin' ya, ya shouldn't be involved, ya shoulda talked ta me before."

"We didn't think of it before," said Tommy.

"And right there is the bitch a life," said Bert. " 'Cause now ya got a problem."

25

Three nervous people slept separately that night in the West Penthouse of the Paradiso.

In the morning, on the balcony, over a breakfast featuring vitamins, trace minerals, and prescription drugs, Murray, looking badly rested and wearing a purple tank top designed for someone with a different kind of body, said, "I think we gotta try LaRue."

The suggestion met with no enthusiasm.

"I think we gotta look 'im in the eye," the Bra King said, "and let 'im know we're not gonna let ourselves be bullied."

"Except we *are* gonna let ourselves be bullied," said the Indian.

Franny's hair was wrapped up in its bright red towel. She was eating a kiwi with a grapefruit spoon. "Not to sound bourgeois," she said, "but has anyone considered the police?"

Tommy gave a derisive snort. "Y'ever read the police blotter in the *Sentinel?* Tourist gets mugged, cops give 'im a victims' rights pamphlet. Guy gets his throat slit in a bar, he gets a pamphlet. Guy gets his arms and legs hacked off, they stick a pamphlet under his chin. Law by brochure. Every day ya see it in the paper."

Murray was drinking coffee. Since Franny had arrived, he'd started seeing things through her eyes, he realized suddenly that his coffee mug was perfect for a rental unit, the kind of cheap generic mug that bounced off tile floors. "That's it," he said, "the paper."

"What about it?" said his ex.

"We tell LaRue, he doesn't back off, we're taking the whole thing public."

"What whole thing?" said Tommy. "My wreck finally goes down, you get hit with an ice cube. This is headlines?"

"There's more to it than that," Murray said.

"Who else cares?" said Tommy.

Franny had finished her kiwi, she now was nibbling blackberries. "That reporter," she said. "The skinny one who talked to you at the cocktail party. Maybe he'd care."

Tommy made a moist and skeptical sound, had to wipe his mouth with the back of his hand. "Like he's gonna go after Barney LaRue for the sake of some nobody Indian."

"Now there's that bitter thing again," the Bra King said.

"Murray—have I been wrong so far?"

This was a tough one to answer, so Murray looked off at the ocean, past the green water to the inky blue where a smudge of a freighter rode the Gulf Stream.

Finally he said, "I'm suggesting a civilized chat with our senator. Anyone got a better idea?"

Franny said, "Be tactful, Murray."

"Come along?" he asked her.

She pictured the politician's smarmy smile, shook her head. "My hair dries, I'm going downtown, see if there's anything not too schlocky in the galleries. You like, Tommy, I'll pick you up some clothes." She ate another berry, glanced with what might have been affection at the Bra King's full and furry flesh as it spilled out the edges of his tank top. "Too bad I wasn't here to shop for Murray too."

◆◆◆◆◆◆

In a tone somewhere between firm and dragonlike, Barney LaRue's receptionist told the two unimportant-looking visitors that the senator was extremely busy and she doubted he would be able to speak with them if they didn't have an appointment.

Murray glanced around the waiting area. It didn't look busy. The unpeopled straight-backed chairs and the scattered magazines gave it the aspect of an abandoned dentist's office. "Would you ask him, please? I think he'll want to see us."

Dubious and annoyed, she pushed a button on her intercom.

When the mellifluous voice of Barney LaRue answered, she said, "There's a Mr. Tampon and a Mister Zimmerman here—"

"Tarpon and Zemelman," said Murray.

"—They don't have an appointment," she scolded.

To her chagrin, the senator instructed her to send them in. She hissed softly at their backs as they went through the door of his office.

LaRue, by contrast, was all welcoming charm this morning. He shook hands warmly with his guests. Eschewing the formality of his desk, he led them to a little grouping of chairs and sofa, where they could sit at ease in the honeyed light that streamed in from the garden.

"So," he said to Tommy, "you're here to talk about your plans for your island."

Tommy looked at Murray. Murray looked at Tommy. It dawned on both of them that they should have rehearsed.

The Bra King made a false start at speech, what came out was something like the forsaken sound a bubble makes when it rises to the surface of a bathtub.

Tommy said, "We're here to tell you your friend Ponte uses pretty shitty tactics."

The senator's face grew no less cordial, but now a blank befuddled look spread across his well-spaced features. "Ponte? I don't believe I know anyone named Ponte."

"Someone named Ponte," Tommy said, "was sitting in your study the other evening. In your chair. Smoking your cigars."

"I'm sure you're mistaken," LaRue said pleasantly.

Tommy licked his lips and stared at Murray. That bitter thing was making his eyeballs throb like boils.

Murray said, "Listen, Barney—"

But the congeniality of the poker table was history now, and the politician interrupted. "I'd appreciate it if you'd call me senator."

"Senator," said Murray, and in the next heartbeat wished he hadn't given in and said it. The concession made him mad, and now he was ready to talk tough. But talking tough takes practice and Murray found that he was no damn good at it at all. "These threats, this pressure," he fumbled. "Tommy and me, we're not looking to make trouble, but what's been happening to us, if it gets out, the publicity—"

"Ah," said Senator LaRue. "The publicity. Yes, that is a matter of concern."

Murray stalled, nonplussed. He hadn't expected it to be so easy. "Awright, then. So what we want—"

"What concerns me," the senator said, in a voice that triumphed not by volume but by suavity, "is Tommy's image."

There was a pause. In the garden, palm fronds scratched, hibiscus leaves shook and blurred the shadows that dappled the office's pale wood floor.

"Ethnic stereotypes," the senator went on. "Nasty things. Hateful. And I would hate to have it said that Tommy here, an emblem of Native Americans everywhere, got so stinking drunk on such an important occasion that he started imagining—"

"You son of a bitch," said Tommy.

"You were drinking heavily," said LaRue. "Forty people saw you drinking heavily. Forty people, some of the most respected people in this community, saw you stagger out without so much as a thank you or a goodbye. It wasn't very gracious, Tommy. I wouldn't think you'd want it in the papers."

The Indian flushed dark as brick, the whites of his popping eyes had turned an acid yellow.

LaRue folded his hands, composed his thin and bloodless mouth, summoned back his wallpaper smile. "And while we're on the subject of your island," he calmly said, "there's something you should be aware of, just in case you're not. You own the land, but the state owns right up to the shoreline. Place isn't worth much if people can't get there. People can't get there unless you dredge a channel. You can't dredge a channel without a special exception from the state. Think about that, Tommy, when you're calling people names . . . Now, is there anything else I can help you with?"

26

Out on the sidewalk, Murray, who never tired of telling people that before moving to Key West he'd been the most moderate of drinkers, said, "I need a drink."

It was around eleven-thirty in the morning. Tommy said nothing, just climbed on his bike and led the way crosstown. They rode through tunnels of bare-limbed poincianas waiting out the spring for a yet-higher sun to bring them into season; they rode past the first frangipanis springing weirdly into bloom, fragrant waxy flowers being dreamed by scaly, leafless stalks.

At length they came to the Eclipse saloon. It was a low and charmless building with a big wood door on which was tacked a 1950's sign that showed a penguin on an ice floe and claimed that it was

COOL INSIDE. The interior was dim and smelled of washrags. The place never closed; between four and eight A.M. no liquor could be served, hard-core patrons dozed or ate soft-boiled eggs. Now, in the lull before the lunch rush, a few of these pickled regulars leaned over the bar in postures that knew no time of day. Waitresses were filling saltshakers and ketchup bottles, a janitor was mopping the scuffed threshold to the kitchen.

Murray slid onto a stool and ordered up a bourbon.

Tommy asked for club soda.

"Club soda?" the Bra King said.

"That son of a bitch," said the Indian.

The drinks arrived. The brown stuff in Murray's glass embarrassed him somewhat, but that didn't stop him from sipping it while he waited for his head to clear and his blood pressure to subside. Air-conditioning tickled his back; people started straggling in for lunch.

Finally he shook his head and said, "I don't know how ya fight these bastards."

Tommy was sucking lime. "Ya fight them by making yourself very small, so small that no one bothers to take a swat at ya."

"I fucked that up for you."

"I never said that."

The Bra King put his bourbon to his lips, didn't in that moment like the taste of it. "Ya hungry?"

"Not really."

"Me neither. Let's have a nosh."

"Knosh? I had one of those once, in Miami."

"That's knish. Nosh is, ya know, a snack, a nibble."

They ordered some conch fritters, and while they were waiting for them, Tommy said, "Murray, can I ask you something? You and Franny, what's the story?"

Murray rattled his drink then blurted out, "I'm still in love with her." He paused, wondered if his own forthrightness would rise up to abash him. To his surprise, it didn't, so he carried on.

"Last time I went crazy, I guess it was about the time I started noticing gray hairs clogging up the shower drain, I dumped her for a brainless model with perfect tits. We divorced, she moved to Florida. Within a year, I was absolutely miserable, I felt like I'd gnawed off my own arm, plucked out my internal organs. Franny, meantime, she'd figured out that being rid of me was the greatest thing that ever happened. She realized what a pain innee ass I'd been all those years."

"Lemme understand this," Tommy said. "You dumped her. She thinks you're a pain innee ass. And now you think she's gonna take you back?"

"I think I got a shot."

The Indian looked down at his soda, stirred the shrinking ice cubes with a swizzle stick.

"The way I look at it," the Bra King went on, "when she was with me, she didn't realize she'd be better off without me, and I knew she didn't realize it, and this made me feel I could act like a schmuck and get away with it. But now that she knows she's better off without me, I think she understands that if I don't act like a schmuck no more, we're really better off together. Does that make sense to you?"

The Indian said no.

"We're mates," said Murray. "Better or worse, we're mates. Franny, I'm not sure she sees it that way. But lemme put it like this—"

But before he could get started, the conch fritters arrived. The Bra King, who was not hungry, picked one up immediately. Hot grease burned his hand, he put the fritter down again, licked his smarting fingers.

He still had his fingers in his mouth when the Eclipse's door swung open, a quick rude rectangle of brightness swept across the murky room, and Arty Magnus, the gangly reporter and city editor for the Key West *Sentinel*, came in for lunch.

The two friends saw the journalist before the journalist saw them. "I think we gotta talk to him," said Tommy.

"LaRue," said Murray. "His clout. It could get really ugly."

Tommy flashed a wry and bitter look through the bubbles of his soda. "It's ugly already." He waved to the skinny writer.

Magnus squinted through the dimness and uncertainly approached. When his eyes adjusted and he could see who he was walking toward, he gave an affable hello. Then he asked if he could join them.

"I was hoping you would," said Tommy. "I think

it's time we had a talk about some of the putrid bullshit that goes on in this town."

The journalist hadn't even got onto his seat yet. "You get right to the point," he said.

"Indians tend to be very direct. That's why there's so few of us left. What can ya tell me about Barney LaRue?"

The bartender came over, gave Arty the kind of hello reserved for steady customers who knew how to behave. Arty ordered a beer and a fish sandwich. The Eclipse's fish sandwich, like that of every other Key West restaurant, claimed to be the best in town and renowned throughout the world.

"LaRue," said Magnus, turning back toward Tommy and Murray. "Old Florida family. Or as old as Florida families get. Great-grandfather made big money, did land deals, swamp drainage, your basic visionary fraud. Granddad was a banker type, dull, talked in capitalist proverbs. Father rebelled, pissed away the fortune, screwed everything that walked, drowned falling shitface off a yacht with his pants around his ankles. Y'ever try swimming with your pants around your ankles?"

The reporter's beer arrived. He took a swig, wiped foam from his upper lip. "As for Barney, nobody really knows why he picked politics. Some people think it was to redeem the family name, erase the memory of his old man's buffoonery. Personally, I think it was to raise the buffoonery to a whole new level."

"What kind of senator's he been?" asked Murray.

"The kind that gets reelected. Hawkish on Cuba. Pro-development while pretending not to be. Doesn't waste tax dollars on poor people."

"Corrupt?"

"Of course corrupt. But not for the money itself, I think. Corruption for sport. Theft as pornography."

Tommy Tarpon finished his soda, wiggled his glass to signal for another. "Did you know he's tied in to the Mafia?"

In his checkered life as journalist and writer, Arty Magnus himself had had some contact, strictly legal, with the Mob. He got a little cagey. "I've heard rumors. I'm not sure I buy them."

"Do you know who Charlie Ponte is?" asked Tommy.

The newspaperman just nodded.

"Did you know he was at LaRue's cocktail party the other night?"

At this, Magnus could not squelch a somewhat unprofessional look of genuine surprise. Tommy told him about the meeting in the study, Ponte's generous offer to build him a casino.

The reporter shook his head. "Barney's got chutzpah, give him that. And you were at this meeting, Murray?"

The Bra King admitted that he wasn't.

"Anyone else see Ponte there?"

"You didn't," Tommy said. "Why would anyone else?"

The journalist remembered his half-eaten lunch, went back to it.

Tommy said, "Then he sank my house."

"He what?"

The Indian explained.

"Any witnesses?"

"No."

"And then his gorilla attacked me with a sno-cone," Murray said, "and hit me with a block of ice and drove off in a Lincoln."

"Did you get the tag number?"

Sadly, the Bra King shook his head.

Magnus ate his sandwich. The sandwich was just getting to the stage where the last piece of the fish fillet always slid out of the frayed and cockeyed roll. Thinking aloud, the reporter said, "If I try and print this—"

"If you try and print it," Tommy interrupted, "LaRue and his friends are gonna tell you I'm a no-good drunk who sees things that aren't there and is a blot on the reputation of Indians everywhere."

Fish slid out the bottom of the roll, it landed on the pickle. "Are you?"

"Am I what?"

"A drunk."

But now the Bra King was getting nervous. He was from New York, he knew from crappy newspapers, he could imagine a scandal that would do nothing but humiliate his friend. He hunkered low on his elbows and leaned in across Tommy. "We're off the record here, right?"

"I never agreed to that," said Magnus.

"Ya mean we're *on* the record?" Murray said.

"I didn't say that either. Look, we're talking, we'll see what happens. I don't go off the record, it ties my hands too much."

"So we're just supposed to trust you?" Murray said. "Why should we trust you?"

The reporter picked up a french fry, pointed it at Murray. "You shouldn't," he said. "Nobody should ever trust a journalist. But sometimes people do. Don't ask me why."

He sipped beer, seemed content to let things drop.

Tommy scratched his head, then decided his neck itched, then his stomach, and he scratched those places too. "Look, I used to drink too much," he said. "Now I only drink a little."

The journalist said, "Since when?"

"Since I ordered this fuckin' club soda," Tommy said.

There was a pause, bar noise flooded in to fill it. With the strange inhalation of restaurants at lunchtime, the Eclipse had gotten packed, its walls seemed to billow outward, it smelled of suntan lotion and cigarettes.

Magnus ate a final french fry, pushed his plate away. "I don't know what to tell you guys," he said. "LaRue, I can't stand him. But the thinness of the facts, the lack of witnesses . . ."

Murray leaned across Tommy, his face was pointed downward toward the bar. There was bourbon on his breath and the beginnings of real fear in his voice. "Arty, I hear what you're saying, but lemme run this by you, give us, like, a reality check. LaRue and Ponte are in cahoots—do you agree with me so far?"

"That's how it sounds," said the reporter.

"And the things that have been happening to us," said Murray, "they've been like nuisance things, warnings."

The journalist agreed.

"And given who we're dealing with," the Bra King said, "it isn't gonna stop with nuisance things."

"No," said Magnus. "If they're serious about persuading you, it isn't."

"So whadda we gotta do?" the Bra King said. "We gotta sit and wait for something really bad to happen?"

Arty wiped his mouth, dropped the napkin on his plate. "Listen," he said, "I'm sorry about this, I really am, but the way it works, when something bad happens, really bad, that's when they call it news."

27

Over the course of twenty-one years of marriage to Franny, Murray had formed a thousand little habits he didn't quite recognize as part of him; he'd invented, and been invented by, a thousand tiny rituals whose importance he never thought about, but which steered him through every hour of every day, and made his life his own and not some other life.

One of these unconscious rituals involved the opening of doors.

When Murray unlocked the door of his home—wherever his home had happened to be—he followed a procedure that was predictable as a sacrament and as crisply timed as music. He fished in his pocket for the key. Holding the knob in his left hand, he stabbed at the lock with his right. He waited for the crisp thunk of the bolt sliding free,

then, precisely half a beat later, having taken precisely half a step into the room, he called out her
name: Franny! The word always came out sounding
exactly the same, though in Murray's throat it could
feel a lot of different ways. On good days it was a
bellow of triumph, on lousy days a crying out for
comfort. But it was always an incantation, a sacred
noise that kept foreign spirits from following him
across the threshold, that separated home from outside world.

Now he slid his key into the lock at the Paradiso
penthouse.

The power of ritual and dusty habit asserted itself
over the power of change and loss. He waited
exactly half a beat, took a half step through the
doorway, and sang out, "Franny!"

Nobody answered.

With Tommy at his shoulder, the Bra King walked
into the room, stopped in the middle of it and
looked around at all four rented walls. He wasn't
worried about Franny, he had no reason to be worried. It was only two o'clock, not even. Franny was
looking at galleries. That was something she liked
to do. So was shopping. So was going off on her
own, chatting with strangers, exploring. She'd be
home when she was ready to come home.

Tommy went to the refrigerator, grabbed a
mango and a pear. "I think I'm gonna go and sell
some shells," he said.

"Now?" the Bra King said. "So late in the day
already?"

Tommy shrugged. "No cash in my pocket. It bugs me. I'm restless."

"Cash?" the Bra King said. "I'll give ya some cash."

"Thanks," said Tommy. "But it's not the same. I like to see the tourists fork it over. I like to see how much it hurts them. I'll see ya later on."

He went to his room, picked up the key to his cart, and left.

As he was leaving, Murray had a thought that shamed him, that made him knock wood to undo it, to clear the slate. Tommy was going off alone, unprotected, on a bicycle, and Murray thought, if something bad is gonna happen, if it has to be that way, let it happen to Tommy, not to Franny. Tommy at least was tough, a pessimist, a stoic; Tommy was his friend but not his wife.

Barely had Murray banished that thought when he was visited by another, even more unpleasant.

Wait a second, it occurred to him, here I am, me, home alone, a sitting duck. Tommy they need; I'm the one that's standing in their way. Something bad happens, chances are *I'm* the one it'll happen to, and it would serve me right, God would punish me for thinking, even for a second, that it should happen to Tommy.

He got up and double-locked the door.

Then he thought, Schmuck! this is crazy, nothing bad is gonna happen, I shouldn't've had a drink with lunch, it's made me gloomy, paranoid.

He found himself pacing. He told himself to calm down, he took deep breaths and held them in; the exercise made him slightly faint but no less jumpy. He opened the sliding glass doors to the balcony and stepped outside. He smelled the clement salty air, looked out at the peaceful greenery, the serene tableau of pool and putting green and tennis courts. Self-consciously, he smiled; finally he could feel his heartbeat slowing.

But the next instant he was ambushed by an image of himself, plump, exposed, and slow, pinpointed in someone's crosshairs, targeted by a gunman hidden—where? Maybe behind the drawn curtains of Barney LaRue's penthouse, a straight shot across the quadrangle; maybe in a car with tinted windows cruising slowly past on A-1A.

His pulse whooshing in his ears, the Bra King dove back into the living room, drew the curtains closed behind him.

He paced some more. Absently, he wandered into Franny's room; through his fear he felt a guilty fascination as he spied upon her neatened bed, her plumped pillow, her herbal cures in brown glass bottles on the nightstand. Her suitcase was open on the floor; Murray felt a lunatic impulse to kneel before it and bury his face in her folded clothes.

Then he thought, My God, I'm fifty-three years old and I'm still sneaking peeks at women's panty drawers. Mortified, he lumbered from the room.

He went to the kitchen, opened the fridge, gulped some juice straight from the bottle. He thought of taking a good hot bath—yes, that would relax him—but the thought of being murdered in the tub, trapped and naked, his laid-open organs soaking like a brisket in the gray and soapy water, was too appalling.

The phone rang.

Murray flinched but then felt joy. He knew it would be Franny, saying she was still downtown, she didn't know where the time went, she was coming home. He moved quickly to the sofa with the nautical stripe, grabbed the handset, said hello.

It wasn't Franny. It was Les Kantor. He sounded all cranked up.

"Murray," he said, "*bubbala*, I'm glad I caught you in."

"Oh hi Les," said the Bra King.

"You sound distracted. I'm catching you at a bad time, wha'?"

"Nah," said Murray, "it's a good time. I'm glad to talk, it'll take my mind off things."

"What things?"

"If I tell ya, Les, it's not gonna take my mind off 'em, is it? What's up?"

"The new campaign," said Kantor proudly. "A whole new campaign to go with this whole new line of bras."

"The bras with the built-in nipples?"

"Right. We're calling it the Perfect Endings line. Whaddya think?"

Murray considered. For a moment, like an untethered blimp, he floated free of his preoccupations. But he didn't answer fast enough.

Kantor said, "Perfect Endings, get it? Like nerve endings, the sex angle—"

"I get it, I get it."

"We played around with a lot of concepts, believe me. The High Points line. The Punctuator."

Murray said nothing. It dawned on him that maybe this was not in fact a good time to be talking, tying up the phone, maybe Franny was trying to get through.

"We're working on a slogan to go with the campaign," said Kantor. "I thought I'd run a couple things by you."

Murray was silent.

Kantor said, "Ya ready?"

"I'm ready."

There was a pause like a drumroll, then Les Kantor put on an announcer's voice and said, "BeautyBreast—Changing the way America buys bras."

"Not bad," said Murray. "But the way they buy— what are we changing?"

"We aren't changing dick," said Kantor. "It's just, ya know, a slogan."

"I don't love it," Murray said. He was staring at his closed curtains, wondering what was happening in the glary and unsparing light behind them.

Undaunted, Kantor said, "Then how 'bout this: BeautyBreast—Because no two are alike."

"Nah, Les. No. Ya don't go around reminding people their tits don't match."

Kantor paused. Murray thought he heard him rustling through a pocket, crinkling the foil on a pack of Tums. "Excuse me," the partner said at last, "but do I detect a certain lack of enthusiasm? Would you rather I didn't keep you in the loop?"

"Les, Les, I'm sorry. Like I said, I got a lot on my mind right now. Shit you wouldn't believe."

"And you don't want to talk about it."

"Another time. Listen, *bubbala*, I gotta free up the phone. We'll talk soon. Perfect Endings—that part of it I think is very good. Very, very good."

He hung up, double-checked that the receiver was secure in the cradle.

He looked at his watch. It was barely after three, and he had the sinking and defeated thought that getting through the afternoon would simply be beyond his stamina. He wished he had some Valium. He didn't, so he popped an extra Prozac.

He lay down on his bed, tried to empty his mind, but the screen kept filling up with scenes of torment and humiliation. He saw Franny bound and gagged, Tommy flayed across his rosewood back. Himself, he was getting slapped a lot, fists and pipes were hammering his ribs.

At length he exhausted himself and fell into a restless doze.

He awoke two hours later, drenched with sweat, to the sound of someone pounding on the door.

Comprehension filled in slowly. He remembered where he was, recalled what he was frightened of. But he couldn't quite remember who had, or didn't have, a key to the apartment. It was Franny knocking; he knew that it was Franny. But hadn't he given her a key? Maybe he'd forgotten. Tommy had a key—or did he?

The pounding paused, then resumed, and the Bra King, drowsy, cottony, plodded to the door.

He was reaching for the knob, when his hand, more savvy in that moment than his brain, suddenly pulled back. What kind of idiot blindly opened a door in this world? It was Bruno behind that door, garlicky and sneering, waiting to deliver a faceful of acid, a boot to the crotch, a fast and final bullet to the chest.

Murray moved quickly sideways, pressed himself against the foyer wall. Standing on tiptoe he leaned in toward the peephole. Silently, he flicked the tiny lever, squinted through the fish-eye glass.

He saw Tommy Tarpon shifting nervously from foot to foot, holding a small brown paper bag. He opened the door.

Tommy swept right past him. "I gotta pee like a pregnant cow," he said. "One more minute I woulda really had a problem."

"Didn't I give you a key?" Murray said to his back.

"You double-locked it, Murray. The key wouldn't go in."

Returned from the bathroom, Tommy set his paper bag on the coffee table, and sat down on the sofa.

"Now look at this," he said, as he reached into the sack. "Two beers, Murray. Used to be, after work I bought a six-pack. I'd finish it then decide what to drink. Today I bought two beers. I'm gonna drink 'em, fuck it. But after that, I go for more, I want you to take a knife and cut my fingers off."

Murray said nothing, and the Indian looked closely at him. Murray was a little green, the rims of his eyes were scarlet.

"You don't look so good," said the Indian.

"Tommy," said the Bra King, "I'm scared."

The Indian popped a beer, brought it halfway to his lips.

"Franny," Murray went on. "I can't believe I let her go off by herself like that."

"They wouldn't bother Franny," Tommy said by reflex, and realized in the next instant he had no reason for believing that.

"She gets hurt I'll kill myself."

"You couldn't have stopped her going."

Murray said nothing.

Tommy pressed. "You know that, right?"

Murray knew Franny. Reluctantly, he nodded.

"Okay then," Tommy said. He closed his eyes and sucked his brew like it was life itself.

28

Around six-thirty, when almost everyone in Key West was migrating toward the island's western flanks to watch the sun go down, Murray and Tommy drove to Duval Street to look for Franny.

It should have been a tranquil hour, or as tranquil as Duval Street ever gets. The light was soft, shadows fluttered down like quilts, and yet enough reflected sun remained to mute the gaudy glare of shop windows. The slackening breeze barely moved the palms; pedestrians were few; the musicians who twanged and howled in the unwalled bars were saving their louder songs for when the rush began.

But Murray Zemelman was not tranquil. Hunched over the wheel of his scratched-up Lexus, he drove Duval from the ocean to the Gulf and back again, desperately peering left while Tommy scanned right. They saw faceless tourists spinning postcard racks, early drinkers weaving down the sidewalks and stumbling into signs with menus stapled on them. They saw pretty men in pastel shirts, tattooed biker women festooned with bits of chain, hookers or beauticians with enormous mouths painted way beyond the outline of their lips. Images flicked past as in a drugged cartoon, and Murray realized he had no chance of spotting Franny from the car.

He parked a couple blocks in from the ocean, on the quiet side of town. He and Tommy got out and walked back toward the fray.

They looked for Franny's bicycle. It was pink, Murray remembered, and it had a milk crate for a basket.

But there were hundreds of rental bikes in Key West, and most of them were pink and had milk crates for baskets. Murray saw them chained to racks, to trees, to picket fences and to chain-link fences, to parking meters and NO PARKING signs and each other. There was something surreal, Chinese, malign, in their alikeness.

The two friends started going into galleries, describing Franny, asking employees if they had seen her. The clerks struck thoughtful postures in front of garish canvases of tropical flowers, tropical fish, and said they really weren't sure, a lot of people filtered through, some of them were short and had curly graying hair, many were dressed in artsy shifts and sandals.

Sunset came and went.

Hordes of tourists put their lens caps on, turned toward land and alcohol, and surged in a slow stampede opposed to Murray and Tommy's progress. Walking became a battle, strangers became obstacles and enemies.

Murray ducked into a department store where he thought Franny might perhaps have shopped for Tommy's clothes. He accosted a salesman near a stack of shirts. The salesman had just come on at six, he hadn't noticed anyone like Franny. No, he couldn't check credit card receipts, there were privacy rules on that. He smirked at Murray: one more tourist jerk whose wife was on a binge, or leaving him, or both.

Back on the street, the sluttish glare of neon grew more brazen in the deepening dusk, the blaring tinny music cranked up like a siren in the bars. People got uglier against the grainy pink and blue and orange light. Murray, in the swelling nausea of his fear, became aggressive, cocked his elbows to preserve a capsule of empty space around him. Someone pushed him; confused, enraged, half-blind with swimming spots before his eyes, he pushed right back. Tommy stepped in front of him, forestalled more trouble with an implacable stare. He grabbed Murray gently by the forearm, coaxed him onward through the hellish carnival.

They found another gallery, climbed a short stone stoop to get to its front door. Inside, Murray asked again after his missing wife. The manager said no, he couldn't place her.

But then a clerk spoke up. He was very young,

his job was wrapping purchases in thick brown paper. Barber's clippers had put pale chevrons on the sides of his narrow head; he had pimples that were very pink against his tanned and freckled cheeks. "I think I might've seen that lady." He seemed a little slow, saliva bubbled as he spoke.

"Yeah?" said Murray. "Talk to me."

"I remember 'cause she left in a limousine. Parked right at the bottom of the steps."

"A limousine?"

"A big dark car, I think it was a limousine. It was parked on the wrong side of the street. Had a driver."

Murray felt faint. He braced himself against a counter, he couldn't speak.

Tommy said, "She got into the limousine herself?"

The kid scratched his clippered head. "A guy met 'er on the landing there. Helped her down the steps."

"Helped her?" Tommy said.

The kid looked baffled by the question, worried now that he was somehow saying things he shouldn't say, getting himself in trouble. He shrugged and scratched a pimple.

Tommy went to Murray, put a hand on his shoulder, eased him toward the door.

Outside, maybe fifteen yards from the bottom of the stoop, a pink bicycle with a milk crate for a basket was chained to a NO PARKING sign.

29

The grab had been made just before three that afternoon. It wasn't supposed to happen like it happened, in fact it was a total screwup.

A skinny young thug named Squeak had been dispatched to Key West by Charlie Ponte. His assignment: join forces with Bruno, kidnap the meddling Jew who was tied in with the Indian, bring him to the boss's Coconut Grove headquarters for a chat. If the chat went well, Murray would be returned in good health, cured of his unwholesome interest in Indian casinos. If the chat went badly, Murray would be dead, and the offending partnership sunk with him in the Gulf Stream, way out where the surging water was a mile deep.

The only problem was that the thugs kept getting hungry and missing Murray.

They lingered over breakfast, and staked out the Paradiso just after he and Tommy had left to see LaRue. When, twenty minutes later, Franny headed out alone, they didn't follow her; they waited. As the day dragged on, however, and they sat in their air-conditioned car parked alongside A-1A, boredom stoked Bruno's appetite.

Around one he said, "I could go for a calzone."

Squeak was a dutiful thug, a nervous thug. His face was concave, hollowed out with worry. His nose and cheeks sunk in, his sharp chin jutted out, in profile he looked like a crescent moon. He frowned at the idea of abandoning their post.

But it was Bruno who was behind the wheel, and Bruno was getting cranky. "Don't gimme that look," he said. "I want a fuckin' calzone."

"But Bruno—" Squeak began.

"Fuck it," said his colleague. "Fucker ain't come out so far, I don't see 'im coming out inna time it takes t'eat a fuckin' calzone. Spinach."

So they went downtown for calzones, and Murray and Tommy came home from the Eclipse while they were gone.

They were back in time to see Tommy leave the condominium by himself, to go sell shells.

Now the gangsters were confused. Just who the hell was home? They were hesitant to go inside the building to find out. The building was big, with many doors, security cameras, alarms maybe. Then again, it was getting to be mid-afternoon, and Ponte wanted them back by evening with a warm body in tow.

"I say we cruise," said Bruno.

Squeak tried to be logical. "After two," he said, in a voice like an ill-played clarinet. "A guy ain't out by after two, chances are he's stayin' in."

"Or else he's out already. Or else he's fuckin' been out all along. This is why I say we cruise."

Squeak shrugged fretfully. They headed downtown and crawled along Duval Street. On the second circuit they spotted Franny. She had big sunglasses on and she was carrying a shopping bag. They trailed her for awhile, watched her go in and out of stores.

"She's gonna meet the husband," Bruno said. "A buck says she's gonna meet the husband."

But there was no rendezvous, and the goons were getting tired of waiting.

Bruno said, "I think we gotta grab 'er."

It worried Squeak to change the plan. "Boss don't want the wife," he brayed.

Bruno picked his teeth. "Wives got influence sometimes. Guys, not always, sometimes, would do a lot to see their wife again."

Squeak scrunched up his face, it made him look like a little boy with an ulcer. "Grabbin' the wife, that ain't the job."

"Got a better idea?"

Squeak didn't, so reluctantly he took his pistol from its shoulder holster and put it in the right-hand pocket of his gray suit jacket. Bruno pulled across Duval Street, idled in front of a small stone stoop. Squeak climbed the steps, stood next to the door. When Franny came out, he grinned and threw his left arm around her, hugged her in a vile parody of affection. His right hand was hidden in his pocket; he pressed his gun against her ribs, let her feel the muzzle. "Sorry, lady," he tweeted shyly in her ear. "Make a noise, you're dead."

Her breath caught in a strangled wheeze, she made no other sound. The upper half of her went stiff with terror, from the knees down she was limp. Squeak half-carried her down the stairs, she looked like she was drunk. Her eyes were wild, unnaturally wide and almost silver, as he prodded her into the back seat of the car, still clutching the shopping bag that held jeans and shirts and underwear for Tommy.

◆◆◆◆◆◆

They blindfolded her in North Key Largo and kept the blindfold on even as she stood in Charlie Ponte's office. So she didn't see the little boss walk slowly up to Bruno, stand on tiptoe, and backhand him hard across the cheek. She did, however, hear the smack. "Wha' for ya bring me a fuckin' woman?" she heard him say.

The big goon answered without resentment, seemed to have absorbed the blow with the dumb patience of a beaten ox.

"The Jew," he explained, "we couldn't find 'im. The Indian, him ya said ya didn't want right now. So we figured—"

"Shut up what you figured," Ponte said. "Ya got

no brain, ya shouldn't figure. Take the fuckin' blinders off 'er."

Squeak untied the black satin sash.

Franny saw cruel yellow light, hard stubbly faces, Ponte's combed-forward mat of frightening slick hair above his shadowed soupy eyes. She thought she heard the faint sound of silverware on plates, smelled butter, hot rolls, seafood. Voluntary visitors to Ponte's sanctum came through the front door of Martinelli's; they walked between huge lobster tanks, through a vast dining room full of people eating lobsters, wearing lobster bibs. Franny had been brought a far less public way—she'd been prodded blindly down an alley paved in oozing cardboard that reeked of decomposing claws and tails and shells, then along a narrow catwalk that flanked a cove of black and stagnant water, and through a narrow metal door with many locks.

Now she stood blinking, trying not to tremble. She was still holding her shopping bag, it was her only link to life before the grab, and Ponte asked her what was in it.

"New clothes for Tommy Tarpon," she said.

Ponte mugged at Squeak and Bruno. "Isn't that sweet. A shame, what happened to his house."

He moved toward his enormous desk, sat down on a corner of it. He was the same height sitting there as standing up. "Cigarette?"

"I don't smoke," Franny said.

He regarded her. The towel-dried hairdo of a liberal. The loose-fitting clothes of a health nut. "No,

I didn't think you did. Well, tough titty, I'm havin'
a cigar."

He took his time unwrapping one, then bit a hole
in the end of it and spit the plug out on the floor.
"What's your name?"

"Franny. Franny Rudin." She strove to keep her
voice steady and unquavering, something told her
that was an important thing to try and do.

"Wanna siddown, Franny Rudin?"

She nodded. Squeak brought over a chair, she
perched on the very edge of it. Ponte lit up, blew
smoke in her direction, watched with pleasure as
she squinted.

Then he said, "Your husband, Franny Rudin—"

"Ex-husband," she corrected.

"Why is he preventing us from using our influence and knowledge to make your friend Tommy
one rich fuckin' redskin?"

Franny said nothing.

"I'll tell you why," said Ponte, knocking off cigar
ash with a pinky. "Because he is a stubborn, meddling, busybody pain innee ass."

"You can say that again," said Franny.

This was not the answer Ponte expected, it took
him a second to collect himself.

"The man's a total yenta," Franny added. Talking,
she felt better.

"Fuck's a yenta?" asked the mobster.

"Ya know," said Franny, "a yenta, he's always
minding other people's business."

"Exactly," Ponte said. "Pain innee ass. An' what's

this ex-husband bullshit? You're living with the man."

"Visiting," she said. "And, for your information, sleeping in a guest room."

Ponte frowned down at his small expensive shoes, the liverish sacs beneath his eyes got darker. He was suddenly exasperated, felt that he was losing the momentum.

"Lady," he said, "I don't care if you're sleepin' inna fuckin' shithouse. The point is this: This husband, ex-husband, whatever—y'ever wanna see the man again?"

"Funny you should ask. That's the exact question I've been thinking about all week."

There was a pause. Behind Charlie Ponte, tiny translucent windows let in faint smears of red and green light. Muted by thick walls, a tray clattered to the tiled floor of the restaurant kitchen. The boss took a deep pull on his cigar, then got down from his desk, walked toward Bruno, and belted him again.

"Ya see why I don't want ya bringin' me no fuckin' woman?"

"Boss, hey," protested Bruno. "I tried ta do good."

"Well, ya did lousy. Pain innee ass broad. The two a them, they deserve each other."

Franny winced at the remark, it had a distressing and insulting ring of truth.

Ponte started pacing, cigar smoke plumed out behind him like steam behind a locomotive. "Now

I got this fuckin' broad," he thought aloud, "now I gotta keep 'er . . . Squeak, anybody inna Odds motel right now?"

The skinny thug said there was not.

"Awright, you'll take 'er to the Odds motel."

"Odds motel?" said Franny. Her voice was letting go, the words came out in a raspy whisper.

Ponte stepped in close to her, put his knees between her knees, leaned down in her face. His eyeballs were yellow and his clothes stank of tobacco.

"Shut up, Franny Rudin. Zipper that fuckin' smart mouth shut."

She did, and Ponte almost smiled, gratified and maybe a little surprised that he could cow her.

"This husband of yours," the boss went on, "ex-husband, whatever, who you are not living with, only visiting and I gather not fucking—let's see how eager he is to see your smart ass again."

30

Numb, despairing, Murray trudged through the glare and noise and beery crush of bodies on Duval Street. Tommy held him by the arm, but still he lumbered into people, stumbled stepping bleary-eyed off curbs. Infernal music knifed into his ears, hard women and gaudy men spun like dervishes before his unfocusing eyes. By the time they reached the scratched-up Lexus, he felt that he had left the earth and landed on some crasser and lewder and more uncouth planet.

"How about I drive?" said Tommy.

Murray just handed him the key. But then, a few blocks off Duval, on the quiet streets that flanked the ocean, he said suddenly, "Wait a second, what we goin' home for? What we gonn' accomplish home?"

Tommy hadn't driven in years. He drove slow but jerkily. Without taking his eyes off the road, he said, "We're gonna see LaRue."

Murray's elbow was propped up on the window frame, breeze was worrying his forearm. Dazedly, he said, "LaRue. That's good, Tommy. We'll see LaRue, we'll give 'im what he wants, he'll get us Franny back."

The Indian said nothing.

The Bra King looked out the window, at ice-white moonlight that spilled across the water and tracked them as they drove.

They arrived at the Paradiso, Tommy almost managed to park between the lines.

Inside the privileged quadrangle, they skirted the pool and the palms, smelled chlorine and closed-up flowers. They went to the East Building, stood in the vestibule. Murray reached for Barney LaRue's buzzer on the intercom.

Tommy deflected his hand. "Use your key," he said. "He doesn't need to be too ready."

They let themselves into the inner hallway, rode the elevator to the penthouse floor, Murray reliving the bafflement and humiliation of his first day in town. The door opened, he saw the nightmarish flopped familiarity of the corridor, everything the same as his but backwards: the same fluorescent fixtures spotted with the same dead bugs, the same number of steps from the elevator to the door, the same vacant little nameplate underneath the peep-hole.

The doorframe had a bell on it, but Tommy didn't use it. He knocked, hard. He badly wanted a drink and his hands were feeling feisty.

After a moment they heard the whisper of steps on carpet, to their surprise the door opened without an inquiry. Pascal was standing there in his splendid red kimono, his face had the off-balance look of a man who was expecting someone else.

"We need to see your boss," said Tommy.

"You can't," the houseboy said. It took only a second for his expression to change to superior and petulant.

The Indian wedged his foot against the door. "We can."

"You can't. He isn't here."

"Where is he?" Murray said.

"None of your business," said Pascal.

Pascal had lots of muscles, he oiled himself and worked out every other day. But he was not a fighter and he did not react when Tommy reached out hard and quick and grabbed two hot handfuls of his robe. The Indian jerked him forward through the doorway, then slammed him back and upward against the corridor wall. He held him pinned up there, his feet barely in contact with the floor. "Where's LaRue, you fucking geek?"

The man in the kimono wriggled like a burned moth, looked down at the mangled silk in Tommy's fists. He seemed more concerned about the garment than himself. "Let me go," he whined.

Tommy pulled, pushed, heard things move inside

the houseboy's chest as his back once again collided with the wall. "Where's your fucking boss?"

"He's in Tallahassee. It's where he works, for God's sake."

"When did he go there?" Murray asked.

"Tell this beast to let me go."

Tommy backed away. Pascal slid down the wall like egg, straightened his kimono. "He left at noon. And now I'm calling the police."

"Do that," Tommy said. "Great idea. And be sure and tell your boss you're doing it. Tell 'im the cops are coming after us and we have a lot to talk with them about."

❖❖❖❖❖❖

The two friends rode the elevator to the courtyard, didn't speak till they were out in the night air that was as moist as fruit and the temperature of skin. Tommy sat on the edge of a webbed lounge near the pool. Murray fell into a plastic chair across from him and glanced down at his own soft arms.

"Me, I've never been in a fight," he absently remarked.

Tommy didn't answer, he was thinking. His pulse was slowing, sweat was drying on his back, and his hands felt somehow better, a brief and rough serenity spread upward from them to his wrists, his elbows, his shoulders.

"Maybe we should talk to Bert," he said.

The Bra King didn't answer right away, and when

he did, it was in a hopeless monotone. "Bert's not gonna help us out. Push comes to shove, Bert's still an old colleague of Ponte's."

Tommy disagreed, but let it slide. "And I thought maybe we'd get in touch with that reporter guy."

Murray pushed some air out past his lips. "Like he gives a shit about anything except his story."

Tommy looked up at the sky, wondered at, without examining too closely, his sudden fragile calm, this tranquility of sober action. Very softly he said, "And there's that bitter thing again. Murray, when ya gonna stop thinkin' the worst about everybody?"

The Bra King didn't answer, just crossed his ankles and slumped down in his chair, dejected in the starlight.

After a moment Tommy said, "Come on, let's go see if Bert's around."

He rose, and Murray followed; he didn't know what to do, except to follow.

They wove through palms and oleanders to the North Building, buzzed the old man on the intercom. It was ten o'clock, he sounded wide awake but deeply surprised to be getting visitors.

He met them at his door in gorgeous silk pajamas, maroon with pale pink piping. He held his dog one-handed, the dog flopped double, like an understuffed sausage. He saw Murray's and Tommy's clenched faces and he didn't greet them, just gestured them into his living room.

It was a busy, cluttered room, unchanged since his wife had died a dozen years before. A brocade sofa was guarded by a glass and marble coffee table with lion's feet. There were China lamps whose shades had pom-poms on them. Gewgaws were strewn everywhere: cut-glass candy dishes, a crystal ball from Lake Tahoe, an ashtray that said Cincinnati. Scattered on the pee-stained carpet were squeak toys that the ancient chihuahua was now too blind to find and too weary to chase around or hump.

The old man motioned his visitors toward the sofa. Murray stepped on a plastic hot dog with a lightning bolt of yellow mustard; it gave a tortured squeal. Bert took a long moment settling into his oxblood BarcaLounger, pushing downward on the arms until the footrest swung up to meet his wizened ankles. Then he said, "What gives?"

Murray tried licking his lips but his tongue was just as dry. "They got Franny," he said. The words freshened his fear, his throat was slamming shut before he'd finished saying them.

"Who got Franny, wha'?"

Murray tried to talk, could not. Tommy took over, told as much as he knew.

"We just tried to see LaRue," he finished up. "LaRue's in Tallahassee."

"Course he is," said Bert. "He's thinkin' alibi already."

"I got a little physical with the houseboy," said the Indian. "He says he's calling the police."

"He won't," the old man said.

"Should we?" said Murray.

The former mobster didn't hesitate. "Ya get the cops involved, Ponte's only play is to make sure the body is never found."

Murray looked like he'd just eaten a bad clam.

"Sorry," the old man said to him. "You asked."

"Then there's this newspaper guy," said Tommy, "this Arty Magnus. Anything he can do for us?"

The host crossed his hands on the front of his pajamas, thought that over. "Sometime maybe. Sometime, if, ya know, you're in a stronger position, ya got a shot at hitting back. But now . . . now ya don't do anything to force his hand."

"So whadda we do?" said Murray.

"Ya go to sleep."

"Fat chance."

"Ya wait," the old man counseled. "You'll hear from 'im, that's how it works. He'll tell ya what he wants, you'll give it to him, chance is not too bad you'll get your wife back. Maybe, if you're very lucky—"

"I'm not feeling very lucky—"

"—If you're very lucky, maybe you'll get your wife back wit'out ya have to give 'im what he wants."

Murray sighed, he sounded like a tire with a nail in it. "I can't imagine," he began.

"Look," Bert interrupted, "ya said you're not gonna be able to sleep. Course you're not. So you'll lay there, you'll think, you'll scheme, you'll try to come up with some way to beat this thing, to win. Innee end, ya won't be able to do it, you'll come up one jump short, like Chinese checkers. But inna meantime it'll make ya feel less bad. It'll help to pass the time, believe me."

"Pass the time," said the Bra King dazedly.

"Like Chinese checkers," said Bert the Shirt. He raised a hand and moved it like a man conducting music. "Jump by jump by jump."

31

Bruno had taken Franny's shopping bag and now, blindfolded again and being led along the splintery catwalk that flanked the Intracoastal, she heard a splash. She pictured neatly folded pants and shirts, their tags and pins still on, darkening with oily water before they sank into the muck.

Waste appalled her, waste was death for things exempt from ordinary dying. "Wha'd you do that for?" she said.

"I got smacked because a you," said Bruno. He pushed her through the alley with its greasy stinking cardboard boxes, its slick crustacean rot underfoot.

"You big baby," she could not help saying, and Squeak came forth with a scraping, tooting laugh, a laugh like the shriek of a gull.

They bundled her back into the car, drove her

somewhere, it took maybe half an hour. She saw nothing except, at the very outside corners of her eyes, where the sash gapped against her temples, a maddening zip and flash of pinkish street lamps streaking past.

They got on a highway and left it again, she could tell by the lean of the ramp and the different sound the tires made when they were going slower. They stopped for traffic lights, roared off, the acceleration pressed her back against the seat. After a time they went quite slowly and crunched briefly over gravel. Then they rode on something soft and silent; then they stopped. She felt the car lock into Park, but Bruno didn't turn the engine off.

Squeak got out and opened up her door. She emerged into a fragrant blankness, it felt like she was on a farm. She smelled fresh sweet water and cut grass and animals and leather and manure. The skinny thug prodded her in some direction, she was walking on a lawn. Bruno drove away. The air got very silent except for the buzz of locusts.

"Three steps up," chirped Squeak. "Then there's a landing."

Her toe found the first stair and she climbed, wondered vaguely if the steps were leading to a precipice, a tiger cage, a shark tank. She felt Squeak brush against her, the nearness of his body was like a lick of clammy water. She heard a key in a lock, the complaint of a rusty hinge.

"Now there's a staircase," said her captor. "Spiral. Narrow. Hold the railing."

The rail was metal, it was cool in her hand, the paint was lumpy. She climbed, reached a platform. Her feet told her it was slatted, like a fire escape. Squeak reached around her, opened up a door, pushed her through it.

"Welcome to the Odds motel," he said.

He flipped a light switch, closed the door behind them, slid a couple of bolts. He took the sash off Franny's eyes.

At first she saw nothing but a hot white glare, then she took in the bleak contours of the chamber she was standing in.

It was not a room, exactly, more like a swollen conduit, a bubble in a metal artery, maybe ten feet long and eight feet wide, with a low oppressive ceiling that bore down like a mortgage. Every surface was painted the same dark dusty green, you couldn't tell where the corners were. Big bundles of wires were strung along the ceiling, tied up with plastic clamps. One entire wall was a grid of peculiar sliding shutters, all of them closed tight, insane in their inscrutable monotony. There was a toilet bowl placed nowhere in particular; it was stained with rust and lacked a seat. There were two cots. One of them was braced against a heavy-gauge chain-link door that led God knew where; the other was snug to a wall into which a pair of thick metal rings were bolted.

"That one's yours," said Squeak, following her eyes. "I lock a wrist and ankle so I can get some sleep."

Franny tried to hold her face together. Her composure was about used up. She wanted some vitamins, some minerals, a soothing cup of tea. She wanted to be home in Sarasota, discussing novels with the ladies. She wanted, even, to be arguing with Murray. Anything but this. "I have to pee," she said.

"So pee," said Squeak. A standoff. Then he said, "Okay, I'll turn around." He made it sound like the most magnanimous thing he'd ever done.

Afterward, he led her to her cot. She lay down and he hovered over her, unlocking the metal rings. He smelled like clothes that have been worn a day too long, there was something talon-like about his thin and veiny hands. His shadow stretched across her like a flight of buzzards.

"You remind me of my son," she said. She didn't have a son, she said it to make herself sound old, to make him feel unsexy.

Clinically, dispassionately, as if he were trussing a veal, he clamped her wrist and ankle, locked the rings around the slender bones.

"You do bondage with your kid?" he said, and he came forth with a demented cackle that rang like a warped gong off the metal walls and floor and ceiling.

Franny turned her face away, closed her eyes, and tried to make herself invisible.

◆◆◆◆◆◆

Murray made the water very hot and took a long soak in the Jacuzzi. Steam swirled up around him, sweat dripped from his eyelashes.

The bath left him faint but not the least bit sleepy. Woozy, wrapped in rented towels, he lay down on his bed and closed his eyes. The room rocked like a boat, his mind sailed along. He pictured Tommy, thought about the brave and sudden purpose in his strength. He thought about Franny, her neat suitcase in the now-vacant guest room, and his eyes filled up with tears. He thought about what Bert had said. Plot, scheme, think. The old man was right—there was a kind of tentative salvation in being able to imagine oneself on top, to entertain notions of triumph, of revenge.

But Murray didn't know how to start. Obstacles were everywhere. His enemies were ruthless, while he was a cream puff and a coward. His enemies had weapons, *were* weapons, and he hadn't thrown a punch since junior high. His enemies were holding Franny, and he was holding nothing.

This mortified him as he lay there: He was wretched, but for the moment he was safe, while his wife, guilty of nothing but coming to visit, was in jeopardy whose grim specifics he couldn't bring himself to think about. Then there was Tommy. When, inevitably, they caved in and gave Ponte what he wanted, it would be Tommy who'd be stuck with the Mafia for a partner, Tommy who would be used, humiliated, eventually squeezed out or even killed. Murray would lose . . . what? Only a diversion he no longer needed. His life had somehow gotten full enough without the new challenge of the casino business.

Still, the whole disaster was his fault, he was like

the guy who got a bar brawl going then sat under a table while others got their teeth kicked in. It wasn't fair. He made the problem, he had to fix the problem. He accepted that.

The night dragged on. He tried to think. He pulled the sweat-soaked towels out from underneath him. His stupor deepened and he may have dozed.

Around three A.M., he sat bolt upright, totally awake. A window had shattered. It was a big window and it was very close, the sound was no mere tinkle but a symphony of wreckage, it hit several notes at once and lingered in a brittle echo.

The Bra King threw a towel around himself and ran into the living room. Tommy Tarpon was already there, kneeling in his underwear above a brown manila envelope wrapped around a rock. The rock was near the bottom of the curtain that covered the sliding door to the third-floor balcony. The carpet there was strewn with shards and spears of glass.

Tommy took off the rubber bands that held the envelope to the missile. The two friends went to the sofa with the nautical stripe, sat down side by side. Tommy fumbled with the clasp, removed a single sheet of paper. It was a ransom note, but not the old-fashioned kind pieced together of words of different sizes in jarring typefaces, snipped from magazines. No, this note came from a computer printer. It was neat and grammatical and seemed to have been written by a lawyer. It said:

Gentlemen:

Thank you for reconsidering your position in regard to our partnership. We may now consummate the arrangement as follows.

You will meet us at 5:45, on the morning of 21 March, on Rickenbacker Beach, on Key Biscayne. The two of you, unaccompanied, will arrive in a single car, park in plain sight of the northernmost lifeguard stand, and proceed on foot to the water's edge. There Mr. Tommy Tarpon will execute a contract setting forth his mutual obligations with First Keys Casinos, Inc., said contract to be witnessed by Mr. Murray Zemelman and Ms. Franny Rudin.

It is of the utmost importance that our business be concluded when and as described herein. We look forward to seeing you on the 21st.

Yours truly,

"No signature," said Tommy.

"There's limits to their chutzpah after all," said Murray.

The Indian leaned back on the sofa, let the note rest on his knee. "Murray, when's the twenty-first?"

The Bra King had to think about it, the days had gotten hazy. "This day just coming up, I think this is the twentieth."

Tommy nodded as though the date required his agreement. He rubbed his chin, then said, "I'll sign—you know that, right?"

"Thanks for saying it."

"I'll sign," the Indian said quite calmly, "and then I'll kill LaRue, and then I'll take a shot at killing Ponte, and then I'll either be dead or go to the electric chair."

Murray's elbows were on his knees, he was tugging at his hair. "No you won't," he said. "I'll think of something."

Tommy didn't believe it for a second. His old pessimism had woken up big and grouchy as a bear, he took a bleak satisfaction from the bleakness of how things were turning out. Sovereign of the Matalatchee, flunkey of the Mob, assassin. "You ready for some coffee?"

"Hm?" said Murray. "Sure."

"We'll have some coffee, maybe we'll go fishing, watch the sun come up."

"Fishing?" Murray said. "I can't go fishing now."

"Do you good," said Tommy.

Murray didn't answer, he couldn't get his face to work. He got up from the sofa, wrapped his towel more snugly around his slack and hairy waist, then knelt down like a mantis and began to clear away the spears and icicles of broken glass.

32

After a long time Franny Rudin fell asleep.

But her sleep was haunted by slicked-haired demons and spiders in suits, leering insects that held cigars in sawtooth jaws, filthy cackling birds flying over her with scaly yellow talons dangling down.

She willed herself awake, struggled up from the gargoyle dreams as from a deep and muddy ditch. Her heart was swollen inside her ribs, she felt her pulse dammed up by the metal rings that held her wrist and ankle.

She lay perfectly still, blinked up toward the ceiling; it was invisible in the utter darkness but even so its nearness had a smothering weight. She lay there and she wondered why this was happening to her. But her conscience was clean, she knew there was no reason, and so she turned her thoughts away; to wonder too much why awful things befell the undeserving was worse than futile, it led to corrosive grudges against life itself, provoked a rage beyond repair.

She tried to think about pleasant things instead. She thought about her garden. She pictured a glass full of paintbrushes, the water turning a milky lavender as the washed-off tints blended and swirled. To her surprise she thought about Murray, about how they used to be. They laughed a lot; they probed; they wrapped in wisecracks their little scraps of understanding, and together they figured out a small piece of the world. Murray—a romantic klutz is what he'd always been. Shooting out light fixtures with errant champagne corks. Getting cramps in his feet at moments of passion. He'd proposed on his knees, let slip an inadvertent fart as he stood up. And always with his schemes, his big ideas— undaunted, untrammeled, and usually nuts. He gave you a headache, Murray did. And yet . . . No, she wouldn't think about it. She was done with Murray. This hell she was going through now—if she survived it, it would serve as a sign, a vivid warning: Go back to Sarasota, a healthy place, a *reasonable* place, a place free of gangsters and ex-husbands.

She heard Squeak breathing. He didn't snore, he wheezed, it was a bent, tormented sound, pinched air following the curves and cave-ins of a nose that had been often smashed. She wondered what time it was, wondered what would happen in the morning. Her thoughts came back to Murray. She banished them, but not before smiling secretly at an image of him falling out of a hammock on their first Caribbean vacation, back when they were young and strapped for cash and working hard to make a life— a life, Franny fended off admitting, that had been the most full of juice and closest to the bone of all the several lives that she had lived so far.

◆◆◆◆◆◆

It was just after four when Tommy and Murray got on their bikes and rode to White Street Pier.

The predawn air was calm and damp and salty. Pinkish halos puffed like dandelions around the street lamps; palms stood still as pictures, darker black against the flat black sky. Unfamiliar stars twinkled overhead, the water was so flat that it reflected them, showed points of starlight intermixed with the glowing trails of phosphorescent creatures scudding on unimaginable missions through the nighttime ocean.

A bum was sleeping on the pier, nestled on a tarp. Feral cats stalked and slunk, searching out fish heads left behind, the chambered bodies of broken crabs. A pelican stood on the railing, blinking out to sea.

Tommy Tarpon got out his casting net, spread the mesh like pizza dough across his fists, made a single perfect throw. The net landed softly, dim green streamers flashed as the weighted edges sank through the living water.

The captured pinfish, spilled out on the pavement, seemed to glow from within themselves, shone a more urgent silver color than they could have borrowed from the sky.

The two friends baited their hooks and fished. They fished in silence, tracked the maneuvers of their doomed minnows, let useless voltage escape from their overheated brains and run down their arms to be doused in the twinkling sea. Time went neither slow nor fast; after awhile they started catching fish, small yellowtails and mangrove snappers. They weren't fishing for dinner, they threw them back. Tommy was trying not to think but now and then he thought about the endless ingenuity of God's dark humor—so many ways to bring dead hopes to life, so many ways to murder them again.

Now and then Murray checked his watch. He wanted to know how the world looked at 5:45 A.M., what they would be surrounded by when Tommy signed his life away to ransom Franny. If, that is, the other side kept to the agreement. But now that he thought of it, why should he suppose they would? A deserted beach at dawn—they could as easily kill him, kill Franny, get Tommy's signature at gunpoint and bully him into a petrified silence. No, the Bra King reflected, that part of it was wrong: They couldn't bully Tommy. Tommy would be a hero, Tommy would win revenge or go down trying. Of course, what the hell good would that do anybody?

Around five-thirty Murray stopped fishing. He leaned his rod against the rail and watched the sky, scanned the universe for answers, stratagems. Chinese checkers, Bert had said. He should think, he should scheme, even though he'd come up one jump short. But what made Bert so sure, god-dammit? The Mafia—okay, they were tough, they were practiced, but were they really all that smart? Were they smarter than him, Murray Zemelman, a big executive, the Bra King?

He looked down at his watch. It was exactly 5:45. On the beach, the unmoving palms still looked black, though the spaces between them were taking on some color now, a murky purplish gray. On the horizon, the sky was just barely floating free of the ocean; the morning's first breeze wrinkled the water like the soft breath of an old woman blowing on a cup of tea. Quite suddenly Murray had an idea. It was a lunatic idea, excessive, extravagant, exorbitant. He didn't trust it but he had it, and it was the only one he had.

The idea made him itch, he scratched himself, walked around in a circle, felt the idea all over, squeezed it like you squeeze a melon. He sat on the rail, stared at the beach, turned the idea around some more, stood up. "I got it," he said.

Tommy had been watching him in silence and with some concern. Now he said, "Got what?"

"Timing," said the Bra King. "The light. The beach. The water. How much ya can see."

"Fuck you talkin' about?" said Tommy.

Murray didn't answer. He was already gathering

up his gear, heading for his bike. "I gotta go lay down," he said. "I gotta count the jumps, I gotta make some calls."

"Ya wanna tell me?" Tommy said.

But Murray didn't hear him. Wobbling, weaving, carrying his fishing rod like a blunt and fragile lance, he was already riding up the pier in the mild unpeopled dawn.

33

Someone pounded on the metal door. The whole chamber clanged like a beaten garbage can.

Squeak was still lying on his cot. The place was dark, though faint scraps of light lined the edges of the strange closed shutters. Franny's captor took a moment, then piped, "Yeah?"

"It's Bruno."

Squeak stood up, fumbled for the bolts. The door fell open, a wedge of dusty brightness tumbled in.

"Christ," said Bruno, "ya still asleep? It's almost nine awready."

"Fuck I got to do but sleep?"

"I brought coffee, donuts."

Squeak turned on the light. The bare bulb threw a rude glare that discovered Franny, stiff, chafed and red-eyed, lying on her back.

"How's the Mouth this morning?" Bruno said in her direction.

Franny said nothing.

"No smart answers today?" the big thug taunted. "Get up, Mouth, have a donut."

Franny detested donuts. Fat-soaked flour spiked with the slow poison called sugar. But she liked the idea of getting up, moving her rigid limbs. She almost didn't mind when Squeak, stale-smelling and hawkish, leaned across her to undo the rings.

She sat up gingerly, rubbed her wrist and ankle. "Any juice, fruit?" she ventured. "Anything like that?"

Bruno shook his head. "Jewish broads," he said. "Wit' them everything is room service. Where's she think she is, the fuckin' Biltmore?"

"She don't know where she is," chirped Squeak.

This struck the two thugs funny; they tittered like baboons.

"Can I have some coffee?" Franny asked.

Bruno handed her a container, she clutched it with both hands. The coffee was milky and sweet, she sipped it slowly, blinking toward the bundled wires that dangled from the ceiling.

"We're here till four tomorra morning," Bruno said to Squeak.

The skinny thug said, "Shit. Then?"

Bruno looked at Franny, bit into a jelly donut before he answered. An ooze of thick red jam appeared at the corner of his mouth, he licked it with a bovine tongue. "Then we take her for a ride."

Franny twitched at that, spilled a little coffee.

Bruno seemed very pleased with himself. "Look," he said. "I think she's scared today, I think we scared the smart-ass comments right outa her. Didn't we, Mouth?"

Franny said nothing, she sat very still at the edge of her cot and tried to keep her coffee cup from shaking.

"Yup," said Bruno, like he'd just proven something deep and satisfying. "The idea a goin' for a ride, she don't like that at all. I think from here on in she's gonna keep that smart mouth zippuhed."

Gratified, he wiped his greasy hands on his trouser legs and reached into the oil-spotted bag for another donut.

◆◆◆◆◆◆

Murray showered, lay down on his bed, closed his pulsing eyes and impatiently waited for the rest of the world to catch up with him, to join him in this brave decisive day.

Around nine he ate two Prozac, washed them down with orange juice. He paced the living room, threw open the curtain that gave onto the balcony. Slender triangles of sundered glass hung precariously in the frame of the sliding door, gave evidence of his enemies' boldness and their violence.

But Murray was no longer rattled, no longer awed, in fact he held their crude and blustering tactics in contempt. He had become nearly certain that everything would soon be under control, that his own gambit, elegant and deft, would surely triumph. This new unflinching confidence—his shrink might have called it a symptom, a side effect, even a delusion—Murray knew was a passage and a transformation.

Walking on tiptoe, he poked his head into Tommy's room; Tommy was asleep with his mouth open, softly snoring.

He moved to the doorframe of Franny's empty chamber, made a silent vow to her suitcase and her clothes: He would bring her back, he would have her back.

He went to his own room, softly closed the door behind him, plumped his rumpled pillows, and began to work the phone.

◆◆◆◆◆◆

For Franny time was thick and empty.

Bruno left. Squeak sat. He didn't talk. He didn't pace. He didn't read the paper. He only sat, and Franny knew from his vacant concave face that he wasn't even thinking. There was something terrifyingly doltish, inhumanly blank, in the way he could sit there for uncounted hours doing nothing whatsoever.

The day grew hot, the metal room got airless as a locked car in the sun.

At some point Franny became aware of things happening outside—whatever outside meant. She didn't hear things, exactly, not at first. She felt a thrum, a change in density, a gathering busyness in the air. Gradually, the thrum became a buzz, resolved itself into something that seemed almost familiar, the pulverized and blended voices of a distant crowd. The buzz rose and fell, sometimes grated and sometimes hit chance harmonies, as when an orchestra tunes up.

Squeak looked at his watch. It was the most enterprising thing he'd done in quite a while. "Won't be long now," he cheeped.

The buzz droned on in a slow crescendo. Then there was a tapering off, a hush.

Squeak stood up from his cot. He walked to the wall of strange closed shutters and opened one a crack.

Franny made bold to follow him across the tiny room, and when he didn't object, she opened a shutter too.

At first she saw nothing but a blinding slash of sun; then she saw a flamingo. It was standing on one leg in a shallow pool and it was drinking water upside down. Around the pool, the grass was very green. It went on for awhile then ended at a low white fence. Beyond it was a swath of rich brown dirt, then there was a grandstand full of loud shirts and polyester jackets, a vast unbroken mat of them that might have been a quilt made in a madhouse.

Franny rubbed her head. She hadn't gotten to wash her hair and she didn't like the feel of it. "Hialeah?"

"Very good," said Squeak. Suddenly expansive, he jerked a thumb toward the bundled wires. "All electric now," he brayed. "Used to be guys would work in here, run the numbers up by hand."

Franny nodded numbly. A bland unmoored acceptance came into her voice, and she said, "I'm a hostage in a tote board."

Her eyes adjusted, she looked across the track, at the prancing thoroughbreds warming up, the tiny jockeys in their screaming silks. She looked out at the thousands of people who could not help her.

"Good view a the finish line from here," Squeak chirped.

When the horses ran, they shook the earth.

34

It was just after two the next morning when Murray and Tommy got into the scratched-up Lexus and headed up the Keys.

At their backs, a red and gibbous moon was setting, the glare of Key West was first muffled, then swallowed up by the humidity. Ahead, the thin ribbon of U.S. 1 lifted over bridges and trestles as it wound from rock to rock; a sparse stream of tourists and refugees was flowing up and down the road even at that bleary hour, people still looking for a place to sleep or drink or find some desperate amusement. Pelicans flew above the power lines, their dipping flight the shape of pendant cable.

"I wish you'd tell me what the plan is," Tommy said, when they were fifteen, twenty miles out of town.

The Bra King shook his head. "Superstition. Like you not wanting me to say the name of our casino."

"Tell me what you want from me, at least."

"I told you. Just stall." Murray's elbow was propped on his window frame, his skin smarted pleasantly from the salt in the air. "Stall," he repeated. "And if it doesn't go well, help me get between the goons and Franny."

The sovereign of the Matalatchee nodded solemnly. That much he could certainly do, would do without being asked. He saw himself running, diving, berserk across the beach, his teeth bared and his arms outstretched, absorbing in a kind of ecstasy the blows and blades and bullets intended for his friends. So much for his triumphant foray into the white man's world.

◆◆◆◆◆◆

The races had ended very long ago. The crowd had dispersed, silence returned, Squeak had subsided once again into stunning insensate dormancy.

Hours dragged. Bruno appeared with Chinese food in greasy white containers. Franny ate two bites with a plastic fork and got a headache from the MSG. She lay down on her cot, the whole place stank of soy sauce.

The two goons shot the breeze. They didn't bother binding her. Her body told her it was getting deep into the night.

At some point Bruno said, "Almost four. We oughta go."

They led Franny out of the metal chamber, walked her down the spiral stairs. Outside, they put the blindfold on, and this had come to seem obscenely normal: You went somewhere, someone tied a sash around your eyes, you were blind until you reached the next abomination.

They drove awhile; they stopped.

A door opened, closed, the car filled up with the smell of aftershave.

"Hello, Franny Rudin."

She recognized the voice of Charlie Ponte. She didn't answer.

They drove. A couple minutes later, Ponte said, "So remember—the redskin signs, then we're outa there. Nothing left behind, everybody in one car."

There was a pause. Squeak was doing arithmetic.

" 'Sgonna be awful crowded," he piped.

"Not with two of 'em inna trunk," said Charlie Ponte. "Very still and very quiet."

Bruno laughed at that, he found it funny when other people died. His laugh was hoarse and breathless, Squeak caught the contagion of it and came forth with a nasal toot whose edges were thickened with phlegm. Franny listened to them laughing and wished they'd made her deaf as well as sightless.

◆◆◆◆◆◆

At twenty minutes after five, the scratched-up Lexus was on the nearly empty causeway that led to Key Biscayne. Street lamps blotted out the stars; the viscous water of the Intracoastal was flat as cooling soup. A map was open on Tommy Tarpon's knee; a thin unpleasant light from the open glove box bounced around inside the car.

They reached the island, drove past sleeping golf courses and the gatehouses of walled estates, past marinas with tall masts clustered thickly as a bundle of sticks.

On the ocean side they found signs for Rickenbacker Beach.

Tommy put the map away, the Bra King drove more slowly. Timing was crucial, they could not be early.

At 5:38 they reached the parking area. Murray pulled off the road and into the vast and vacant lot. White lines, painted in diagonals like the skeletons of fish, gleamed vaguely lavender in the starlight. Ahead, the beach was black. There was no seam between the land and water, nor between the water and the sky.

Murray cruised. His headlights discovered three tall lifeguard chairs, each with a little rescue boat poised next to it like a dog at the feet of its master. The chairs were perhaps two hundred yards apart; in the darkness they seemed as monumental as Mayan pyramids. He idled toward the north end of the lot; he found a dark Lincoln parked just beyond the pavement, hidden in a little copse of palms. He pulled in near it, switched off the ignition. It was 5:42.

With the engine off, the world seemed as quiet as if it had never been created. Murray tried to take a deep breath, the locked muscles between his ribs wouldn't let the air come in. He tried to speak, could not. He reached out to put a hand on Tommy's shoulder; Tommy pulled him into a quick and awkward warriors' embrace. They got out of the car.

Fearlessly, the Indian approached the Lincoln, confirmed that it was empty. Then the two friends started walking across the beach, toward the northernmost lifeguard chair.

Damp sand slowed their steps, the scratch of it and the faint hiss of dissolving sea foam were the only sounds. They labored closer to the platform; its spindly contours came gradually, dimly into focus, but still they saw no people. Murray peered out to sea. His gaze was thwarted, mocked by the humid darkness, he had no idea how far his vision penetrated before it failed.

They plodded on. And suddenly four mismatched silhouettes popped up from behind the little rescue boat. Murray wanted to run to Franny, convince himself she still existed. But he disciplined his steps, remembered that he had to be deliberate.

Very close now, he saw that Bruno and Squeak had guns out, the barrels glistened dully in the starlight. Franny looked brittle and dry, her eyes were sunken, the sockets sharp and bony.

Charlie Ponte said, "Hello, Chief. Hello, asshole."

Murray said to Franny, "Are you all right?"

She looked at him and nodded, the nod was very small.

The thugs stood with their backs to the ocean; Murray stealthily stared past their shoulders. Ponte reached into his silver zippered jacket, pulled out a stapled sheaf of papers and a pen, handed them to Tommy.

"Sign this," he commanded.

Tommy knew his job. "I'd like to read it first," he said, though in the dimness it would have been a struggle.

"There's nothin' to read, Tonto. We run the casino, you get twenty grand a month. Like we agreed. Now sign the fuckin' thing."

"Don't," said Franny.

Bruno turned toward her, his gun at the level of her forehead. "Shut up, Mouth," he said.

Murray, in a trance of panicked bravery, grabbed the big man's arm. "Don't fucking touch her."

"Shut up alla yas," said Ponte. "Sign the fuckin' papers, Chief."

The Indian fumbled with the pages.

"It won't make any difference," Franny said.

"I said shut up. He signs right now or everybody's dead."

Murray peered toward the horizon. There was beginning to be a boundary between the sea and sky, a lifting. He wanted badly to believe he saw vague but moving shapes against the paler black.

Tommy flipped through to the last page of the contract, found the dotted line, shook his wrist free of his shirt cuff. He raised the pen, moved it to the paper, and dropped it on the beach.

"Fuckin' jerk," said Squeak.

With a quick and unseen foot Tommy buried the pen in the sand.

Ponte's thugs squirmed and shuffled in their pointy shoes. They were primed to kill, the delay was as infuriating as sex withheld.

Tommy crouched, felt around, buried the pen a little deeper. Ponte cursed under his breath. His thugs rocked on their avid knees, slapped the muzzles of their guns against their palms.

The eastern sky was purple now, against it Murray saw what he'd been waiting for. He bit his lip then squatted next to Tommy and fumbled in the sand, tried to keep the thugs' attention fixed on the ground in front of them. Against the rush of blood in his ears, he thought he could already hear the plunk and whoosh of oars. Dimmer still came the tiny whir of an electric motor, a small propeller turning with such exquisite slowness that the blades would barely blur.

The two friends were still crouching, feeling for the pen, when the first floodlight exploded into life.

"What the fuck?" said Ponte, wheeling, then crossing his arms in front of his face as if fending off a splash of acid.

The floodlight sent a blue-white fireball across the beach, everything it touched stood out stark as bone, movements were jerky as a flip-book. For a moment the thugs were blinded, then they thought that maybe they had lost their minds. A Viking ship was landing.

It had a high prow, painted gold and carved in the shape of a scaly serpent; many pairs of slender oars were powering it slowly so that its keel now scraped along the shore. Working the oars were forty women wearing horned and furry helmets, and pastel bras with built-in nipples.

Squeak looked at the women, saw bare midriffs, cleavages smooth as the seam on plums, and said, "Jesus Christ Almighty."

Next to the Viking ship was a powerboat whose cockpit was piled high with lights and booms and cameras.

Ponte saw the cameras, counted more bodies than his troops had bullets, and whispered hoarsely, "The pieces, stash 'em."

The lovely Vikings disembarked, sashayed up the beach in tiny skirts made out of pelts. Instinct told the mobsters to turn their backs on the floodlights that tracked the oddly clad women and made them gleam like excited angels carved in soap. As the thugs cringed, the models joined hands and formed a wavy line that led on toward the Bra King.

"Sign the fucking contract," Ponte said again, but the command was whiny now, despairing, forceless, Tommy Tarpon just shot him a look that was solemn, judging.

Barely noticed, giddy with hope, Franny Rudin took her shirt off.

It so happened she was very small on top, she didn't care for bras, she wore an undershirt, boyish but for a tiny pink bow that lay against her sternum.

She made a dash and joined the Vikings. They opened ranks for her, welcomed her into the chain.

Ponte's collar was pulled up to his ears, he stood hunched and stupefied in the breaking dawn.

The bosomy Vikings surrounded Murray and Tommy, pulled them away from Bruno and Squeak like cowboys cutting steers.

From the power boat, through a raspy bullhorn, came an authoritative voice: "Beautiful. Now put the crown on him."

Moving at a ritual pace, the Viking Queen approached the Bra King, bearing his foil-covered cardboard trademark. Murray, the pulse still slamming in his neck, lowered his head to receive the honor. But before the model could anoint him, Franny gently but firmly took the crown away. Murray, soupy-eyed, looked at her; she pursed her lips, paused a moment, put on a disbelieving pout that was almost a smile, and crowned him.

They moved in a protective circle back to the boats. The Vikings climbed aboard their ancient ship. Murray and Franny and Tommy scrambled onto the power boat.

An engine fired—not the small electric motor, but a beast of many horsepower. Towing the Vikings in their bras, the boat roared off just as the sun lifted from the sea, striping the sky with pale bands of red and green and yellow.

Charlie Ponte, looking jaundiced in the sallow dawn, said to no one in particular, "That didn't happen."

Squeak said, "Jesus Christ Almighty."

The little boss moved toward Bruno, backhanded him across the cheek. "Ya see what happens, ya bring me a fuckin' woman?"

When the boats were out of gunshot range, they slowed, and Murray said, "Vikings? Ya send me Vikings? I asked for pirates."

"The notice you give me," said Les Kantor, putting down the bullhorn. "I did the best I could."

"So what happens now?" said Franny.

Murray went to scratch his scalp. He'd forgotten he was still wearing the Bra King crown, the fake gold foil scratched his wrist. "I dunno," he admitted. "I haven't thought that many jumps ahead."

FOUR

35

At North Key Largo the models put their shirts on and were loaded into a bus back to South Beach. The Viking ship was dispatched to the Miami prop shop where it had been rented.

Then Les Kantor steered the power boat to a small marina looking out across Card Sound, and, by pink light through lavender clouds, he and Murray and Franny and Tommy sat down to breakfast among the fishermen. Murray still had his crown on, he forgot about it till the waitress looked at him funny, then he put it on the table next to him.

They sat on a wooden deck above the water, squinting at a day that seemed a whole new era, an age away from what they'd just escaped. It was wonderful, miraculous almost, this mundane business of having breakfast, feeling safe, being able to order what you wanted. Franny had juice, melon, a double stack of unbuttered whole wheat toast.

"So how's the footage?" said the Bra King, washing Prozac down with coffee. "Ya think it's any good?"

"The footage stinks," Les Kantor said. "Forget about the footage." A fastidious man, he was eating a Danish he'd cut into four pieces; he paused to wipe cherry glaze from his salt and pepper mustache. "Only good thing about the footage, it gives us something to show the IRS, we deduct the whole thing as a business trip."

"You're beautiful, *bubbala*," Murray said. "Always thinking."

"And what about you?" said Kantor. "You thinking, Murray? You thinking about giving up this casino *mishigas* and coming home?"

The Bra King mulled that over, glanced sideways at Tommy, watched a cormorant tuck its narrow head and dart down for a fish. "Coming home? Ya mean New York? Nah, Les. That's over."

"But Murray," said his ex. "This casino thing. You can't still want—"

"It doesn't matter what I want," Murray interrupted. "I've been noticing that lately. It matters that we get this settled."

Tommy was eating sunnyside-up eggs. The yolks were high and perfectly jelled, they reminded him of Vikings. "It's not settled yet," he thought aloud.

"No, it isn't," Murray agreed. "We got Franny back but now they're mad. We made 'em look dumb."

"They are dumb," said the Indian.

Les Kantor finished up another wedge of Danish, wiped his fingers on his napkin. "Look, a woman was kidnapped, for Chrissake. Why don't you go to the police?"

Murray fingered his fake gold crown, resolutely shook his head. "Call me a shitty citizen, I think that's a lousy bet. Maybe Ponte's got 'em in his pocket. Maybe LaRue pulls strings. Maybe they're just incompetent, they piss around long enough for us to disappear."

Franny's appetite was suddenly gone, she put down a piece of toast edged with crescents the shape of her teeth.

"We can't go back to Key West," Tommy Tarpon said.

"No," said Murray. "I guess we can't. They'd find us in a—"

"That's not what I mean. Your car's still on Biscayne."

This seemed one more exasperation than the Bra King could process. He slapped his coffee down, a little of it spilled into the saucer. "Car's been nothing but aggravation. Well, fuck it, it's just a car. "

"He's right though," said Les Kantor. "Key West wouldn't be safe."

Murray thought that over, looked out at scudding pelicans, gently bobbing boats. He grabbed a toothpick from a plastic holder and said, "*Shlemazel.*"

Les and Franny nodded as though the comment were neither more nor less than obvious.

"*Shlemazel?*" Tommy said.

"*Shlemazel,*" Murray repeated, louder, so it would be easier to understand. "A guy with lousy luck. Like, other people, they come to Florida, they get a beautiful tan, their blood pressure goes down. Me, I come to Florida, I lose my car, I plunk down twenty grand for a penthouse I'll get murdered if I go to."

"Ah," said Tommy. "*Kamana wamputi.*"

"Meaning?" asked Les Kantor.

"He who falls from horseback into dung."

"That's Murray," Franny said. Absently, she again picked up a piece of toast, nibbled at the crust. "So where *are* we gonna go?"

◆ ◆ ◆ ◆ ◆ ◆

"Fuck you, Bahney."

The senator was not awake yet, had reached for the clamoring phone on the Tallahassee nightstand without even cracking an eye. He said, "What time is it?"

"You're in trouble, friend."

"What?"

"The fuckin' tribe you were gonna deliver, you ain't delivered dick."

Swimming up toward consciousness, sliding his shoulders higher onto pillows, LaRue said, "Charlie, I have no idea what you're talking about."

Clarity of speech, even in the best of times, was not what Ponte was best at. Now, back at his desk in Coconut Grove, he was hammer-tongued with rage. "A hundred fuckin' grand on the casino bill, I see squat for that, ya tell me sorry. Another fifty up front for this fucking Indian. Easy, you say. Easy my ass."

"I told you one Indian, one Jew amateur."

"Bahney," said the mobster, a grudging regard edging into his tone, "you don't know these fucking people. You made it sound like you know them, and you don't."

The politician made a miscalculation, tried to tweak the other man's pride. "I handed you this person, Charlie. You can't close the deal, what do you want from me?"

"I want my fucking tribe."

"I did what I said I'd do."

"And I'm telling you you didn't."

LaRue scratched his chest through silk pajamas, said wearily, "So Charlie, just what is it you'd like me to do?"

The truth was, Ponte didn't know. He swiveled in his big chair, looked with distaste at the early morning light squeezing through his fortress windows. Then he swiveled back, listened half a second longer to the faint but irritating sound of the politician's breathing, and dropped the phone back into its cradle.

◆◆◆◆◆◆

Les Kantor, his small ears and high forehead turning bright red as the unaccustomed sun reared up toward its zenith, whisked them down the Keys in the rented power boat.

Flaco, the old sponger, was to meet them ten, twelve miles above Key West, at a forgotten place that had once been called the Sand Key Marina. It had a falling-down dock whose planks were sprung like the keys of a mangled xylophone; its derelict gas pump was a column of rust caught in a stranglehold of vines. The place was reached by way of a winding overgrown channel that an uninformed boater would never find.

Tommy guided Kantor through it; the sleek and gleaming speedboat scratched its way between the mangroves. Flaco was already waiting in the small still basin. His skiff looked very meager, very frail. It sat low in the water, loaded to the gunwales with the provisions Tommy Tarpon had asked him to gather: fresh water, fruit, bread, rice, matches, line and net and fish hooks, blankets and utensils.

"And beer?" Flaco had asked, when they'd spoken on the phone.

Tommy had paused, and in the pause he'd tasted hops and malt, felt the tart astringent draw of a cold one on his tongue. "No," he'd said. "No beer."

The two craft were side by side now in the sun-shot water; the grizzled Cuban, wordlessly efficient, was holding them together.

Murray put a hand on Kantor's shoulder, thanked him.

Kantor just shrugged. Then he said to Franny, "Look, it's none of my business, but you don't have to be as pigheaded as my partner. You could fly with me to New York, double back to Sarasota . . . "

Franny stood there in the sunshine. The boat was rocking softly, somewhere a gull was screaming. Cutting loose from the danger and the craziness, cutting loose, again, from Murray—it was awfully tempting. Returning to safe, normal Sarasota; really rather dull Sarasota . . . Momentarily she lost her balance, she couldn't tell if it was the motion of the boat or her own contrary leanings. She grabbed a gunwale, surprised herself by saying at last, "No, I was never one for leaving in the middle of a show. I'm staying."

She boarded Flaco's skiff.

Still shaking his fastidious and sunburned head, Les Kantor roared off, heading back to the safe and normal business of selling bras.

The old Cuban waited for his wake to settle, then moved at a temperate pace toward Tommy's island, Kilicumba, that place of flies and snakes and gators, a place where nobody could find them and they could steal some time to rest and think.

36

When they were out in the back country, skimming through the flat and lucent water over barracuda and eagle rays and propeller scars and random tufts of turtle grass, Murray said, "This island—it's not gonna be what you expect, ya know."

"What do you think I expect?" said Franny.

"Ya know—a desert island. Beach, coconuts, waterfalls."

"Murray, I've lived in Florida half a dozen years. I don't expect that, Murray."

"Oh," the Bra King said, and he vaguely wondered why it was that everyone else's expectations of life and fate and the world in general seemed saner, more measured, and more accurate than his own. "Am I nuts?"

Franny thought it better not to answer, just looked

across the green water to the featureless low islands that seemed to float a few inches above the surface, weightless, vagrant, resolutely dark in even the most searing sun. She was nestled among the provisions, her head was pillowed by a sack of rice. It was white rice, stripped of its nutrition, and she asked Tommy if it would be safe for Flaco to go sometime to the apartment and retrieve her vitamins. Tommy looked at the boatman and the boatman nodded yes. He knew the Anglos pretty well. He knew that no one would really look at him, he'd be taken for a maintenance man, a gardener.

They neared Kilicumba, Flaco zigzagged toward it with an airtight logic known only to himself.

They scraped aground at the kidney-shaped notch in the mangroves, and Tommy Tarpon jumped nimbly overboard, sinking, this time, only to his ankles. He dragged the skiff ashore, then, abruptly, like a man having a religious revelation, he dropped to his knees at the water's edge. In another instant he was rolling in the muck like a hog.

He rolled on his back, he rolled on his belly, he squirmed like a fetus on either side. When he was finished rolling he picked up big dollops of limestone goo and slapped them on his neck and face and hair. By the time he was done, nothing was left uncoated but his eyeballs and his lips, they stood out weirdly against the khaki mud, he looked a little like Al Jolson.

Murray and Franny gaped. "Tribal ritual?" she asked.

"Survival," Tommy said, dripping grainy marl. "Keeps the bugs off. I recommend it."

Murray said, "Me? I don't think so."

Franny shyly shook her head.

But the mosquitos and *wakita malti* were coming forth to meet them. They swarmed, they buzzed, they dive-bombed necks and ears, flicking out their feeding tubes like switchblades. Franny and Murray shook themselves, slapped themselves, wiped away battalions of blood-bloated insects. In twenty seconds they'd leapt overboard and were wallowing.

They wiggled, they squirmed, the mucky pleasure of it freed them of the burden of their dignity, sucked tension out of them and made them slaphappy. They were exhausted, giddy with relief and with the fear that still lingered beyond the relief. Now they were breaded like veal cutlets.

Franny sat cross-legged at the water's edge, drizzling wet sand on her head. "Fancy spa," she said, "people pay big bucks for this."

Murray opened up his shirt, rubbed muck into his chest hair. He massaged his face with it like it was shaving cream.

Wordlessly, Flaco started unloading the boat.

Then he led the way through the underbrush, past the gator holes, toward the clearing with the middens. The trail he'd cut a month before was already overgrown; once again he had to bushwhack. Lizards scampered from rock to rock, toads squirted under their rotten roof of fallen mangrove leaves. Carrying provisions, muck drying on them like a thin crust of cement, Tommy and Franny and Murray trudged along, their eyes on the perilous and shadowed ground in front of them.

They reached the clearing. The place worked its nameless ancient magic, loss and mystery drugged the air and for a moment there was silence. Afternoon sun lit up the west faces of the pyramids of shells; they had a pearly gleam and gave off a smell of iodine.

Franny said, "People lived here."

She said it very softly, the simple words seemed to come out with no breath behind them, as if they hadn't been spoken, but only thought. No one answered. Everyone put down what they were carrying. Flaco left, promising that he'd return tomorrow.

Tommy looked for a place where the porous limestone rock was not too jagged or too lumpy, and there he laid out blankets. Murray set down the canteens of water, the tin mess kits with their rattling spoons. Franny found a shady place for the fruit and the rice and the bread.

The activity broke the clearing's spell, and Murray, overtired and disoriented, started rambling. "A Jew going camping, whoever heard of a Jew going camping? Jews go on cruises. Jews go to hotels. Camping, it's like a very Christian thing. The last Jew who camped, I think his name was Moses."

No one picked up on his patter.

Tommy said, "I'm going fishing."

Franny lay down on her blanket. Limestone flakes

cracked off her as she shifted toward a position of some comfort. She was asleep almost immediately in the dappled light of late sun through arcing mangroves.

Murray yawned and lay down near her. He longed to put his arm around her, to cradle her back against his chest, but he did not. He looked at her hair, spiky with dried mud, smelled the salty ground beneath him, and fell into a nap.

◆◆◆◆◆◆

Frustrated and miffed, Ponte's thugs had taken a certain glee in destroying Murray's car. They knocked out windshields with their gun butts, snapped off the little pig's tail of cellular antenna, slashed tires with long knives produced from socks, used can openers to scrape off long curls of champagne-colored paint.

That, however, was as much fun as they would have that day. Charlie Ponte sent them on a slow and glary ride back to Key West to stake out the Paradiso.

"Jesus, Boss," Squeak had piped, "they're not gonna be so stupid to go back there."

"Ya never know how stupid people are gonna be," said Ponte. "Say they're stupid enough to go there and we're too smart to follow. Who's stupid then, huh?"

So, sleep-deprived, stale-breathed, itchy in their clothes, the thugs spent many hours in the Lincoln.

They parked next to the promenade, watched the mute condominium, its windows opening here and there, its curtains meaninglessly blinking. They watched the sun begin its westward dive, leered with envious scorn at the wholesome bikers and joggers and walkers, and at some point Bruno caught himself drowsily staring at the undulating backside of a man as he skated smoothly by. Fearing that Squeak had noticed him watching, he muttered, "Faggot. Hey, did you see the tits on those models?"

◆◆◆◆◆◆

Murray and Franny woke to the sound of crackling twigs and the flickering light of wood flames in the dusk.

Tommy was tending a fire, boiling rice. Three mangrove snappers, dappled brown and white, skewered through the gills, were slow-cooking in the fragrant smoke.

Murray looked at Franny. She had just opened her eyes, her eyeballs looked very big and white against her mask of muck. Frogs were croaking, thwarted bugs buzzed and rattled. Quite close by, there was a furtive splash, an alligator bedding down in a turgid puddle made homey by a coating of slime.

"Don't say I never take ya anywhere," the Bra King whispered.

Franny tried to smile but her face was more or less cemented in a neutral look. She blinked. Only now did she feel rested enough, safe enough, to call up the memory of Bruno with his brainless cruelty, Squeak with his raptor hands—to let the vile taste of captivity bubble up inside her and filter out. Her throat closed; her body felt suddenly cold. "Hold me a minute," she said to Murray.

He sidled toward her on his blanket. They had a very odd embrace, a hug as of two burned cookies. Crumbs fell off them as they moved together, brittle crust caved in when pressed. Murray reached for his ex-wife's hair, stroked the curled stalactites.

"Dinner's almost ready," Tommy said.

They dined by last light, their backs against the sloping side of a midden. They had rice on tin plates, fish eaten whole, the leaved flesh nibbled off the backbone. Embers flew from Tommy's fire, wafted away on gentle currents of salt air.

The warm food made Murray feel talkative and confident. "So, Tommy," he said, "how d'ya want it to be?"

"Hm?" Tommy was thinking about beer. What harm would there have been in having a couple, just a couple, with the rice and the fish and the fire?

"Our casino," the Bra King said. "How d'ya picture it?"

Tommy sucked a fish bone, cocked his head. He didn't answer fast enough, and the Bra King rambled on.

"I mean, I've seen pictures of some of these Indian bingo joints, and, due respect, they look like shitholes. Airline hangars. School cafeterias, with those long plastic tables. You don't want it to look like that, do ya?"

Tommy ate rice, stared past the fire to the edge of the clearing where firelight played on mangroves, where somehow, long ago, ancestors whose lives were nearly as foreign to him as the lives of ancient Greeks or Hebrews, had arrested the greedy march of jungle to reserve this small space for themselves.

"Of course," continued Murray, "if you're going for volume, ya go for volume. But this location, the exoticness, the remoteness, it cries out to be exclusive, upscale. No bingo. No slots. Just the more elegant games. Baccarat. Roulette. A dock for yachts. A mahogany launch, antique, captain in a braided hat, bringing high rollers out from town."

He paused to nibble fish, pictured green felt and red carpet against the dimming purple of the western sky.

His ex-wife said, "What a fantasy life."

The Bra King took this as a compliment. "And you don't know the half of it. Tommy presiding. Me behind the scenes. Women in gowns, men in black tie. A string quartet in the lounge——"

"A bullet in the brain," said Franny. "Do we have to talk about this right now?"

"Gotta talk about something," Murray said, though no one else seemed necessarily to think so.

Franny coaxed flesh off the backbone of her fish. "Then how about we talk about this wonderful place."

Murray blinked off toward the mangroves, the

gator holes, the fetid milky puddles. "What about it?"

Franny leaned back against the midden. The shells still held the heat of the day, they soothed her neck and shoulders. She looked up, thought she saw a shooting star moving with unnatural slowness through the sky, then realized it was a single egret flying past, a thousand feet above them, its white belly reflecting the glimmer of the flats. "It's beautiful here," she said.

"Beautiful as a place that never happened," said Tommy Tarpon, who for some reason had been thinking about his lost houseboat with its little fridge, its tilted lawn chairs bolted to the deck, its absurd but comforting attempts at comfort. "Wonderful. Rare. Like no place else. But for the longer haul, I'd take the penthouse any day."

37

They tossed on the hard ground all night, they twitched at bugs in their noses and their ears, and in the morning they swam, or tried to.

By early golden light, they waded out from the notch in the shore, picking their way carefully, looking for firm footing. But the bottom was level as a table, the water grew no deeper as they waded. Their eyes sleepy, they walked out two hundred yards and still it was as shallow and warm as a kiddie pool.

So they sat down on the bottom and washed as best they could. Yesterday's muck flaked off their clothes like paint chips from a rotten canvas; off of skin, it softened to a murky cloud and swirled away. Ibis flew by overhead; tiny houndfish, fleeing many terrors, skittered past on madly flicking tails.

It was wonderful, it was rare, and yet . . . And

yet, in the distance, squat and undetailed, Key West loomed as a monument to ease and pleasure. Murray, his flesh sore, his back complaining, sat there in the knee-deep sea and remembered what civilization was about: Mattresses. Towels. Bars of virgin soap, big and firm as bricks. Gizmos with timers that made coffee before the dull throb of a caffeine headache kicked in.

They waded back to shore. They wallowed, smeared themselves with muck. Wallowing had already come to seem a normal part of the day's toilette.

Tommy got a fire going, boiled up some coffee grounds. The resulting beverage tasted mostly like aluminum and smoke. They drank it without milk, with unadorned bread gone dank and soggy, and with each caustic sip and each pasty bite the romance of camping wore thinner.

"Okay," said Murray, washing down his Prozac with yesterday's stale water. "Let's figure how the hell we're getting outa this."

"Even here?" said Franny. "Even here you need the pills?"

"Thank God I remembered them," the Bra King said. He shifted his butt on the stony ground, tried to find a position that didn't hurt. He looked at Tommy. Tommy was sitting cross-legged. He looked comfortable. He probably wasn't, but he looked like he was, and this made Murray grumpy. "How the hell can you sit like that?"

"S'gonna be a long day," the Indian said gently. "Let's not get cranky."

"I'd give ten thousand dollars for a bath," said Murray.

Franny had started nibbling a mango. She nibbled it very carefully, because they had no dental floss out there, a mango string between the teeth could make her life a living hell. "I think we need a plan," she said.

Very calmly, Tommy said, "We have a plan."

"We have a plan?" said Murray.

"I thought of it yesterday when I was fishing. It's very simple. Maybe not that simple. Basically I sign some papers."

Murray took another swig of coffee, wished he hadn't, grimaced. "I don't want you to sign any papers. The whole idea was getting things to where you didn't have to sign."

Tommy shrugged. Behind him, morning sun broke free of slabs of cloud clustered low near the horizon, sprayed crisp and grainy light across the clearing.

Murray said, "Come on, Tommy, we're not looking for a martyr here."

The Indian shrugged again and said, "I wasn't planning on martyrdom. Character assassination, maybe. Human sacrifice, maybe. Martyrdom, no."

He put down his tin cup of lukewarm coffee and got up to do a little fishing.

◆◆◆◆◆◆

Sometime after noon, the three bored and breaded campers heard the faint whine of Flaco's ancient motor in the distance. Halfheartedly shaking off their torpor, they rose and walked lightheaded along the bushwhacked path. From the notch in the shore they watched the little skiff approach, and at some point, through the knife-edged glare, Murray saw a second figure in the boat. The figure was squat and silver-bearded, wearing horn-rimmed glasses, a bowtie, and a jacket that, on closer inspection, would prove to be made of tweed. The man's furry knuckles gripped the gun-wales nervously, on his face was a look of befuddle-ment or disbelief.

The little boat scraped aground. The new arrival stood up gingerly. He gaped at Murray. Murray gaped at him. Then he said, "*Oy.*"

The Bra King frowned. "I knew you were gonna say that, Max."

"You look like a savage," said his psychiatrist.

"Don'tcha say hello to Franny?"

Lowenstein stared at the muck-coated female with the popping eyes and limestone hair. "Good God, it is Franny."

"And this is Tommy," Murray said.

"We talked on the phone," said the sovereign. "I *am* a savage."

The shrink was having some trouble with his footing, his feet were wedged between a big water jug and the sack that held bread and fruit and Franny's vitamins. "Murray, what the hell are you doing here?"

"What the hell are *you* doing here?" the Bra King countered.

But before Max Lowenstein could answer, the bugs had found him, he started shucking and swatting, fending and dodging like a tired fighter.

"This is why we wallow," Franny said. "You really have to."

"I had a dream," the shrink explained, smacking and flinching. "Anxiety. That prescription, like I shouldn't have given it, something terrible would happen."

"What's so terrible?" said Murray. He lifted his shoulders, and fissures spread through his coating of mud.

"So I hopped a plane," Lowenstein went on. "I can't wallow, these are my only clothes."

"Take 'em off," said Franny.

The shrink weighed the statement's motivation. But a plague of insects was on him, they landed in a blurred mass on his neck and wrists and forehead, and soon he was sweeping off his jacket, kicking off his loafers, stepping out of his corduroy pants. In striped boxer shorts and an old-fashioned undershirt with shoulder straps, he stepped uncertainly overboard and rolled stoutly in the muck.

While he was rolling, Flaco explained, "I find him in the lobby. He looking for a Zemelman. He seem hokay. I feel him, you know, for gun, for knife."

Tommy nodded.

"I also see big car parked outside," said Flaco. "Two *pendejos*, mean. I think they maybe not hokay."

Tommy nodded again, then he asked Flaco to

go to the office of the Key West *Sentinel* and gather up the reporter Arty Magnus; and to have him contact Bert, the old man with the little dog; and to bring them both to Kilicumba as soon as he could. Flaco asked no questions, made no protests, just handed over the provisions and Max Lowenstein's suit of northern clothes, and poled his little skiff off the bottom.

Meanwhile the psychiatrist wallowed. He rolled, he shimmied, he reflected on his day. He'd had his crotch patted by an old Spanish fisherman; the wife of a patient had suggested he disrobe. At length he sat in the inches-deep sea, and in his corpulence and his sagacity he looked like Buddha.

Murray stared at him, said, "Jesus, Max, I'm really touched you came."

◆◆◆◆◆◆

From a pay phone on the promenade, Bruno called his boss.

"It's been a day, a night, and most of another fucking day already, and we ain't seen shit," he said.

Charlie Ponte drummed fingers on his desk. He'd slept in his own bed last night, changed his underwear, what the hell did he care? "Give it more time," he ordered.

Bruno's nylon socks were crusty, his athlete's foot was driving him insane. "How about we break in, wait for 'em inside?" That way he could wash between his toes at least.

"Too risky those places," Ponte said. "Alarms, closed circuit. Then ya first got headaches."

There was a standoff. Bruno shuffled his tormented dogs against the hot sidewalk, looked at women facedown with their tops undone, sunning on the beach.

Finally Ponte said, "Maybe you'll take over LaRue's place, keep an eye from there."

The big thug loved that idea. Foot powder. A liquor cabinet. Television. "That gonna be okay with him?"

"Fuck what's okay with him," said Charlie Ponte. "I'm fed up with that dog turd anyway. Call me back an hour or two, I'll have it all set up."

38

"Jesus Christ," said Bert the Shirt, looking at the mud-smeared group in the notch of the shore, "youse look ridiculous."

The old man was sitting in the bow of Flaco's skiff, his ancient chihuahua nestled in his lap. Behind him stood tall thin Arty Magnus, a cheap pen and spiral notebook clutched in his hand, and behind both of them was a lowering sun that sent a weirdly even copper sheen across the water.

"The bugs," said Murray. "You'll join us, you'll see."

"Nuh-uh," the old man said, as Flaco dragged the little craft toward shore and the blood-feeders began to swarm. "Dignity, my friend. There has to be a line. I haven't met the lady. Charmed, I'm sure." From a trouser pocket he produced a huge silk handkerchief, the same soft lavender as his shirt; almost daintily, he wrapped the cloth around his hair, tied it underneath his chin. "And who's the gentleman in his underwear?"

"This is my psychiatrist," the Bra King said. "His name is Max."

Max nodded graciously from behind his smoking pipe.

"Psychiatrist," said Bert. "Y'opening a casino or a nuthouse?" The skiff scraped bottom, and slowly, carefully, he stepped over the low gunwale. He was holding his dog the way some people hold a prayer book, all he needed was the square black shoes to look like a Sicilian grandmother on her way to church.

Arty Magnus, wearing shorts and sandals, climbed nimbly overboard, waded calf-deep and coated his bare legs with marl. He slapped some on his neck and looked around at the unbroken shoreline, the strangling vegetation. "S'gonna be quite a feat opening anything here," he said.

The others followed his eyes, saw beauty or impediments, challenge or futility, according to their dispositions.

When Bert was securely up on land, he said, "So Murray, ya come up one jump short. Ya save the missus and now you're stuck out here. This is what I call one jump short."

No one disagreed.

Tommy led the way past gator holes and severed vines back to the clearing, where low sun threw blockish and ominous monoliths of shade on one side of the middens. They sat. Bert's dog smelled nature or history and began to tremble.

Murray told the new arrivals the details of Franny's captivity and rescue and the flight to Kilicumba.

Bert sadly shook his kerchiefed head. "Ponte," he said. "He wants to think he's a businessman, but he's still a thug at heart."

"A selfish child," Max Lowenstein put in, "justifying his pathology."

"LaRue's just as bad," said Arty Magnus.

"How'd you like the pleasure," Tommy Tarpon said, "of announcing that to the whole wide world?"

The journalist said nothing. Unconsciously, he licked his chops.

"Ever hear of a company called First Keys Casinos?" the Indian went on.

Magnus shook his head, waved bugs away from his ears.

"It's Ponte's front. Mentioned in what I guess you'd call the ransom note. A little digging, I'll bet you find the link."

"What's it got to do with LaRue?" the reporter asked.

"He was supposed to pressure me into signing on with them."

"Got proof?" said the reporter.

"There he goes again," said Murray.

"He's conscientious," said the shrink, blue whorls escaping from his mouth. "Too much, it's obsessive."

Tommy said, "If LaRue handed me a large cash payment to get the contract signed, would that persuade you he's involved?"

"LaRue himself?" said Magnus. "Never happen."

"If you saw it with your own eyes?" pressed Tommy Tarpon. "Senator as bagman. If you had an exclusive on the story?"

"He'd never risk that kind of exposure," said the journalist.

Tommy paused. Some pelicans flew past just above the level of the mangroves, you could hear the soft whistle of their wings. "I think he might," the sovereign said, "if the choice was even greater risk."

"Aha," said Lowenstein, "the classic double bind."

"Ponte wants that contract signed," said Tommy. "We've seen how far he'll go to get it signed."

"Go on," the reporter said.

"My position is this. I'm ready to sign now, but only if LaRue himself is witness. I want him implicated. I want him to have a stake in making sure nothing bad happens to my friends or me."

Now Bert the Shirt spoke up, there was something grimly oracular in the way the voice issued forth from shadowed features underneath the silk *babushka*. "Guy like Ponte, don't kid yourself someone's name on a piece a paper is gonna protect ya."

"Did I say I believed it?" Tommy said. "I said that's my position."

The psychiatrist shifted on the lumpy ground, swiftly checked that the fly of his shorts had not gapped open. "A construct," he said. "A situational construct."

Bert hugged his nervous chihuahua, leaned back against the midden. The slowly cooling shells gave off a smell of salt and iron. "And how does Ponte find out what your position is?"

Tommy just looked at him.

Murray said, "Never hurts to have a friend in the business."

"Now wait a second—" the old man began.

Franny said, "They kept me locked up in a tote board, Bert. You have to help us."

"I'm asking you to have two conversations," Tommy said.

Bert waved bugs from in front of his silk-framed face. "Two? Now it's two?"

"Someone's gotta call Ponte," Tommy said, "and someone's gotta talk to LaRue. He's probably still in Tallahassee."

"Ponte'll call LaRue," said Arty Magnus.

The Indian stood, paced the shady trough between the middens. "Exactly. And that conversation will be a lot more interesting if the two of them have different information."

Max Lowenstein sucked his pipe. "Cognitive dissonance," he murmured.

"And then some," Tommy said.

"I don't think I understand," said Bert the Shirt.

Striding between the shell heaps, slipping from

red light to purple shadow and back again, the sovereign of the Matalatchee spun out the details of his stratagem. Bert listened hard, stroking his dog like the dog was his own chin, and when Tommy finished, the old man's face was neutral as a saucer. "I'll talk to them," he said.

After a silence, Arty Magnus said, "Ponte's headquarters, it's at this lobsters-and-mobsters kinda place—"

"I know where it is," said Bert, a little testily. "It's supposed to be a secret."

"It isn't," said the journalist.

A gull screamed in the distance. There was a damp and furtive rustling in the shrubs.

Tommy asked Magnus for the loan of some paper and a pen. "You want your exclusive," he said, "be ready for Flaco at one tomorrow. Come prepared to spend a while in the mangroves." Then, almost as an afterthought, he said to the psychiatrist, "You can leave, Max, if you want. You can go back home."

Lowenstein shifted on the hard warm ground, flecks of muck dropped off him like tiles from a ruined mosaic. "Actually," he surprised himself by saying, "I'd like to stay."

The sun hit the horizon, bugs and birds and frogs saluted it with a sudden rasping crescendo. "Good," said the Indian, masterful on his ancestral lands. "Maybe we'll find a little job for you."

39.

It was Bruno who opened the door of Barney LaRue's penthouse, and now Bert was confused. Briefly speechless on the threshold, he stared at the gigantic goon, saw that he was barefoot, that his feet were heavily powdered, that the powder had left ursine footprints as he'd trudged across the living room to the entryway. A whirring whine revved up, and in a moment the old man saw Pascal, crab-walking in Bruno's wake, expunging his traces with a handheld vacuum cleaner.

" 'Lo, Bert," said the big man, with a grudging cordiality. They were slightly acquainted, comrades in theory but seldom allies of late.

"I'm lookin' for Bahney," the old man said, as the little vacuum was switched off.

"What about?" said Bruno.

There was a whiff of threat in how he said it, just enough for Bert to know he ought to lie. But his reflexes weren't what they once had been, a heartbeat passed before he said, "Gin rummy game."

"He's still in Tallahassee," Pascal told him. He was dressed in red tights and seemed very put out by company.

"Ah," said Bert, holding his dog tight against his wizened stomach. "Ya got a number for him there?"

A reedy voice piped forth from the living room. "Ya don't play gin rummy by telephone. You're not fuckin' wit' us, are ya, Bert?"

"Squeak, now why would I do that?"

"We're lookin' for a neighbor a yours," said Bruno. "Guy wit' the penthouse across the way. Seen 'im?"

Bert scratched his cheek, tugged an earlobe. "Not since ya took his wife to Hialeah."

"Fuck you know about that?" said Bruno.

Bert spoke calmly to Pascal. "Gimme a number for Bahney. Write it down, my memory's shot."

"You know where they are, don'tcha Bert?" said Squeak.

Bert didn't answer.

Bruno said, "Where are they?"

"Like I said, my memory's shot."

The big thug leaned closer to him, his powdered toes curled for purchase in the rug. "We got ways t'improve an old man's memory."

"An' I'm sure they're very clever ways," Bert said,

as Pascal reached in and handed him the number. "But me, I'm goin' home now. I'm gonna call LaRue about a gin game. Then I'm gonna call Cholly, 'cause his number I remember. Then I'm gettin' inta my pajamas. Ya wanna come torture me, murder me, whatever, come right in, the door is open."

◆◆◆◆◆◆

"Why me, Don Giovanni?" said Bert the Shirt, as he labored across the pee-stained carpet to his BarcaLounger, halfconsciously sidestepping rawhide bones and rubber burgers. "Why do I always get put inna middle?"

He put the chihuahua on its unspeakable dog bed, the creature looked up through milky eyes, gave a sympathetic twitch to its whiskers.

"One a these times," the old man rambled, "someone's gonna end up gettin' really mad at me. I'm too old for havin' people mad at me. It wears ya down, Giovanni."

The dog put its chin on a paw as scrawny as a chicken wing. Bert sighed, settled back in the cradling chair. He picked up the phone and dialed.

"Hello, Martinelli's," said an oily voice.

"This is Bert the Shirt. Put Cholly on."

"There's no one here named Cholly," said the maitre d'.

"Cut the shit. Everybody knows."

There was an affronted silence on the line.

"Awright, awright," said Bert. "Ya want passwords? Calf head. Gnocchi. *Stringozzi*. Now ya happy? Gimme Cholly."

The line went dead. In a moment Charlie Ponte picked it up.

"Same old Bert," said the Miami boss. "Always fuckin' wit' guys' heads."

"I'm doin' you a favor," said the Shirt. "Your headquarters, you might as well hang a sign."

"You call to tell me that?" said Ponte.

"I call with a message from your Indian."

Ponte's silence turned interested. Then he said, "How you know about my Indian?"

"Your Indian is about as secret as your password, Cholly."

"Where is he?" demanded Ponte.

"Your boys already asked me that," said Bert. "I wouldn't tell them either."

"Whose side you on?"

"Right now I'm onna side a no one gettin' hurt. Here's the message: The Indian's ready to sign."

In his large bare office, Ponte tugged at the zipper of his silver jacket and almost smiled. "He's finally wising up."

"He's got a coupla conditions," said Bert.

"He ain't in a position to have conditions."

"He has them anyway. Up front he wants fifty grand to replace his houseboat."

"Fuck his houseboat," Ponte said.

"Come on, Cholly. What's fifty grand? You'll give 'im the money, you'll let 'im save face."

"And that's it? Fifty and he signs?"

"He wants one other thing. He wants LaRue to bring the contract and to witness it."

There was a pause.

Bert explained. "He thinks his friend, the Jewish guy, would be safe if LaRue's name was on the paper. Ya know, implicated, like."

The little mobster found this droll. "Like I'd hold off doin' what I gotta do for the sake a that douchebag politician?"

"What could I tell ya?" said the Shirt. "The Indian, he's got this sense a loyalty, he thinks that other people have it too."

"Asshole," Ponte said.

"So it's a go, or what?" pressed Bert.

Ponte thought it over, not for long. "Yeah. Okay."

"I'll call LaRue," said Bert. "I'll tell 'im what he's gotta do. He isn't gonna like it, Cholly."

"Fuck what he likes," Ponte said. "I'll make sure he does it."

◆◆◆◆◆◆

"I have no idea what you're talking about," said State Senator Barney LaRue, speaking from his apartment in the capital. It was a discreet one-bedroom where he behaved discreetly, as was demanded in that part of the state.

"Look," said the Shirt, "ya helped Tommy get this island, ya wanna make a couple bucks off it yourself. Waya the world. I unnerstand. But inna meantime, the only way the deal is gonna happen—"

"The deal has nothing to do with me," the senator insisted.

"If that's your story," Bert said, "you stick to it. But Tommy Tarpon will only sign if you are there to witness, and if you bring a hundred thousand dollars to replace his houseboat, which got sunk to the bottom a the ocean during a period when negotiations weren't going well."

"Bert, listen," said LaRue, his mellifluous baritone getting slightly pinched, "I couldn't possibly lend my name—"

"Bahney, I'm not here to convince you. I'm delivering a message, this is all. There's a gentleman I'm sure you've never met, even though his colleagues are camped out in your penthouse. His name is Cholly Ponte. He feels very strongly that this contract should be signed."

The senator sat up straighter in his chair, tried to muster a stentorian tone. "I will not be put in a position—"

"I'm sure you won't," said Bert. "But Mr. Ponte has the papers and the cash, and I think it would be best for everybody if you could bring them to the Cow Key Bridge tomorrow at five."

"There is no way," the politician began. But he was interrupted by a soft click on the line. "Shit," he said, "I've got another call coming in."

"I'm sure it isn't Cholly Ponte," said the Shirt, "because I know you do not know the man. But just in case it is, explain the conditions, ask him to front the hundred grand, and give him my regards."

40

Next morning on Kilicumba, four badly rested people waded, washed, and wallowed in the muck. Above them, frigate birds wheeled with the tiniest adjustments of their long forked tails, flocks of ibis commuted from the secret precincts of their rookeries to their daily business of finding food.

Back in the clearing, Tommy took himself to the far side of the middens and scrawled on the notebook pages borrowed from Arty Magnus. Max Lowenstein discreetly withdrew into the mangroves to attempt to move his bowels.

Murray Zemelman tried to start a fire. He'd seen Tommy do it, he didn't understand why he was having so much trouble. He made a teepee of sticks; the sticks fell down. He got some twigs to light, they gave off soft puffs like someone smoking a cigar and then they died.

Franny was measuring water and coffee into a dented can. She looked over her shoulder to make sure Tommy was out of earshot, then whispered, "Murray, d'you think he knows what he's doing?"

Blithely the Bra King said, "I have no idea."

Franny shook her head, mud cracked into facets on her neck. "That goddam casino."

Murray tried to strike another match, it made a soggy squeak against the phosphorous. "Franny," he said, "if it wasn't for the casino and everything that's happened, you and me, we wouldn't have gotten together again."

She blinked silt from her eyelashes. "And what a tragedy that would be."

A fast and deep emotion knifed through Murray, filled him like a flash flood in a canyon. "It *would* be," he said. "A tragedy is exactly what it would be. Fighting fate. That's tragedy, right?"

His former wife started to say something, then bit her lip and went back to her coffee grounds and water.

Murray said, "At least give me the satisfaction of saying you're glad you came to see me."

She put the can down on the ground, stood there with her hands on her hips. She looked at her ex, this man no longer young, hardly handsome, covered in limestone. He looked like an animate boulder, a rock formation come to life. Except rock formations weren't needy, whiny, grandiose, hypochondriacal lunatics. "I am glad," she said. "That's the sick part."

"Did someone say sick?" Max Lowenstein asked, emerging from the foliage in his underwear, an unrelieved look on his face and a blur of flies around his matted beard.

◆◆◆◆◆◆

Flaco appeared around nine. He brought real coffee in a thermos, and salty Cuban bread still warm from the oven. He took the pages Tommy Tarpon had written on, and he shuttled back across the flats to town.

The sun moved up the sky. Birds and bugs and gators eased into a breathless stillness, hoarded their strength against the heat of the day. The island captives hunkered down and chatted in shrinking scraps of shade.

At some point Max Lowenstein said, "So level with me, Murray—how many pills you taking?"

"Two a day," the Bra King said. "Sometimes, I feel stressed, exhausted, three."

The psychiatrist said, "*Oy*. Murray, three is not for a human being. Three is for a catatonic horse."

"What could I tell ya? I take the pills, I feel better, this is all I know."

"Shnockered, used to be all I knew," Tommy volunteered.

"Used to be?" Lowenstein said smoothly. He lit his pipe. "You used to drink and stopped?"

Tommy didn't meet his eye. "For now."

"There," said Franny. "You see?"

"See what?" Murray said. "Now wait a second. You can't compare—"

"Of course you can," said the psychiatrist.

"Why is everyone ganging up on me?" the Bra King said, and he went into a sulk that no one had the energy to pull him out of.

He was still pouting when, shortly after two, the skiff returned, bringing Arty Magnus.

The gangly reporter had a paramilitary look about him. He was wearing stout black boots and camouflage fatigues; in a small pack he carried a helmet of mosquito netting, his spiral notebook, a miniature cassette recorder held together with duct tape, and a manila envelope, which he handed over to Tommy.

"Find out anything about First Keys Casinos?" the Indian asked him.

"Registered in the Cayman Islands," Arty said. "Officers include a lawyer who once defended Trafficante, and an accountant who was questioned but never indicted on a charge concerning a loan from the Teamsters' pension fund. The Teamsters, it so happened, were big donors to LaRue's campaign that year."

"Convinced?" said Tommy.

"Intrigued," said Magnus.

Flaco interrupted. "The *pendejo senatore*," he said. "I go back for heem now?"

◆◆◆◆◆◆

Cow Key Bridge was part of the only road that linked Key West to North America, and at five P.M. it carried heavy traffic. Rented convertibles and hand-buffed Harleys and hollowed trucks sped by, making I-beams tremble and rivets sing. Beneath the modest span, timeless currents spilled between the ocean and the Gulf; pelicans and egrets, oblivious to the clamor and the stink, fished the fertile shallows in the slanting sun. Flaco leaned across a gunwale and staked his boat at the base of the embankment that sloped down from the roadway, and waited for Barney LaRue.

Soon a car pulled onto the shoulder, and the politician—tall, annoyingly handsome, wearing a suit and carrying a briefcase—appeared above the guardrail. Unexpectedly, he was sandwiched between two other men, nasty men, men that Flaco recognized from the big dark Lincoln parked outside the Paradiso. The boatman, with a subtle shifting of his weight, leaned in against his push-pole, said, "One man only goes."

Squeak said, "Don't tell us, ya fuckin' spick."

"Then no one go," said Flaco.

Bruno, half-lunging, half-sliding down the gravel incline, made a move for him. With an astonishing lack of hurry, Flaco poled away from shore, just far enough to be unreachable. "We waste time," he said to LaRue.

The politician looked sour and disgusted. On the flight from Tallahassee to Miami, he'd been assailed by misgivings that put a bad taste in his mouth, a taste of blood and chalk. In Coconut Grove, he hadn't liked the look on Charlie Ponte's face when the gangster handed over the briefcase full of cash, hadn't liked the way his upper lip twitched back from his teeth. Nor did he like the sprawl and smell of Ponte's thugs camped out in his apartment. Now LaRue was abashed and weary; that was as close as he would come to admitting he was scared. "He's right," he said to Squeak and Bruno.

"Don't fuckin' tell us who's right," said Squeak. "You got that briefcase, we're supposed ta go along."

Discomfort put a snide edge on the politician's arrogance. Recklessly he said, "Look, you tried it your way, you fell on your face. Now back off and let me settle this."

The two goons, balancing with difficulty against the slope, looked at each other, unable to think themselves beyond the stalemate. Slow but resolute, Flaco poled back to the shore. As traffic whined and herons flicked their snakelike necks for fish, Barney LaRue angled down the gravel in his expensive shoes and stepped alone into the skiff.

Bruno sat on the embankment, balled his right fist, nestled it in the vastness of his left palm. "Don't tell Ponte," he said to Squeak, beneath the roar and ring of traffic, "but I almost hope that fucker fucks it up."

41

On Kilicumba, they heard the little boat approaching across the still and echoing flats. They heard the motor cough and die, heard the soft scratch of fiberglass on marl.

Arty Magnus tied his helmet of mosquito-netting securely over his head and face, and buried himself in the dense light-blotting mangroves that edged the clearing.

Murray and Franny and Max looked to Tommy for instructions. But he had nothing to say to them. He stood there in his crusty clothes, he inhaled concentration and exhaled silence. He crossed his arms against his chest, spread his feet out shoulder-wide, set his mouth and turned down his eyes in an expression that was solemn, judging. Very Indian. Except now it was no pose put on for the tourists, but the stubborn core of something desperate, undaunted and unyielding.

Flaco led LaRue to the middens.

It was just after six. The light was soft and golden, shadows were long, distorted, with fainter shadows stretching from their edges. Under his poplin suit LaRue was wearing a blue oxford shirt and a yellow silk tie, he looked like what he was—an ambassador in time of war, dispatched under deep duress from a very different nation.

He glanced quickly at the island exiles caked in mud, made no effort to mask his civilized contempt. Briefly he stared at Max Lowenstein, smoking his pipe in his unspeakable boxers. "And who the hell are you?"

The shrink said, "I'm visiting from New York."

"Crazy goddam Yankees," said the senator. He handed over the briefcase that held the contracts and the cash, said, "All right, let's get this over with."

Tommy put the satchel on the ground beside him. "Why?" he said. "You in a hurry?"

Bugs, waking up hungry as pygmy bears, were beginning to swarm into their sunset orgy. Mosquitoes flocked to the senator's unprotected neck, *wakita malti* tapped into the faint blue veins of his slender wrists and elegant hands.

"This is sordid," he hissed.

"You don't like being Ponte's errand boy?" said the Indian.

LaRue felt tiny punctures in his flesh, tried very hard to hold on to his self-possession, to resist the urge to swat and shimmy. "I don't like being used," he said.

"No one does," said Tommy. "Funny you never noticed that before."

The politician said, "Take out the contracts, please. Two copies. You sign, I witness."

Tommy picked up the briefcase, opened it. In the silence the snap of the clasps was very loud. He looked with no great pleasure at the bundled fifties, then removed a manila envelope that lay on top of them. Setting the briefcase down again, he slid out the contracts and started to read.

"For God's sake," said LaRue, "you know what's in them."

The Indian said nothing, kept reading. Moths and beetles streamed in and out of shadow. LaRue gave in and swatted and slapped.

"Calamine works pretty good for that," said Murray.

"Tea tree oil's better," Franny said. "Organic."

Tommy finished reading. Still clutching the papers, he started stomping softly on the ground, sending forth a high and reedy humming as he did so.

"Just sign the goddam contracts," said LaRue.

Tommy stood still and stared at him. "You're in my country now," he said. "Here we have respect for certain ceremonies."

He went back to his stomping and his rocking and his humming, to Murray he looked like an old Jew *dahvenning* on Yom Kippur. His voice rose gradually, mysterious syllables passed his lips, his

feet began to cover ground, to trace out the perimeter of the clearing. Loudly now, his voice no longer
a private moan but a keening to the heavens, he
sang out ancient chants as he bowed and swooped
and wove his way between the middens. Deep in
secret communion, he disappeared behind them
for a time, the haunting vibrato of his voice poured
down like chilly rain from unseen clouds.

Very softly, Franny said, "I think he's asking his
ancestors to forgive him. I think I read that somewhere."

"Jung," said the psychiatrist. "Reconciling the
forebears. An archetypal impulse."

LaRue twitched and scratched and felt his rising
welts.

Tommy danced back into view, his priestly movements tracked by a red and eerie shaft of light that
trickled weakly through the mangroves. His tempo
slowed, his volume fell, his fluid movements grew
sporadic, jerky, as when a wind-up toy has nearly
spent its tension. His face somber and serene and
drained, he finally came to rest in front of Barney
LaRue, stood closer than LaRue wanted him to be,
and said, "Now we sign."

The senator pulled his face away, quickly produced a pen from the pocket of his shirt.

Tommy flicked back his muddy cuff and signed
the documents. The politician witnessed them,
brusquely gave the Indian a copy.

"Isn't it traditional to shake hands now?" Tommy
said.

Barney LaRue had no intention of shaking hands.

Instead, he took two quick steps back, flicked his eyes to the left and to the right, set his feet at marksman's width. A travesty of a smile grabbed at the corners of his mouth. He said, "And now you're going to give the money back."

Bugs buzzed. A gull cackled. Franny couldn't quite hold back a sharp indignant sound. Tommy looked at the senator, at his right hand that was buried in the hip pocket of his jacket.

Flaco was standing at the edge of the clearing, his stringy form was slightly stooped. The Indian said to him, "You didn't pat him down?"

The old Cuban, shamefaced, shook his head and said, "*Oy.*"

LaRue said calmly, "I'll take the money. Our Spanish friend will bring me home."

Moment by moment the light was fading. Shadows lost their edges, colors went dry and curled like dying flowers. Tommy stalled, said, "There's too many of us."

With his left hand LaRue waved bugs from before his eyes. "There'll be fewer if you don't do as I say. Back off from that goddam case."

Tommy thought that over. He held his ground a moment, then grudgingly fell back.

LaRue smirked. "The lady," he said. He pointed at his feet. "The lady puts the briefcase over here."

Franny couldn't get her legs to move. The middens gave off a salty smell, the mangroves threw a rude whiff of generation and decay.

The politician's hand was twitchy in his pocket. He said, "Don't try my patience, people."

Murray stared at him. In the dim illusive light he studied the place where the jawbone tucked beneath the ear. Begging his eyes to speak to him truly, the Bra King focused on the tiny spot where LaRue's last shred of honesty resided. He wanted to believe he saw a tinge of pink. He made his lunge.

The attack was slow and unathletic, it took Murray much too long to close the small space between his adversary and himself. Franny had time to shout; Max had time to reach for her. Tommy joined in Murray's charge, the world went dead and waited for the crack and whine of the gun, the air itself seemed to flee the path of the imminent bullet.

Like a fat old linebacker dreaming, Murray threw himself at the politician's knees, closed his eyes and wondered if he was about to be shot in the back of the head. But the explosion didn't happen, and in the next instant Tommy finished off the tackle, brought LaRue down with a grunting thump against his ribs and a long groan on the hard and nubbly ground.

Pinning the senator's flailing arms, the Indian said through hard-clenched teeth, "Take the gun away."

Murray, kneeling on the limestone, was breathing with great effort, wheezing. "You crazy? You think I would've done that if he had a gun?"

Tommy stared down, solemn, judging, at the blandly handsome face of his defeated enemy, and briefly understood the appeal of taking scalps. But the bitterness and the violence had somehow all drained out of him, he looked at LaRue less with hate than sorrow, said, "You're pathetic, errand boy. Now straighten out your suit and go deliver the papers."

The Bra King stood, nonchalantly dusted off his hands, and bragged, "I can always tell a bullshitter."

42

His suit no longer perfect, Barney LaRue followed Flaco to the skiff. He was too depressed to swat at bugs, they swarmed around him like he was a piece of rotting meat.

Arty Magnus freed himself from the shrubbery. Tommy walked between the middens, returned with some papers and a manila envelope and handed them to the reporter. Then he started gathering twigs and branches to make a fire, to have a little light and cheer until Flaco returned to bring them home.

Sitting with her back against a midden, Franny said, "That chant, Tommy—were you summoning the spirits of your ancestors?"

The Indian poked the fire with a stick, gave a short and rueful laugh. "I don't know the words to summon them," he said.

"But what you were singing—?" began Max Lowenstein.

"I have no idea what I was singing. It might as well have been a Chinese menu."

When they heard the sound of Flaco's motor, they left the clearing without ever looking back.

By the time they reached Key West, a crescent moon was slouching toward the horizon, the sphere's dim bulk nested in the bright arc like a pocked gigantic egg. At the foot of White Street Pier, wet and tangy seaweed lay in rippling silver mounds. Flaco's skiff, heavy-freighted now, lumbered over the pillowed vegetation until the weed had swallowed up both sound and forward progress.

Arty and Tommy stepped overboard, hauled the craft ashore. The others stepped out on the beach, savored a breeze that was as damp and sweet as the steam from fresh-baked pastries. It was miraculous: There were no bugs, no encroaching mangroves. Palm fronds swayed. There were flowers on the air, the scents of spice and powder brought a feeling of oasis, an unspeakable gratitude that here was a place of comfort and refreshment.

"I wanna kiss the ground," the Bra King said.

"Who's stopping you?" said Franny.

Murray looked down at the beach, thought about the taste of sand. "I was speaking figurative." Then another thought tweaked him. "You sure it's safe to go back?"

"No," the Indian said blandly. "But I think we

have a little window. I think it's safe as it's gonna get."

"The fatalism of the tropics," said Max Lowenstein.

"Easy for you to say," said Murray.

Tommy was carrying his stash of money in an oily rumpled paper bag. He reached in, pulled out ten thousand dollars, handed it to Flaco. "For everything you've done."

The gift called forth from the old Cuban a burst of loquacity. "Too much," he said.

Tommy pressed the money into his reluctant hands. "Get a new boat, Flaco. That thing's a goddam deathtrap."

Murray glanced back at the craft that had just carried them across five miles of water. "Now ya tell us."

Arty Magnus, gangly and itchy in his camouflage fatigues, was eager to be gone. "They'll hold the presses till midnight," he said. "I'm going to the office."

He headed downtown. Murray and Franny and Tommy and Max walked the other way, along the street that flanked the ocean, toward the Paradiso.

For awhile they strolled in reverent silence. The street was lined with casuarinas, wispy, droopy trees that threw shadows like no others, crosshatched shadows that seemed made of satin net. Tree frogs croaked. Lights switched off and on in houses.

After a time Tommy said, "Our casino, Murray. Now you can tell me what it would've been called."

"Would've been?" said the Bra King.

Tommy exhaled, ran a hand through his hair, dried muck crumbled off it. He said nothing.

The Bra King held a silence like a drumroll, gestured like he was sweeping huge letters across a bright marquee. "Lost Tribes Casino."

They took a few more steps. He went on.

"Get it? A place for all the exiles. Always open, never closed. Free drinks for the bitter. Bottomless coffee for the depressed. A place for Indians. Cubans. Jews. The unhappy. The slaphappy. Anybody who's a refugee."

"For people who've been dumped," said Franny.

"Or lost their mates," said Murray.

"Or forgot the words," Tommy said, "to talk with their ancestors."

"You'd have the whole wide world in there," said Max.

They walked. Dogs barked, renewing their claims to home. Cats slunk around the warm tires of parked cars.

"So there isn't going to be a casino?" Franny said.

"Did you ever think there would be?" said the sovereign of the Matalatchee.

No one answered because no one knew who, if anybody, was really being asked.

A moment passed, the returning foursome shed crumbs of limestone as they walked. Then Tommy said, "Max, I have a job for you."

The psychiatrist coughed, dust shook off his undershirt. "What kind of job?"

"We'll have to talk to Bert."

◆◆◆◆◆◆

"Put the briefcase onna fuckin' desk," said Charlie Ponte.

There was something in the way he said it, something dismissive, bored almost, that instantly shattered the confidence LaRue had struggled so hard to regain. Sitting in the Lincoln with Bruno and Squeak, he'd had a couple of silent hours to erase his humiliation on Kilicumba, to reinflate his arrogance. He would come out on top. Of course he would: he always had before. They'd called his bluff—so what? His own name was on the contracts now, and that could be a trifle awkward. But even in the face of a full-fledged scandal, what did he have to lose? His honor? Drummed out of office, he'd live in heinous luxury on Bimini, Eleuthera. Some punishment! But now he looked at Charlie Ponte's sallow face and the cockiness leaked right out of him. He understood he was no longer needed. The Indian was sovereign. The papers had been executed. What was LaRue now but a guy cut in for five percent, a liability? He put the briefcase on the desk.

"Now siddown," the mobster told him.

Squeak brought a chair. LaRue perched on the edge of it.

Ponte said, "There's something I been wanting to tell you for a long time, Bahney." He was pacing in back of his desk, on his short legs it took several steps to walk the width of it. "Know what it is? . . . I hate your fuckin' guts."

He said it like he was spitting in the other man's face, and the politician flinched as though he had in fact been spat on.

"Other guys," the boss continued, "ya do business with them, okay, it's unnerstood that everybody's tryin' to make a buck, but there are limits to how much ya grab, certain rules for how ya do it. You, you're a sneak, a creep—"

"I didn't come here to listen to—"

"Shut up," said Ponte. "I'm just starting. You're a whore, Bahney. But you're too small t'unnerstand the importance of giving away a freebie now and then. The goodwill, y'unnerstand. You don't have the character for that. With you, it's gotta be grabbing every second, God forbid ya miss an opportunity. It's ugly, Bahney. Really ugly."

He broke off, stopped pacing, leaned in toward the briefcase on his desk. He snapped open the clasps, they rang like a whining ricochet. He lifted the top, saw nothing inside but a manila envelope.

Without hurry, he came around his desk, walked right up to Bruno, and backhanded him hard across the cheek. "Fuck ya give 'im time to stash the other fifty?"

Bruno didn't budge, didn't rub his face. "He had ta stash it 'fore he got to us," he said. "Once he's wit' us, I don't see 'im having time ta stash the fifty."

Ponte went back around his desk, stared a moment at the cashless briefcase. He turned his attention to the senator once again. The senator looked confused. Ponte smiled horribly, leaned over on balled fists. "Well, fuck it, I don't care about that fifty."

"What fifty?" said LaRue.

Ponte mugged up at his thugs. When he looked back at his visitor his eyes were very narrow.

"The Indian didn't ask me for a hundred grand," he said. "The Indian wanted fifty."

"Bullshit!" said LaRue. He tried to say it forcefully but his voice cracked and it came out as a whimper. "Bert specifically said to me—"

"I known Bert a long time," Ponte cut him off. "Bert's a friend a mine. You calling Bert a liar?"

"Then the Indian put him up to it," said the politician. "The fucking Indian set me up!"

Ponte frowned, considered, scratched his chest through the shiny fabric of his silver jacket. "Nah," he said, "it doesn't wash. How many times you told me, Bahney, that who we're dealin' with, we're dealin' with a stupid drunken Indian. A smart guy like you—you tellin' me a stupid drunken Indian is smart enough to set you up?"

LaRue opened his mouth; no words came out. His Adam's apple shuttled up and down, his eyes bulged like he was choking on a bone.

For a moment Charlie Ponte savored his discomfiture, then made a soothing gesture. "Bahney, Bahney, don't get your bowels in an uproar. That fifty grand, fuhget about it, I fuhgive it."

The politician, sweating now along his perfect hairline, stared at him in silence.

"I fuhgive that fifty grand," the little boss continued. "Ya know why? To teach you a lesson. A lesson in graciousness. A lesson in class. A gentleman, Bahney, he doesn't scrape after every nickel and dime. A good businessman, he doesn't have to. Ya make the right deals, y'earn the honor and the privilege to be a sport. Like this casino: the money it's gonna spin off, Bahney—aren't you embarrassed to grab a measly fifty grand?"

There was nothing for LaRue to say, he sat there sweating in his bruised and dirty suit, the salty sweat tormented all his bug bites. Bruno and Squeak were flanking his chair, squeezing in on either side of him, their nearness made him faintly nauseous.

Casually, almost as an afterthought, Charlie Ponte picked up the manila envelope, slid out the signed and witnessed contract. From a pocket of his silver jacket, he produced a pair of half-round reading glasses; they gave him a weirdly studious aspect.

He began to read. He looked puzzled; then concerned; then enraged. With fingers transformed suddenly into awkward claws, he rattled his way to the last page of the document. He read, re-read, paused a heartbeat to bite his lower lip and remove his glasses. Then he sprang up from his chair, threw himself across his desk, and grabbed on to Barney LaRue's silk tie.

He grabbed the tie and shoved the knot up as tightly as he could, his small hard fist wedged beneath the politician's chin. Trapped blood swelled veins in LaRue's neck, his face went scarlet and taut as an abscess. A thin gurgling sound escaped his imploding throat, until Ponte let up on the noose and started slapping him around the nose and eyes.

LaRue tried feebly to fend off the blows, but his arms were pinioned by the goons. They dragged him to his feet. Ponte came around his desk and punched him in the groin, kneed him in the lips when he doubled over.

"Fucking asshole," the boss hissed into his distorted face, and the victim didn't understand what had gone wrong.

Reeling, tasting blood and snot, too sorry for himself to grasp that the calamity he'd courted for so long was coming due, he opened his bloody mouth to ask a question.

Bruno's fist crushed the words back down his gullet. "I got smacked because a you," the big thug said. He hit the reeling figure a second time, knocked him backwards until he slammed into a wall then crumpled to the floor.

Charlie Ponte paced a moment, caught his breath, plucked at the collar of his silver jacket. He went back to his desk, barely touched a corner of the document LaRue had brought, as though the pages held some dread contamination.

He looked with loathing at the beaten figure in the twisted tie, then said to Bruno, "Lose 'im. Lose 'im forever. Then we see about the fuckin' Indian and his jerkoff friend."

The two thugs dragged the politician through the narrow dockside door, raked him over the splintery catwalk, tossed him like a sack of rice into Ponte's speedboat that was tied up to the wharf. The engines whined then roared, and they headed for the Gulf Stream, where the surging water was indigo and a mile deep.

◆◆◆◆◆◆

Some time later, Max Lowenstein, washed, shampooed, wearing his tweed jacket and carrying a small suitcase, walked into Martinelli's restaurant, took a deep slow breath, and approached the lectern where the maître d' was leaning on the reservation book. He flicked his eyes to the left and to the right, cleared his throat, and said softly, "Excuse me, do you have *stringozzi?*"

The maître d' looked at him sadly, tiredly, said, "Everybody knows. I'll take ya back."

He led the way past a pair of enormous lobster tanks, through a dining room still half-full of late eaters wearing lobster bibs, into a raucous kitchen where lobsters flailed like scorpions as they were dropped into boiling vats. At the back of the kitchen he knocked on a door.

Bruno, very recently returned from murder, opened it, looked at the visitor, said, "Who the fuck are you?"

"I have a message from the Indian," blurted Lowenstein.

"It better be good," said Squeak, in a voice like a misblown horn. "The Indian's nuts are hangin' by a thread." He patted the psychiatrist down, paused a moment at a hard thing in his pocket. It turned out to be his pipe. He led Lowenstein through another door to Ponte's inner office.

Under a single bare light bulb, the little boss was sitting at his desk. His hands were splayed in front of him, his skin was yellow, he looked like a man with a bellyache, waiting in secret anguish for a belch. He glanced up, stretched the liverish sacs beneath his eyes. "What now?" he said.

On legs that were none too steady, the visitor approached. He put the little suitcase on the desk, opened it. "The Indian's returning this," he said.

Ponte blinked, looked at the bundled bills, at the nervous bearded man that brought them. "No one ever gives back money," he murmured, wonder in his voice.

Lowenstein said nothing.

"How d'you come into this?" Ponte asked suspiciously.

"The Indian's friend, I'm his psychiatrist."

Ponte scratched his plastered hair, mugged over at his goons. "Psychiatrist. I'm starting to think I need a fucking psychiatrist."

"It's a serious commitment, therapy. There's fifty thousand dollars there. Every penny."

The mobster stared again at the money, dumbfounded at the perversity of its reappearance. Finally he said, "The fuckin' aggravation I been through, the money doesn't pay for that."

Lowenstein knew that sometimes people had to

say things, it didn't mean you had to answer them. He let Ponte's words settle, then resumed. "The Indian says you didn't get what you were paying for, there's no reason you should pay. He returns the money as a token of respect. Chief to chief."

Ponte drummed fingers on his desk. "Respect is a good thing. A casino is a better thing."

"I presume you've read the papers LaRue was carrying."

"I haven't seen LaRue in weeks."

There was a silence marred by kitchen noises: hissing water, rattling trays.

Ponte resumed, pointing a finger. "The Redskin fucks me, goes into business with someone else, I'll kill 'im."

"He knows that. He accepts it."

"He fuckin' better," said the mobster, but he felt himself off-balance now, like a man who throws a roundhouse punch and encounters only air.

"He wants no quarrel with you," said the shrink. "Your differences before, he says they're like the smoke from yesterday's fire. What I would call finished business."

Ponte looked at the money, looked at his fingernails, glanced furtively at his goons and wondered what more he could say to remind them he was still master of the situation. "Chief to chief?" he said at last. "He said that?"

"Exact words."

"Fuckin' A." Then he thought of something else that cheered him up. "And the stubborn bastard don't even have a place to live."

"No, he doesn't," said the shrink.

Ponte shook his head, picked up a sheaf of bills, put them down again, said, "Ah shit. Cigar?"

"You don't mind, I'll smoke a pipe."

The mobster unwrapped a corona, bit and spit the plug, held his lighter out for Lowenstein, who bent across the desk and drew in the offered flame.

Ponte puffed, exhaled a violet haze, squinted philosophically. "Psychiatrist. Sweet Jesus. You noticed it's a crazy fucking world we live in?"

"I've noticed our ideas about what's sane and normal are very flawed and very fragile. So Mr. Ponte, we smoke in peace?"

43

Next morning, in the West Building penthouse of the Paradiso condo, three people, ecstatically clean, were lolling in their separate beds, when there was a knocking at the door.

Murray Zemelman pulled on a robe, walked across the living room where a breeze was blowing through the shattered glass, and was reaching for the door-knob when it occurred to him that it might be prudent to check the peephole. Flattening himself against the foyer wall to peek, he saw a bulbous chihuahua, distorted by the lens, its glazed and milky eyes enormous, its twitching nostrils cavernous and wet. Holding the dog, a newspaper in his other hand, was Bert the Shirt, who this morning was resplendent in a tunic of teal blue linen, with a newly opened frangipani blossom protruding from the pocket.

Murray opened the door.

Bert said, "I'm out early with the stupid dog. Not wakin' youse, I hope? I thought you'd wanna see this."

The Bra King motioned him in.

Franny appeared, barefoot and yawning. She was wearing a smock of yellow seersucker. Her eyes still had sleep in them, her hair was curled as the towel had left it the night before, her skin was scrubbed to the pink of a painted cherub.

Tommy's voice came booming from the other bedroom. "Murray? Loan me something to put on. These clothes, I'm burning them."

Bert said, "A regular roomin' house you're runnin' here."

Franny went to put up coffee. Murray found a pair of shorts and a cranberry tank top to lend the Indian.

They gathered on the balcony, sipped java that did not steam against the already toasty morning. Bert put the newspaper on the table, and the others jockeyed for position to read it. Across the top was a banner headline. It said: INDIAN ISLAND TO REMAIN UNDEVELOPED. Then, in smaller type, STATE SENATOR LINKED TO REJECTED CASINO; TIES TO ORGANIZED CRIME SUGGESTED.

Tommy scanned the words, and didn't smile, just crossed his arms against his chest and peered out past the balcony railing, to the pool, the palms, the beach, the sea.

Murray turned the paper toward himself. Franny

seized a corner of it and changed the angle. Murray twisted it again. Finally Franny grabbed the thing and read aloud. Under Arty Magnus's byline, it said:

"*Kilicumba Island—In a bizarre ceremony involving tribal rituals, switched documents—*"

Murray cut in, "That meshuga dance between the middens—"

Franny shushed him, read on. "*—and a satchel of cash delivered by a well-known politician, it was decided here today that the lands recently ceded to Mr. Tommy Tarpon, last surviving member of the Matalatchee nation, would perpetually remain in the state left by Mr. Tarpon's forebears.*

"*The decision came despite intense pressure from representatives of a consortium known as First Keys Casinos, Inc., whose officers include several men with suspected connections to South Florida's alleged Mob boss, Mr. Charles Ponte of Miami. Revealed as one of the group's allies is state senator Barney LaRue, who visited Kilicumba, bringing with him a $50,000 cash payment in a last-ditch effort to persuade the Matalatchee chief to sign a contract authorizing First Keys to build a gambling casino on his property.*

"*However, the document actually signed by Mr. Tarpon—and witnessed by Senator LaRue, who was offered ample opportunity to examine the papers— was a very different piece of business.* Continued on page seven."

She riffled through the soggy newsprint.

Bert stroked his dog enthusiastically, said, "Now here's the part I like."

Franny sipped some coffee, then resumed. "*Obtained exclusively by the* Sentinel, *the document consists of three pages of personal ads, and a short statement penned by Mr. Tarpon. That statement is here reprinted in its entirety:*

"*'When Kilicumba was part of the white man's world, it was considered worthless, a mangrove dot among ten thousand others—and so it was a small thing to return it to me. But once it was mine, it took on great worth in the eyes of certain people, who decided, as the powerful have always decided, to take it back again. I am indebted to these people for teaching me a useful lesson: that the surest way to safeguard something is to protect it from becoming valuable, to find a worth in it that is a private worth, and that seems worthlessness to others.*

"*'I therefore decree, that now and for all time, Kilicumba shall not be changed or built upon. Access to it shall remain difficult. Its unbearable insects will not be disturbed, its impossible shoreline will not be improved. If the occasional visitor should venture upon it and be moved, the Tribe welcomes him. If it is never visited again, it does not matter.'*"

Franny stopped reading, let the paper fold shut on the plastic table. "Tommy," she said, "that's fantastic."

"Is it?" said the Indian. He was gazing absently down at the Paradiso's placid courtyard, beginning to fill now with early sunbathers and swimmers of laps and people reading magazines.

"Of course it is," said Murray.

"Ya did the right thing," said Bert the Shirt.

"You won," the Bra King said. "And you found your own way to win."

"I guess," said Tommy, sounding unconvinced. He sipped some coffee, leaned back in his chair. "I just feel all chewed up. I mean, three months ago, I was just a guy who sold shells, drank beer, went fishing. Nothing ever happened to me."

"Then you met Murray," Franny said. She said it with the compassion of a fellow-sufferer.

"Then I met Murray," the Indian echoed.

"Jesus," said the Bra King, "ya don't have to make it sound like catching cancer."

No one made it sound like anything better, so Murray went on in his own defense.

"Come on now, Tommy, ya met me, ya drank like a fish and were bitterer than horseradish."

"At least he had a home," put in Bert the Shirt.

"He has a home now," Murray shot right back. "He's living here with us."

"Us?" said Franny.

"He's always pulling that us shit," Tommy said.

"Now wait a second," said the Bra King. "One thing at a time. Ya met me, you were like paralyzed with bitterness. True or false?"

Tommy's tongue explored the inside of his face. Grudgingly, he said, "True."

"Thank you," Murray said. "And now, what about now? Tell me yes or no."

"Don't put him on the spot like that," said Franny.

But Tommy didn't seem to mind. He leaned back, pouted, ran a hand over his chest and stomach like he was feeling for a tumor or a wound. "Less," he said.

He sounded surprised and for a moment he pondered that surprise.

"I still think white people are fucked up," he went on. "But now I know it's not my problem. I had my chance to jump into the game, jump in big time. How many people get that chance? The chance to look it right in the eye and say screw it, I don't want it."

Triumphantly, Murray looked around the table.

Bert d'Ambrosia stroked his drowsing dog. "But he still don't have a place ta live."

"Will ya let it go already?" the Bra King said to him. "Since when are you such a *nuhdge*?"

"Forty thousand's enough for a houseboat," Tommy said. "A nice one. That's all I wanted out of this—to get back to where I started from."

"Toxic Triangle?" said Murray.

"Primo waterfront," said Tommy.

"And LaRue?" said Franny. "You think there'll be a scandal?"

There was a pause. A south breeze carried the smell of iodine from the ocean. Palm fronds scratched and rattled, there was soft splashing from the pool. Across the Paradiso's edenic quadrangle, the senator's penthouse was dark, its curtains drawn.

Old Bert petted his chihuahua. "Bahney's beyond shame," he said. "I'd be very surprised if at this point Bahney even cares about a scandal."

44

They finished their coffee. Bert got up to leave. Tommy, embracing his old life with the chastened gratitude of a man returned from a bold but calamitous furlough, resolved to hitch his cart of shells to his rusty bike and reclaim his spot in the shade of the southernmost banyan.

Murray walked them to the elevator, and when he came back he found Franny kneeling on the floor of her room, folding clothes into her suitcase. He watched her just a moment before she noticed him, watched her small efficient hands, noted the calm pleasure in her face as she composed a neat mosaic of cotton and linen.

She looked up and said, "You think he'll be satisfied, doing what he did before?"

Murray shrugged. "Ya think about it, it wasn't

bad. His own boss. Outdoor work. Who knows, maybe we'll find a business, go into it together."

"You tried that," Franny said.

"So maybe we'll try again. Ya know, he needs me to look out for him."

Franny let that slide. "And the drinking?" she said. "You think he'll go back?"

Her ex-husband shrugged again. A shrug seemed the most honest answer to questions about the heart and mind of another human being, even when that person was a friend, a man whose tribal recollections and forgettings were not so very different from one's own.

A moment passed. Murray looked at Franny, kneeling in her yellow smock. Her room was narrow, it had a single bed, it was like a child's room, or a nun's, it made him shy, he felt rude and blockish standing in the doorway. He heard himself say, "Franny, I really wish you'd stay with me."

She said nothing, just bit her lip and kept on folding clothes.

"We're meant to be together," he said. "Isn't it obvious? Ya don't just turn your back on that."

"You did," she said.

"I was a schmuck. You're smarter than I am."

She didn't disagree.

"Can't we try at least?" he said. "Put me on probation."

She kept packing.

"I'd do anything, Franny. I'd go anywhere. I'd . . . I'd give up Prozac."

Franny primped the shoulders of a pale blue shirt, laid it next to a pair of khaki shorts. "You already have," she softly said.

"Excuse me?"

His ex-wife kept on folding. "You haven't had Prozac since I've been here."

Murray's stomach churned inside his bathrobe. His jaw flopped open like the jaw of a skeleton, his eyebrows rose like they were pulled with wires.

"First thing I did," she went serenely on. "I opened the capsules, flushed the Prozac, put in zinc."

The Bra King felt dizzy. He stared vacantly into the room. Walls no longer met at corners, the ceiling seemed to tip. He shuffled numbly across the carpet and sat slumped on the edge of Franny's bed.

"Zinc," he whispered. "Zinc," he said, more firmly. "Zinc?!" he hissed. "I'm fighting the Mafia, making split-second judgments on matters of life and death, on *zinc*?!"

"Don't exaggerate," said Franny.

Murray sat there, as utterly at sea as an executive who's just been fired.

"Although," his former wife conceded, "the way you rescued me, that was pretty clever."

"I thought so," Murray whispered.

Franny started packing sandals and sneakers, packed them soles-out, like a border, around the edges of her suitcase.

"But ya know," the Bra King mused, "it's weird, Prozac or no, I haven't felt depressed in awhile."

"Because you've been too busy," Franny said, "to take your temperature every fifteen minutes."

Murray leaned forward, put his elbows on his knees. "No," he said, "it's because you've been here."

His ex-wife looked at him over her shoulder, rather grudgingly. "Very flattering," she said. "Probably untrue. But Murray—worrying about your moods, taking care of you, this is not my mission in life."

He pushed his lips out, thought that over. "You sure?"

Franny looked exasperated, made small adjustments in her already perfect packing job.

"I mean," said Murray, "think about it. Bras. Casinos. Crooked politicians. Gorillas throwing snocones. What I'm asking—be honest now—I'm asking, ya look around, ya see this craziness, this nonsense, people making themselves miserable over stupid things—ya see all that, and are ya really sure there's anything more important, more worthwhile, than that two people, they should take care of each other?"

Franny said nothing, lowered the lid of her suitcase. Piled clothes kept it from shutting tight, it needed pushing down but she didn't push it.

"Really, Franny—can you look me in the eye and tell me you've got something more important to do than be my wife? 'Cause I'm telling you, I know it plain as the nose on my face, I've got nothing more important than to be your husband."

She half-turned on her knees, the carpet rubbed her skin. "Murray," she said, "you're driving me crazy."

"So what else is new?"

"After everything you've put me through—"

"Right, Franny. After everything, here we are, you and me."

He reached a hand out toward her. She looked at it, smiled at it as at a daydream, didn't take it.

"Listen," he said, undaunted. "I have an idea. This room, this . . . this dormitory—this is no place to talk about our future. How about we continue this discussion in the bathtub?"

She sat back on her haunches, sighed. *This Murray*, she thought, as she had thought with wary stubborn fondness a million times before, as many times as she had rehearsed her reasons for never seeing him again.

"Steam," he said. "Relaxation. Warm jets on the lower back. We'll unwind. We'll plan a vacation."

"We're on vacation," Franny said.

"We'll plan a better one," said Murray. "I'll run the water. Whaddya say?"

She said nothing.

But Murray didn't need an answer. Prozac or no Prozac, brain juices were gushing, jolts of hope made his movements angular, decisive. He stood, went to his room.

Franny looked down at her suitcase. One push, one little push, would be enough to slam it shut.

Murray peered through the window of the master

aying like island dancers, fronds
like hiked-up skirts. He walked
made bed, turned on the water good
the gigantic jetted tub.

nny got up from the floor, sat on the rumpled
ace where Murray had been sitting. She stared
across the narrow room, spilled her thoughts against
the blankness of the wall. She thought about the
losses that you couldn't help and the losses that
you could.

Murray watched the water swirl, saw the heat rise
up to fog the mirror. He took his robe off, hung it
on a peg, and gingerly stepped in.

Franny winced just slightly, thought about the
hurtful things that people sometimes did, the
unthinkable mistakes, how much they mattered,
and how much they didn't. How big a loss, how
big a damaged part of your own life, could you cut
away before you'd cut off more than you could ever
find again?

Murray leaned back in the hot and roiling water.
He was confident and he was terrified, he knew
his wife would come to him, he knew that she
would leave. He closed his eyes, counted to ten,
opened them again. In his mind he saw her stepping
through the doorway, her face wreathed in steam
and forgiveness, her hair curled very tightly by the
damp. He pictured her; he hoped; he waited, and
the hot caressing water rose around him like a
swiftly flooding tide.

IF YOU LOVED
TROPICAL DEPRESSION,
BE SURE TO CATCH
LAURENCE SHAMES'S
NEWEST NOVEL,
VIRGIN HEAT,
COMING IN MARCH 1997
FROM HYPERION

Paranoia doesn't sleep; a guilty conscience looks over its shoulder forever.

Ziggy Maxx, nearly a decade after he took that name and the new face that went with it, still hated to be photographed, still flinched like a native whenever a camera lens was aimed at him.

Cameras were aimed at him often. A bartender in Key West, he was a prop in a million vacations, an extra in the memories of hordes of strangers. He was scenery, like the scabbed mahogany tree that dominated the courtyard at Raul's, like the purple bougainvillea that rained down from its trellis above the horseshoe bar. The bougainvillea; the beveled glass and polished teak; the burly barkeep in his mostly open shirt with faded palm trees on it—it made a nice picture, a travel poster, almost.

So people shot Ziggy with Nikons, Minoltas, with cardboard disposables that cost ten bucks at any drugstore. They'd raise the camera, futz with a couple seconds, then they'd harden down and squint, exactly like a guy about to squeeze a trigger. If the barkeep wasn't quick enough to dodge and blink, to wheel discreetly like an indicted businessman, the flash would make green ovals dance before his throbbing eyes.

Every time he was captured on film he felt the same archaic panic; every time, he had to soothe himself, to murmur silently, Hey, it didn't matter, no one would recognize the straightened nose with the dewdrop septum, the chin plumped and stitched out of its former cleft, the scalp clipped and sewn so that the hairline, once a prowlike widow's peak, was no a smooth curve, nondescript. Hell, even nine years after surgery, there were hungover mornings when he himself didn't recognize that fabricated face, thought his bathroom mirror had become a window with a dissipated stranger leering through it, begging for an aspirin.

Still, he hated having his picture taken. The worry of it, on top of the aggravation from his other job, sometimes gave him rashes on his elbows and behind his knees.

The guys with videocams, they were the worst.

Like this guy right here, thought Ziggy, glancing briefly at one of his customers. Typical tourist jerk, fifty-something, with a mango daiquiri in front of him and a Panasonic beside him on the bar. Shiny lime-green shirt. The round red cheeks of a clown, and a sunburned head peeling already under thin hair raked in oily strings across the hairless top. Next to him, his wife—pretty once, with too much makeup, too much perfume, sucking on a frozen margarita, her lips clamped around the straw as though claiming under oath that nothing of larger diameter had ever penetrated there. Tourists. It was early April, the ass-end of the season, and Ziggy Maxx was sick to death of tourists. Sick of being asked where Hemingway really drank. Sick of preparing complex, disgusting cocktails with imbecilic names—Sputnik, Woo Woo, Sex on the Beach. Sick of lighting cigarettes for kindergarten teachers from Ohio, Canadian beauticians; nice women, probably, but temporarily deformed and made ridiculous by an awkward urge to misbehave.

A regular gestured, and Ziggy reached up to the rack above his head, grabbed a couple beer mugs, drew a couple drafts. His furry back was damp inside his shirt; Key West was then poised between the wholesome warmth of winter and the overripe, quietly deranging heat of summer. By the thermometer, the change was subtle; still, it was all-transforming. Daytime temperatures went up only a few degrees, but they stayed there even after sunset and straight on through the night. The breeze diminished, the air sat there and congealed, grew freighted like a soggy sheet with remembered excess. Sober winter plants died back, were overwhelmed by the exorbitant rude growths of the tropics—butter-yellow flowers as big and brazen as trombones, the traveler palm whose leaves were taller than a man, weird cactuses that dreamed white blossoms in the middle of the night.

When the wet heat of summer started kicking in, Key West seemed to drift farther out from the familiar mainland, became ever more an island. Ziggy Maxx had lived here six years now, and he'd noticed the same thing every year: less happened in the summer, but what happened was more strange.

Another tourist caught his eye. Ziggy's glance slid off the face like it was a label in the no-frills aisle, fixed instead on the jerky slogan on the tourist's T-shirt: WILL WORK FOR SEX.

The tourist said, "Lemme get a Virgin Heat."

Ziggy stifled a grimace. Of all the idiot drinks he hated to make, Virgin Heats were among the ones he hated most. Fussy, sticky, labor-intensive. Substitutes for conversation, they drew people's attention away from each other and toward the bottles and the bartender. The building of a cocktail like a Virgin Heat sent people groping for their cameras.

And sure enough, as Ziggy was setting up the pony glass and reaching for the Sambuca, he saw out of the corner of his eye that the man with the sunburned head was readying his videocam. Ziggy flinched, turned a few degrees. He poured the thick liqueur, then felt more than saw that the camera was sliding off his manufactured face to focus on his busy hands. An artsy shot, the barkeep thought, with something like relief. Another jerk who'd seen too many movies.

Ziggy made the drink. He made it with riffs and flourishes it never dawned on him were his alone.

Although he wore a short-sleeved shirt, he began by flicking his wrists as if shooting back a pair of cuffs. When he inverted the teaspoon to float the Chartreuse on the 'Buca, he extended a pinky in a gesture that was incongruously dainty, given the furry knuckle and the broad and close-cropped fingernail. Grasping the bottle in his right hand, he let his index finger float free; mangled long ago from an ill-thrown punch, that bent and puffy digit refused to parallel the others. He didn't bring the bottle directly to the glass, he banked and looped it in, like a plane approaching an airport. Slowly, with the pomp of mastery, he poured a layer of purple cassis over yellow Chartreuse, green crème de menthe over purple cassis. He topped the gross rainbow with a membrane of grenadine, then delicately laid in a cherry that sank with a portentous slowness, carrying with it a streaky red lascivious rain.

He slid the drink across the bar to the tourist who had ordered it. "Five dollars, please," he said.

He took cash, glanced around. The videocam had been switched off, for the moment everyone was happy.

A light breeze shook the bougainvillea on its trellis, the papery flowers rattled dryly. A woman, a nice woman probably, from Ohio, Michigan, New Jersey, fumbled in a big purse for a cigarette. She didn't have a match, she looked at Ziggy. Damp inside his faded shirt at the beginning of that season when things got only damper and only stranger, he snapped his lighter and cupped his hands and lit her up. She smiled, then blew twin streams of exhaust through her nose. If she was out to misbehave, and if she could stay awake till closing time, and if she didn't get a better offer in the meanwhile, maybe she would misbehave with him.